Claire —
wishing you handsome
heroes & happy ever after!
Tessa :)

PRAIRIE DEVIL

A COWBOYS OF THE FLINT HILLS NOVEL
(Book 6)

TESSA LAYNE

D1247641

Shady Layne Media
www.tessalayne.com

WELCOME TO PRAIRIE!

Where the cowboys are sexy as sin, the women are smart and sassy, and everyone gets their Happily Ever After!

Prairie is a fictional small town in the heart of the Flint Hills, Kansas – the original Wild West. Here, you'll meet the Sinclaire family, descended from French fur-trappers and residents of the area since the 1850s. You'll also meet the Hansens and the Graces, who've been ranching in the Flint Hills since right before the Civil War.

Sharing a property line with the Graces are the heroes of Resolution Ranch, the men and women who've put their bodies on the line serving our country at home and abroad.

Prairie embodies the best of western small town life. It's a community where family, kindness, and respect are treasured. Where people pull together in times of trial, and yes... where the Cowboy Code of Honor is alive and well.

Every novel is a stand-alone book where the characters get their HEA, but you'll get to know a cast of secondary characters along the way.

Get on the waiting list for Prairie Fever and the rest of the Cowboys of the Flint Hills
tessalayne.com/newsletter

PRAIRIE FEVER
(Book 7 in the Cowboys of the Flint Hills Series)

Playing doctor has never been so sexy.

Confirmed bachelor Gunnar Hansen, has successfully resisted the matchmaking efforts of Dottie Grace and her posse of granny wannabe's. There's no room in his life for love, or for starting a family of his own. Not when his hands are full running Hansen Stables and heading up the board of Prairie's new medical clinic. But everything turns upside down when the socialite who ditched him at the altar years ago turns out to be Prairie's new doctor.

Four years ago, fresh out of medical school, Suzannah Winslow took a gamble on a sweet-talking cowboy who left her high and dry… and pregnant. With her residency behind her, and an offer to become Prairie's first and only physician, she can finally provide her daughter with stability she's longed for. She has no interest in taking a second chance on a silver-tongued cowboy full of empty promises. Even if his smile still melts her panties.

But Gunnar has other ideas, and when he mounts a full-scale campaign to win back the woman he lost, will little Lula Beth become his unlikely ally or the wedge that drives them apart for good?

Do you like a dose of military with your cowboys?
Meet the Heroes of Resolution Ranch

Inspired by the real work of Heroes & Horses… Chances are, someone you know, someone you *love* has served in the military. And chances are, they've struggled with re-entry into civilian life. The folks of Prairie are no different. With the biggest Army base in the country, Fort Riley, located in the heart of the Flint Hills, the war has come home to Prairie.

Join me as we finally discover Travis Kincaid's story and learn how he copes in the aftermath of a mission gone wrong. Meet Sterling, who never expected to return to Prairie after he left for West Point. Fall in love with Cash as he learns to trust himself again. Laugh with Jason and Braden as they meet and fall in love with the sassy ladies of Prairie. Same Flint Hills setting, same cast of friendly, funny, and heartwarming characters, same twists and surprises that will keep you up all night turning the pages.

A HERO'S HONOR – Travis Kincaid & Elaine Ryder
(On Sale Now)
A HERO'S HEART – Sterling Walker & Emma Sinclaire
(On Sale Now)
A HERO'S HAVEN – Cash Aiken & Kaycee Starr
(On Sale Now)
A HERO'S HOME – Jason Case & Millie Prescott
(Coming June 2018)
A HERO'S HOPE – Braden McCall & Luci Cruz
(Coming 2018)

Help a Hero – Read a Cowboy
KISS ME COWBOY – A Box Set for Veterans
Six Western Romance authors have joined up to support their
favorite charity – Heroes & Horses – and offer you this sexy
box set with Six Full Length Cowboy Novels, filled with
steamy kisses and HEA's. Grab your copy and help an
American Hero today!
*All proceeds go to Heroes & Horses**

Visit www.tessalayne.com for more titles & release info
Sign up for my Newsletter here
tessalayne.com/newsletter
Hang out with me! Join my Facebook Reader Group –
Prairie Posse
facebook.com/groups/1390521967655100

CHAPTER 1

NERVOUS ENERGY THRUMMED through Colton Kincaid's hands as he turned his pickup onto the long driveway leading up to his family's farmhouse on the outskirts of Prairie, Kansas. Ten years. Ten years since his big brother Travis had turned him out on his ass without so much as an "I'm sorry." Ten years since his next-door neighbor and the closest thing he'd had to a mother, Dottie Grace, had driven him to the Greyhound station in Manhattan, bought him a one-way ticket to a ranch in Steamboat Springs, Colorado, and given him a hundred bucks with the admonishment to spend it wisely.

The contents of his stomach churned, threatening to empty all over the inside of the cab. He should have known better than to mix truck stop coffee, beef jerky, and nacho cheese chips, but hell if he hadn't been nervous making the ten-hour drive over from Steamboat. Colton Kincaid, rodeo star. Scrapper and hell-raiser. Nervous?

It shamed him to admit it, the power his brother still held after ten years of not speaking, of not calling even once to check up on him. So who was the fool? In about three minute's time, he'd finally have the answer. Colton's breath hitched just beneath his sternum as the truck crested the rise, a flood of memories hitting him as the old farmhouse came into sight. Someone had repainted the barn. The farmhouse looked ten years older, the paint faded and cracked. Some things never changed. The yard was packed with trucks and SUVs, maybe thirty in all. So he hadn't missed the wedding. At least he didn't think so. Travis's messages had said three, and it was three-oh-five. Not that he'd been to many weddings, but they never started on time, did they?

Colton slid the truck in at the end of a long line and cut the ignition. A northerly breeze carrying the scent of withered prairie grass and fried turkey hit his nose as he hopped down. North wind in the Flint Hills always brought cooler weather, but for now, it looked like the perfect afternoon for a wedding. He jammed on his Stetson and wove through the vehicles, heart thundering more erratically with every step closer to the front porch. A vivid memory arose, of Travis standing backlit by the solitary porch light, arms folded, expression cold and unfeeling. Colton's mouth went dry and a shiver ran up the back of his arms. It had been an early frost that night ten years ago, and Travis had turned him out with only a frayed jean jacket for warmth. The words they'd exchanged had been just as cold, but Colton had been too far gone to notice either until Lydia Grace had shaken him awake from where he'd let sleep obliviate him on her front porch. Ten years, and he could recall the burning look in her eyes like it had been yesterday. Would she be here? Surely her parents Dottie and Teddy would be.

He paused, boot on the top step. Maybe now wasn't the time. Maybe he should turn tail and slink back to Colorado. To the life he'd built without Prairie, without family. Ten years was a long time for apologies to stack up. Travis's last voice message jangled in his head. "I know it's a long shot. But I promise you're welcome here. No judgment."

No judgment. But could Travis account for the thirty or

2

forty-some pairs of eyes on the other side of the door? Travis might not judge him, but what about the rest of the town? Colton's stomach churned perilously. Shaking his head, he reached into an inside pocket for a shot of liquid courage. He might not booze it up the way he had, once-upon-a-time, but if ever there was a time…

He twisted the cap off the flask and took a long draw of the rye whiskey he'd brought with him, wiped his mouth, and squared his shoulders. He could be a pussy about this or he could man up and face his past. If it all went to shit, he could turn around and drive straight back to Steamboat. But if it didn't? Wasn't it worth taking a shot? Travis was the only family he had left. Steeling himself, he rapped hard on the door.

On the other side, a chair scraped, a muffled voice spoke low, but Colton could barely hear it over the pounding of his blood. After what felt like eons, the door creaked open and dozens of pairs of eyes turned on him, some with surprise, some narrowed. He searched for Travis and found him, gripping the elbow of a pretty young thing with big blue eyes in a simple white dress. This must be Elaine. And the boy next to her must be her son Travis had mentioned, Dax. Colton gulped and removed his hat, all the speeches he'd prepared vanishing into the ether. "I hope I'm not interrupting."

The startled silence unnerved him. Colton's chest burned. He never should have come. But fuck it, he was here now, and he wouldn't back down, not until this played out until the bitter end. He flashed a grin to the faces in the room, and his eyes collided with a blue-green pair in the back of the room. He'd know those eyes anywhere. But it had been so long, he couldn't tell. And instead of long hair wrapped in a ponytail, it was sleek and short, swinging against her jawline. Lydia? Or her twin, Lexi? Back in the day, it had been easy to tell them apart. Lexi'd always been wrapped up saving animals, the environment, or some other crusade of the week, and hadn't ever paid him much attention. Lydia had been the more buttoned-up of the pair, and had tried to save *him*. Sweet, good Lydia. He owed her an apology too. Judging from the way his pulse quickened, it had to be Lydia. But the look in her eye didn't say buttoned-up. Not by a long shot.

Travis stepped forward, eyes guarded. "Colton."

"Travis." The tension wound around them, pulsing between them like a living, angry dragon. Someone coughed. A chair squeaked. The buzzing in his ears grew louder, drowning out the sound of his breathing.

And then – Travis stepped forward and pulled him into a bear hug, pounding him on the back. "You're just in time." He spoke hoarsely, like a sweetgum burr had lodged itself in his throat. "Just in time."

A rush of hot emotions surged through Colton, taking his voice. Relief, primary amongst them. He returned the hug, awkwardly giving his brother a pat. They were the same size now, both men. Each hardened through the pressures of life. Colton cleared his throat. "I'll just stand in the back."

"Wait." Travis laid a hand on his arm. "Stand with me?"

Had he lost his mind? Ten years gone, and the first thing he asked was this? Shit. Travis really did mean to bury that hatchet. Colton nodded once, keeping his face neutral. No need to let everything hang out in front of the assembled group. There'd be plenty of time down the line to hash things out. The room let out a collective sigh as he took his place next to his brother. Throughout the brief ceremony, Colton kept his eyes trained on a spot between Travis's shoulder blades, hearing but not registering any of the words until the little boy next to him shouted. "Now I have a dad *and* an uncle."

Laughter and applause erupted around him. This was too much. Travis turned back to him, his arm around his bride, and flashed him a happy smile. Colton's throat grew prickly. He'd never seen Travis like this. Happy. It threw him off-balance. This was anything but the reunion he'd imagined. Chaos reigned as attendees spilled out onto the porch, and others began shifting chairs in preparation for the Thanksgiving feast to follow.

A hand tapped his shoulder. "Colton Kincaid, I never thought I'd see the likes of you again," Dottie Grace gushed, eyes sparkling with pride.

The years had been good to her. She still oozed vitality. Her hair was streaked with gray. There were more wrinkles around her eyes and stress lines around her mouth. But still the same old force of nature. "Look at you. All grown up and devilishly handsome." She shook her head, smiling. "I know it means so much to Travis that you're here." She wrapped her arms around him in a vice-like grip.

Colton's voice grew thick as he tried to explain himself. "I always meant to contact you." But he'd been too ashamed. And by the time he'd earned a little success, too many years had passed.

"Hush, now. We're glad you're home."

Home? Maybe to them. Not to him. But no use in contradicting Dottie, especially on Thanksgiving at a wedding celebration. He scanned the room again, looking for the sassy pair of blue-green eyes. "Did I see Lydia?"

"You did. Home for the holidays." Dottie's tone of voice shut down further conversation. As if to say, *I'm glad you're home, but stay away from my daughter.*

Huh. He guessed some things would never change. Him not being good enough for the likes of the amazing Grace sisters, at least one of them. Flashing Dottie the smile that always earned him a slice of pie from the diner counter, he spoke sincerely. "It's good to see you, Dottie. And... thank you for everything you did for me... back then. I didn't deserve half of it."

Compassion filled the woman's eyes and she cupped his cheek. "You didn't deserve half of what was heaped on you either. I'd have done it for anyone. I'm glad you've made something of yourself. Made us all proud. Now if you'll excuse me, I have a feast to help set out."

Someone handed Colton a beer, and he lingered by the mantel, feeling more like a stranger than a man in his childhood home. His phone vibrated in his pocket. Who in the hell would be contacting him on Thanksgiving? Of course... he didn't even have to check his phone to know who it would be. The only question was which Carter would be interrupting him? When the phone buzzed again, he risked a look. A picture of him with some lady he vaguely remembered flashed across the screen along with a text from thorn-in-his-side, Samantha Jo Carter.

Really? Taking up with *married* women now? wtf?!?

Colton bit back a curse. Leave it to Sammy Jo to assume the worst just because some drunken wife had to hashtag the shit out of a photo and slap it up all over Instagram. How many times had he reminded his sponsors they *wanted* him to accept photo-ops from the ladies? Until it came back to bite them in the ass. Colton struggled to remember that night, but came up short. He studied the face in the picture again. Wife of a competing sponsor? Maybe from Frontier Days? How in the hell was he supposed to keep track of every lady who bought him a drink or asked to dance? He couldn't fucking win. And he wasn't dignifying any text from Sammy Jo with a response. Plenty of time to deal with her and her dad and uncle at the NFR's. He'd be at their beck and call for most of that run anyway. No need to let them ruin his first trip back to Prairie.

But all thoughts of issues with his sponsors vanished as soon as he laid eyes on Lydia in line by the makeshift bar. She wore some kind of a clingy sweater dress that skimmed her knees and left everything to the imagination. Lydia Grace had always been cute. But cute wasn't standing in front of him. Oh no, she'd matured into a luscious, curve-laden woman from the slender column of her neck, to her shapely hips, all the way down to her pretty ankles obscured by girly boots. As if feeling his gaze on her, she turned, and for the second time, their gazes collided with the force of a bull hitting a barrel-man.

CHAPTER 2

COLTON WAS STARING at her again. She could feel his eyes boring into her backside. Seeing straight through her dress to the red lace thong she'd chosen on a whim. If she couldn't embrace her wild-side at a wedding, she should just give up. Find a nice accountant and settle down. No more flamboyant, temperamental designers who stole her ideas. Or opera singers. Or *cowboys*. No more projects. No one who needed fixing and the love of a solid, steady woman. Problem was, every time she went on a date with a nice young financial advisor, or someone who hailed from the Upper East Side, it was boring. B-O-R-I-N-G.

Confining. Total yawner.

And by dessert, she could see her future spinning out before her in an endless sea of teas and charity events, two-point-five kids and a labradoodle. Or worse, a teacup Chihuahua. And eventually, even though it was only the first date, Lydia could tell she'd be the one asked to give up *her* life. *Her* passion, to stand by her man. And, she just… couldn't. Her friends in New York might consider her provincial, but her mother was a successful businesswoman, and her three sisters smart and kicking ass in their own professions. Where did she fit in?

She drank green tea, not Cosmos. She slept in flannel pajamas, not buck naked. Her idea of being scandalous was staying so long at MOMA that security had to escort her out ten minutes past closing. Or losing herself in the stacks at the public library and discovering some treatise on fifteenth-century alchemy. She wasn't a clubber. She didn't take pills washed down with a gin fizz. But she didn't spend nights playing scrabble and reading Sylvia Plath, either. Too Gertrude Stein for Prairie, too plain Jane for New York.

She stepped up to the makeshift bar. "Old Fashioned, please." One thing was certain. Tonight, she was breaking the mold. She was going to have a cocktail. Maybe even *two*. Celebrate the fact she'd just cut off ten inches of her hair and kissed her dream job goodbye. She glanced back over her shoulder while she waited. Damn. Colton's eyes bored straight into her, sending liquid fire right to her core. One thing hadn't changed in ten years, his effect on her. One look from him and she went weak in the knees. But this time there was heat in his eyes. Appreciation. She stood a little taller in her boots. Let him look. Let him finally realize what had been in front of him but that he'd stupidly ignored. She brushed away a flash of anger. Water under the bridge. She was a different person now. Stronger.

Colton? Not so much. He oozed dangerous. Bad-boy. Wild-child. Ten years, a half-a-foot, and forty more pounds of muscle had only amplified that. She'd heard through the grapevine that he rodeoed. And it showed in the way he moved. In the way his muscles bunched under his shirt. And yes, she was not ashamed to admit, in the way his ass filled out a pair of dark Wranglers. Something about the way a pair of worn jeans hugged rock-hard muscles set a heat in her belly in a way worsted wool and chinos never did.

She accepted her cocktail and took a sip, keeping her eyes on Colton as he crossed the room to stand before her.

"You cut your hair." His voice sounded like too much smoke and whiskey. A shiver of attraction raced down her spine. A voice like that would rough up her sensitive parts in the most delightful way.

"You cleaned up," she answered tartly. Better to keep Colton Kincaid at arm's length. Or at least try.

He raised an eyebrow. "You look good, Lyds."

"Don't call me that," she whispered, heat from the Old Fashioned and not his gaze, warming her belly. At least that's what she tried to tell herself.

His mouth curved temptingly up. "Why not? Too many memories?"

Oh, hell. She was going to need another cocktail. Or three. Memories of taking his keys, of watching in despair as he disappeared behind the barn to get stoned with one of his buddies. And worst, of kissing him goodbye. Of pouring all of her idealistic seventeen-year-old emotions into a kiss he'd ultimately rejected. She gulped down the rest of her drink and licked the remainder off her lower lip. She registered his sharp intake of breath. Let him look. Let him think about everything he'd tossed away the night he'd left Prairie. "Yeah," she muttered when she found her voice. "I guess you could say that."

"Can we talk?"

"I think I need another cocktail if we're going to talk."

His eyes shot skyward.

"I'm not a goody-two-shoes."

"Nobody ever called you that."

They didn't have to. She knew what his friends had thought of her, how they'd referred to her as Libby-Lyds, short for Librarian Lydia. She gave him a bright smile. "I'm glad you're back, Colt. I know how much it means to Travis.

Mama, too," she added after a pause. "I'm glad to hear you're doing well." She turned to escape to the kitchen, too flustered to think straight.

"Wait, Lydia." He caught her arm, eyes pleading. "Save me a dance?"

Several of the men were already outside, lighting a big bonfire for those willing to brave the cold November air. They'd even set up a small sound system, running electricity from the barn. She lifted a shoulder, smiling coyly. "Maybe?"

"Maybe?" he challenged, a knowing smile brightening his face. This was the Colton she remembered, had a hard time resisting. The young man full of swagger, doing what he wanted, when he wanted, damn the consequences. "Afraid you won't be able to resist my charms?"

She couldn't help it. A laugh rose, and she gently socked his shoulder, not missing the solid mass underneath her fingers. "Hardly likely. I think you're the one who needs to resist *my* charms," she flirted back.

He captured her hand, held it pressed against his shoulder. His voice dropped. "Maybe I don't want to."

His look said everything, made her mouth go dry. A spark of desire burst to life between her legs. She clenched her thighs against the warming tingle. No. *Nononono.* She would not give into these sensations. It didn't matter that this might be her only opportunity to take a walk on the wild side. To break in her red lace thong, to see what love 'em and leave 'em felt like. Lord knew, she'd been on the receiving end of that equation more times than she cared to count. What did her roommate in New York always say? Go big or go home? There was no one bigger or badder in Prairie than Colton Kincaid. And if she wanted to shed her good-girl image once and for all, take advantage of the condoms she always carried in her purse but never used, banging him at his brother's wedding reception would certainly be a good way to start.

She cocked her chin, and stared right at him. "That so?" She held his gaze one, two, three beats, then reclaimed her hand. "I'll see you 'round, Colton." She turned and made her way to the buffet set up along the far wall. *Do not look back, do not look back.*

She did.

He still stared at her like he had x-ray vision. Her lady bits responded as if he did.

CHAPTER 3

C OLTON STOOD IN the shadow of the bonfire, a glass of whiskey in one hand, a half-smoked Cuban in the other. Lydia Grace was a contradiction. The look she'd given him as she walked away had made him instantly hard. Made his balls ache for sweet relief. Contrary to the bad-boy reputation he cultivated in the rodeo world. It had been a long time since a pretty lady had warmed his bed. Too long, his dick yelled at him.

But he wasn't home for a quick lay. Hell, if he wanted that, he could hit any bar on a Tuesday night along Lincoln Avenue back home and find a willing companion. One thing was certain – Lydia Grace was not the kind of woman you scratched an itch with. Her goodness oozed out of her. Even when she tried to put on bad-girl airs. Lydia Grace would never be anything but good. Even if her sexy curves drove him wild, she was out of his league. And he'd received Dottie's warning plain and clear – Lydia was off-limits. *Not* for the likes of him.

He took a puff of the cigar, letting the sweet tobacco swirl in his mouth. Too bad. His instincts told him Lydia's sensuality was largely untapped, and likely ran deep. He might be wrong about so much in his life, but he was rarely wrong about women.

"Earth to Colt," Parker Hansen, who'd been just a year

ahead of him in school, scoffed. "You're either thinking about a woman or your bank account."

"What if I asked you that same question?" That was a cagey answer, but if he admitted to Lydia's brother-in-law he'd been imagining what was underneath that soft dress she wore, he doubted he'd still be standing.

"Hell, I'm still a newlywed. I'm supposed to think about nothing but my wife all the time."

"That how it works?"

Parker smiled the smile of a satisfied, content man. "Wouldn't change it for the world."

Parker had been a rabble-rouser. It was no surprise he'd ended up in a risky profession like fighting fires. Also not surprising was that he'd paired off with Cassidy, Lydia's older sister. She and Parker had egged each other on all the time when they'd been young. Funny how even after ten years, some things never changed. Melancholy poked at him. Catching up with folks this afternoon had been fun. But it hurt, too. They'd moved on with their lives. Settled down. Some even with kids, now. And rightly or wrongly, he still saw them through seventeen-year-old eyes. He'd been surprised to learn that one of his old buddies was now in the state pen for distributing drugs to minors. Colton shuddered. In the throes of his misbehavior as a teenaged delinquent, he'd never thought of his actions as bad... And yet, if Travis hadn't given him an ultimatum and kicked him out, would he have ended up the same way? He sipped on his whiskey, pondering.

"You ever think you'll settle down?" Parker asked.

Colton kicked the dirt. "Prob'ly not. Rodeo life is no life for a wife and family. And I'm not quitting until I win World Champion."

"What happens when you do?"

Colt gave Parker a sardonic smile. "Guess I'll be in the market for a wife, then."

"But in the meantime, you'll leave a string of broken hearts across the west." Cassidy wrapped her arms around Parker's waist, perching her chin on his shoulder. "Am I right?"

Colton quirked a smile and toasted the couple. "I don't kiss and tell." The words had barely left his mouth when Lydia joined him.

Her laugh cut through the night air like music. "That's new."

"What's new?" Cassidy turned to look at her sister.

"Colton. Kissing and telling. I think at one point he had a girlfriend in six towns."

At least the darkness hid the flames that shot up his neck. "Aww, you can't hold that against me. I've learned a few things since then."

"Like how not to get caught?" she teased.

But he didn't want teasing. Not now. And he didn't want her thinking ill of him. "Like maybe I'm secretly a one-woman man."

She laughed, genuinely amused. "I'll believe that when pigs fly over to mama's food truck and line up for bacon."

Her joke cut the tension, made everyone laugh. "You always did have the best zingers," he said after Parker and Cassidy took their leave.

She grinned back at him, and his chest went funny. "Had to, to survive in our house."

"Dance with me?"

"Lose the cigar."

Without taking his eyes off her, he tossed the cigar.

"Give me your drink."

"It's straight whiskey."

"And?" She held out her hand.

He handed over the plastic cup and she downed the remains in one gulp. Damn if that wasn't sexy as sin. He extended his hand, and she stepped into his embrace, easily following his lead as he moved them to the edge of where the other couples danced by firelight. It was the perfect night for a bonfire. Cool and crisp, mid-forties. Perfect for snuggling. For a moment, neither spoke, they swayed to the beat of Lady Antebellum in the firelight. Then they both filled the silence at once.

"You first," Colton said with a laugh.

Lydia tilted her head back, studying him. "I heard you rodeo. And you've done well."

He shrugged. "I guess you can say that. I started off in saddle bronc, but the last two years, I've made a run for best All-Around Cowboy, and it's hard to do that in a single event. So I expanded to bareback and bullriding."

"Why not do a timed event like steer wrestling or tie-down roping?"

He grinned down at her. You could take a girl out of the country... "Honestly? Takes too much precision. Costs too much. In the rough stock events, it's just me and the ride."

"Man against beast," she said with a roll of her eyes.

"Exactly. And when I was eighteen and sleeping on the ground, or in the back of a truck, I knew if I just held on, I'd have a fighting chance to make enough money to get to the next town."

Her eyes went wide. Even in the dim light, he could see the effect his words had on her. "First few years after I left were hard." Brutal. If it hadn't been for Dottie securing a ranch-hand spot for him with a friend of a cousin who lived in

Steamboat, he'd have ended up homeless.

"I had no idea," she murmured. "I always wondered."

Colton's heart twisted painfully. He'd always regretted not staying in touch with Dottie, and by extension, her. But he'd been young and cocky and full of himself. And had a chip on his shoulder the size of a fourteener. "But enough about me. I want to hear about Libby-Lyds. What have you been up to?"

She scowled at him. "More than finding cheap thrills in the next town."

Sassy. He deserved that. He'd been an ass to her. He'd take her barbs as long as she stayed in his arms and kept talking to him.

"Because those touchy-feely metrosexuals you date are a better bet?" He dared her to disagree with him. "Let me guess. You're one of those girls who just likes to be held all night long in your white flannel nightie."

She stiffened in his embrace. *A-ha.* He had her there. She could deny all she wanted, but he had her number.

"Judge me all you like, but at the end of the day, who's living and who's playing it safe?" He shouldn't goad her this way. But he'd scrapped and fended for himself, and so what if he enjoyed life along the way? He'd always been completely upfront with the women he'd bedded. No feelings, no commitment. Only pleasure.

Her eyes snapped to his, lit with anger and something else. Something hotter. "And maybe you've misjudged me. Maybe I'm one of those girls who takes what she wants and wears a red lace thong."

Before he could respond. Before he could even think of a quippy comeback, she'd tugged on his neck, raised on tiptoe and pressed her mouth against his.

She'd kissed him once before. So long ago, she probably didn't recall, but he did. He'd thought about that kiss off and on through the years, the only kiss, however brief, that had been delivered like he mattered.

This kiss? Was way more. Hotter, angrier.

She tasted of whiskey and sin wrapped up in soft curves and apple pie. With a low groan, he snaked an arm around her and pulled her flush against his body. Her sweetness molded against him with a heat that made his head spin. Any number of people would tan his hide for the way he was kissing her, but he didn't care. Her tongue slid against his, and he received it willingly, drinking her in, letting the sensations pull him heavenward, out of his skin, out of his past, and into a future of possibility where he was worthy of someone as special as Lydia Grace.

CHAPTER 4

W HAT WAS SHE doing, kissing Colton? At the moment, she didn't care to answer that question. His comments burned her up, hit too close to home. She'd simply wanted to prove she'd shed the good-girl persona he and his friends had pigeon-holed her with. But he tasted too damned good, of sweet tobacco, whiskey, and so enticingly male that she couldn't stop herself. Didn't want to stop. His mouth on her was like fire. No downtown banker had ever kissed her like this, with total possession. Like they weren't standing in a crowd at the edge of a bonfire. Where, if they were seen, there'd be plenty to gossip about at her mother's food truck in the morning.

He let out a possessive sound, wrapping an arm around her and pulling her tight, and took over the kiss. It was like a bomb went off in her brain, laying waste to all thought, leaving room only for feeling. Cascades of sensation settled in a warm rush at the apex of her thighs.

Maybe it was the booze, or the fact that three days ago her career had been upended, and she had nothing left to lose. She'd already lost her job and her dignity. What was the worst that could happen if she let go? She'd spent her entire life worrying about what was next, and where had it landed her? Unemployed and back in Prairie. She was wearing a red lace thong, dammit. She was going to live in this moment and let it carry here wherever it willed.

Colton lifted his head, his breath coming in harsh, uneven pulses. "You sure you wanna tangle with me, sweetheart? I'm pretty sure your mama would tan my hide if she found us together."

She tilted up her chin defiantly. "I'm not planning on telling mama," she muttered huskily, pulling him in for another kiss, because who in their right mind would want to stop kissing him? He'd unleashed a heat inside her that wouldn't be quenched with anything but more of him. All of him.

His hand drifted lower, cupping her hip, and she pressed against him, fully aware of his arousal. Colt lifted his head again. "You sure you're not drunk?"

"Only on your kisses," she quipped. "And I want more." Lordy, did she want more. His hands on her breasts, between her legs. His mouth on her. His reaction when he saw her with nothing but red lace. Grabbing his hand, she glanced around, then gave a tug, heading in the direction of the barn. Once they were out of the pull of the bonfire, they were encased in darkness. No one would notice them now. Not with the booze and the music.

"What are you doing?" he whispered urgently.

"What does it look like?" She reached the barn door and gave a push, relieved that it glided open with minimal sound.

As soon as she stepped in, her nose filled with the scent of sweet clover and horse. It had been ages since she'd set foot in the Kincaid barn, but if she recalled correctly, the tack room was immediately to her left. With the bravado that only came from recklessness, she stepped left, crossing her fingers that she wouldn't walk into anything in the dark. Luck was on her side, and as they moved deeper into the tack room, moonlight coming through the window on the far wall cast everything in blue and black shadow. She turned back to Colton and looped her hands around her neck. "Much better."

His hands came to her hips, pulling her close. "What do you want, Lydia?" he asked, voice rough.

"You," she answered simply. God's truth. She wanted to take her fill. Please herself for once.

"Why?"

"Why not? It's a wedding. We're here... I like how you kiss," she answered boldly, pulse pounding. The scandalous nature of what she was proposing made her skin tingle all over. She liked this newer, wilder self and tipped her chin to receive his kiss. His tongue slid against hers, teasing and seductive, but his hands stayed firmly planted on her hips. Dropping her arm, she rucked up her dress on one side, exposing her thigh, inviting him to touch her.

Colton let out a strangled groan. "Are you trying to kill me?"

"Quite the contrary."

"I'm trying to be a gentleman here."

Taking a step back, she whisked off her dress, thankful she'd chosen a stretchy knit material with no buttons, no clasps to catch or tear. "I don't want you to be a gentleman, Colt."

His face went taut. All angles and planes in the dim light. She stood before him, heart pounding erratically, waiting for him to move. Hope flickered, then faltered as the moment stretched between them. When he finally moved, it was to caress her with the barest graze of skin on skin. The back of a finger drawn down from her collarbone over the swell of her breast. Her nipples strained against the silk of her bra, aching to be touched, pinched. "Perfection." His voice dropped, coming out rough and hard, like gravel.

He stood so close, she could feel the heat radiating off him, warming her skin against the cool night air. Colt continued a feather-light perusal down her torso, fingers gliding just inside her panties. Her breath caught, and she held herself still, nerve endings vibrating with anticipation of his next move. His fingers swept through her slick swollen folds, and she bit her lip to keep from crying at the ecstasy of it.

Colt lowered his head to her neck, breath skating in heated whorls across her skin. "You have no idea how much I want you," he murmured.

If it was half as much as she wanted him, then she had every idea.

"How gorgeous you are in the moonlight." He slipped his fingers from her, and gripped her hip as he peppered her collarbone with hot kisses. "But we can't do this."

His day's growth scraped her flesh like fine sandpaper, sending tongues of fire rippling down her limbs. She dropped her head back, giving him access to her neck. "Yessss," she hissed on a breath.

In the recesses of her brain, his words registered. "No."

She lifted her head, confused. "Wait. What do you mean?" Her heart yo-yoed sickeningly.

Colt groaned and pressed his mouth to her temple. Then he stepped back, hands clasping her bare shoulders, voice laced with regret. "You deserve more than a fifteen-minute fuck in the tack room."

Mortification incinerated her insides. At least the darkness hid her flaming cheeks. "But I... you..." What had she done? Hot tears pricked her eyes. Was she so pathetic that even the town bad boy would reject her? That would be a resounding *yes.* Never had she wished more fervently for the earth to swallow her up. Or a flying horse to spirit her away. She clenched her stomach, fighting to keep the quiver from her voice. She would *not* let Colton see her humiliation. "I see." By a miracle, her voice stayed even. She swallowed as she bent for her dress, and turned her back as she slipped it over her head.

"I'm sorry."

Colt sounded like he wanted to say more, but really, what else was there to say when he'd already rejected her? Further explanation would only draw out the discomfort for both of them. Best to make a quick getaway and preserve what little dignity she had left. Smoothing her skirt and rolling her shoulders, she turned. His face didn't show a shred of emotion, but his sheer physical presence overwhelmed her, his body tense and hard. He'd always been good looking, but now? The utter masculinity of him was breathtaking, even in her humiliation. "No." She shook her head. "I'm sorry. I-I misread... I-I'll see you around." She flashed him an empty smile and brushed past him before he could hear the catch in her throat.

"Lyds, wait," he called after her.

Shaking her head, she kept moving, slipping out the door. The cold air pricked her lungs as she skirted the bonfire and blindly followed the fence line between the Kincaid and Grace properties, until she reached the old gate one of the families had constructed decades ago. Once the gate clicked shut behind her, she let the tears come. She'd never be able to show her face around the Kincaids again.

CHAPTER 5

H OLY SHIT. COLT ran a hand through his hair and stared up at the wooden slats comprising the ceiling in the tack room, trying to wrap his head around what had just happened. How long had it been since they'd snuck into the barn? Fifteen-minutes? Maybe? And in that short span of time, she'd managed to shove his whole world off its axis.

She must have been intoxicated.

It was the only explanation for why she'd come onto him like that. Not that he'd minded. Hell, if it had been any other woman, his pants would have been down around his ankles in a hot second. But this was *Lydia*. The embodiment of goodness. Everything he wasn't. His cock jerked against his jeans chastising him for his restraint. "Yeah, yeah. I'm an idiot." He shook his head and let out a ragged sigh.

As long as he lived, he'd never forget the way her creamy skin glowed in the moonlight. And how slick her pussy had been. *For him.* And fuck, her kisses. He'd never been more surprised, or turned on. But he was pretty sure if word got out, that there'd be a long line of folks lined up to take their shot. It wouldn't matter to them in the least that *she'd* been the one to come onto him. All they'd see was that the town's biggest disappointment had tapped the good girl everyone loved and respected.

Colt puffed his cheeks and let out another slow breath,

trying to pull his galloping heart back to a walk. He smiled bitterly into the dark. This. This was why he never wasted time being honorable. It sucked. So much easier to live in the moment, screw the consequences, and move on before things got emotional.

He lived by one rule – no regrets.

Okay, yeah, he *definitely* regretted pushing Lydia away. But he'd regret the consequences of *not* pushing her away more. He might live for fun, but he wasn't an idiot. Everyone in town knew why Travis kicked him out ten years ago. And although wild horses couldn't have dragged the admission from him then, he was mature enough now to see that Travis had done him a favor. Probably saved his life. One of many conversations he and his brother needed to have in the coming days. But not on his wedding day.

Giving the tack room one last look, he turned and made his way back to the bonfire. He scanned the faces halfheartedly. Lydia wouldn't be among them. *Go after her* his conscience pricked. *Talk to her.* Someone put a whiskey in his hand. The party was breaking up, and he made his way back to the house, pulling up a chair to the large table that had been returned to the center of the room. Conversation floated around him as one by one, Travis and Elaine's closest friends joined them at the table. Colt didn't feel like joining in. He was more interested in the contents of his glass, but he also wasn't going to be rude to his brother on his wedding day. As he swirled the ice and amber liquid, his mind kept returning to Lydia. The curve of her hip in the palm of his hand. Her sweet, plump mouth. He was an idiot for letting her go. He was a bigger idiot for wanting more. He was a fucking rodeo champion, for chrissakes. Women slipped their hotel keys and more into his shirt pocket when they congratulated him with a wink and a smile on a good ride. He'd never wanted more, needed more, from any of them.

It irked him that she thought he was easy. Lydia had been the only one to see through his shenanigans, the only one brave enough, or stupid enough as he thought back then, to challenge him to be a better person. A better man. Hell, he'd only been a kid when he left, but he was a better man now. Wasn't he? He owned a ranch. Had a great career. Discovered he was a smart businessman. Okay, so he still might be a little wild where the ladies were concerned, but who could blame him?

Why would Lydia want a quick hookup? That wasn't her. He puzzled on that as he brought the whiskey to his mouth, letting the burn sharpen his focus. Prairie's new police chief, Weston Tucker, who Travis had introduced as a former military buddy, was talking. "Have you given anymore thought to Resolution Ranch?"

"What's this?" Brodie Sinclaire asked. Brodie was a few years older than Colton, but had been just as wild in their youth. He'd been surprised to learn Brodie had been married nearly a year.

"Nothing." Travis waved a hand. "Just a harebrained idea of Weston's to get the ranch running again and turn it into a place to help veterans land on their feet."

"Using animal husbandry, like what Hope does, and working with a counselor I know," added Weston.

Hope Hansen leaned in. She'd married Ben Sinclaire at the same time last year. "You know," she said, tapping a finger on the table and glancing over at Ben. "I've been thinking along those same lines. Using what I've been teaching you with others. Would you be interested in collaborating?"

While not the only single guy in Prairie by a long shot,

Colton's insides twisted with the realization that life in Prairie had continued without him. Yes, he'd walked away without a backward glance, and with the exception of Hope's brothers, who he'd run into at the NFR's in Las Vegas a few years back, he hadn't seen or heard from any of them. Again, his conscience pricked at him. Would things be different, would *he* be different if he'd tried to re-establish contact once he'd cleaned up his act? Would people see him in a more positive light? Would *Lydia* see him in a more positive light?

His thoughts flicked back to the conversation at hand. His brother really wanted to start a ranch for veterans? An honorable idea. A good idea. He knew a few rodeo hands who'd served overseas. Solid guys, who struggled. The ones that found a purpose upon returning home seemed to do better. The guys he knew were some of the best horse handlers on the circuit.

Colton stared at the enthusiastic faces surrounding the table. How long had it been since he'd been a part of something bigger than himself? Had he ever? He studied the ice in his glass, focusing on the way it caught the light. An ache pushed against his ribs. He'd been looking out for number one his whole life. Had never lifted a finger around the ranch. Had driven his dad, then later Travis to distraction with his bad grades and substance abuse. "I'd be willing to invest a portion of my earnings," he offered quietly.

Conversation stopped as everyone turned to stare. He locked gazes with his brother as they engaged in a silent tug-of-war.

Travis shook his head dismissively. "No way. I can't let you do that." All eyes swung to Travis, then landed back on him as the silent volley continued. Travis cleared his throat. "I appreciate the offer. But you only just got home. I don't even know how long you're staying."

He didn't know either. He was on a day to day basis at the moment, at least until the NFRs in a few more weeks. "Silent partner only. I'll stay out of the way." Colton countered firmly.

Travis's expression went from chagrined to doubtful to hopeful when his wife chimed in. "You know I can help with managing the books, among other things."

Colton's heart gave a painful squeeze at the way they stared at each other, love on their faces. He shut his eyes against the thickening in his throat. No one, not one person, had ever looked at him that way. With adoration. He pushed aside the momentary longing. He had everything he needed, a roof over his head, money in the bank, fame. There was no place in his life for touchy-feely shit. It only complicated things. He lifted his glass with the others as Weston offered a toast. "To Elaine and Travis, may your love infuse this ranch with new life, and bring second chances to those who need it most."

Second chances. Is that why he'd returned to Prairie? For a second chance? He wasn't sure he liked the murky feelings it stirred up. Colton pushed back from the table a little too forcefully as soon as the bride and groom kissed. "I think it's time for me to head out."

Travis made a face. "You only just got here."

"Stay with us," "We have room," a chorus of offers sounded.

Heat raced up his spine. This was too much. Everyone was being too nice. He waved them off, flashing a smile. "No need. I booked a place in Manhattan."

"Jamey'd tan my hide if I didn't insist you stay at the lodge with us," Brodie offered. "Manhattan's too far."

Colton shook his head. He didn't feel like making small talk, and he'd had enough swapping stories of the old days to last him a good long while. "Thanks, kindly. But I'll take a raincheck."

"You're coming back tomorrow?" Travis asked, the hopeful look returning to his eyes.

Colton nodded once. "Sure. We'll talk then."

CHAPTER 6

A S FAR AS Colt was concerned, eleven a.m. was still too early to show up at the ranch. If it were him, he'd be pissed as hell at anyone who dared show their face before two in the afternoon the day after his wedding. But Colt had already enjoyed a hearty breakfast at The Chef in downtown Manhattan and successfully avoided the holiday shoppers lining up at the local Wal-Mart, ready to knock their Christmas lists out before lunch. And he'd managed to avoid not one, but two phone calls from Hal and Harrison Carter. It irked him to no end that they assumed he'd jump every time they called. They might be his biggest sponsor, and while he couldn't afford to lose them, especially after offering to help Travis with Resolution Ranch, they didn't own him. He was his own man, and there would be plenty of time at the NFRs to hash out any differences they had over a steak and a few beers.

The drive back to Prairie from Manhattan had been pleasant enough, and the bleached gold grass and leafless trees that peppered the Flint Hills this time of year offered an equally dramatic counterpoint to the high sagebrush flats and dramatic granite cliffs of Northern Colorado.

Wild horses would trample him before he'd admit he was lonely, but casting about with time on his hands left him uneasy and at loose ends. Colt threw his truck into park in the vacant lot behind what used to be Dottie's Diner and looked around. He didn't recognize Prairie anymore. The Prairie he'd known, whether he loved it was debatable, was gone. His conscience pricked at him again. He'd been in Texas when he'd gotten word of the tornado that ripped through Prairie. For a dreadful, heart-stopping moment, fear had turned his blood to ice, until he'd seen his brother on national television describing what had happened. But he'd shied away from taking action, figuring he'd be branded as an opportunist for crawling out of the woodwork after being gone so many years. Instead, he'd sent an anonymous check to the foundation.

But seeing his hometown like this? Stirred him. Unsettled him, triggering an unfamiliar ache beneath his sternum. Maybe it was just breakfast. Or maybe it was his conscience telling him he'd been an asshole and he had a lot of making up to do. He could start by taking a walk over to Dottie's food truck. He admired Dottie's grit. She might have been way too up in his business when he'd been a rowdy kid, but no one, not even him, had ever dared cross her. And in the end, her big heart had saved him.

Hopping down from the truck, he jammed his hands deep into the pockets of his jacket and headed for Main. No surprise, the line at the food truck stretched halfway to the picnic tables scattered nearby. He scanned the crowd for Lydia, wishing for the umpteenth time he'd figured out a way to get her number. More than anything, he wanted to see her. Make sure she was okay. Maybe take her on a walk. Hell, who was he kidding? He wanted to pick things up where they left off. His balls still ached from last night. He hadn't even been able to take himself in hand as he'd lain wide awake counting the ceiling tiles. It felt sacrilegious. He might give in if the need became too great, but what he wanted more than anything was to bury himself balls deep in her sweetness and know she meant it. That he was something more than a pressure valve being released. Maybe that was asking too much.

Dottie stood at the counter when it was his turn to step up. She gave him an indulgent smile. "We have pumpkin pie and coffee with whipped cream on special today. Can I interest you?"

No one made pie like Dottie. "Of course you can." He gave her his best smile and jumped in before he lost his nerve. "Know where I can find Lydia today?"

Dottie gave him a hard stare. "Whatever for?"

His stomach traded places with his tonsils. "I... wanted to make sure she got home okay."

"She did. She was still asleep when I left."

Dottie must have x-ray vision into his soul. There was no reason for her to make things this hard for him. Unless she'd already firmly placed him in the 'not for my daughter' category.

"I... ah... also want to talk to her about a pair of boots." An angel must have nudged his memory, as the conversations he'd overheard last night about Lydia's shoemaking popped into his head. "I swear. Just talk."

"Boots, huh? Well, you've come to the right woman. No one makes shoes like my Lydia." Dottie gave him the stink-eye as she wiped down the narrow countertop. "Talk better be all you have in mind, Colton."

He held up his hands in surrender. "Wouldn't dream of anything else, Mrs. Grace." At least not that he'd admit to her. "Can I give you my number to pass along? In case she's interested in talking?"

Dottie smirked, but pushed across a piece of scrap paper and a pen. He quickly scrawled his number and pushed it back. "I'll see she gets this," she said and handed him his pumpkin pie and a cup of coffee. "On me today," she smiled down at him. "I always knew you'd get on the right track and make something of yourself if you had the chance. I'm so proud you came home for Travis's wedding."

But not so proud that he was good enough for her daughter. That stung.

"You headed over to see the newlyweds?" Dottie asked.

Colton nodded, still chewing on Dottie's warning.

"Here." Dottie reached down, pulled up a folded paper bag, and handed it through the window. "I know how it is at a wedding. You never get to eat your own food. I saved them a cream pie. Travis's favorite. And make sure Dax doesn't eat it all. I swear that little boy is a bottomless pit," she complained with a twinkle in her eye.

"He's not the only one," Colton winked as he accepted the bag. He'd been a bottomless pit growing up, too. How often had Dottie saved a cookie or a slice of pie for the kids who'd stopped by the diner after school?

Fifteen minutes later Colton pulled onto the long drive that led to the farmhouse. No nerves today. It might not feel like home. Probably wouldn't ever, but at least the anxiety was gone.

This time the door opened before his fist touched the wood. "IT'S UNCLE COLT," Dax shouted, wrapping him in a kiddie bear-hug. Had the kid been waiting for him?

"Morning to you, too, kiddo." He ruffled the boy's hair, the tight, queasy sensation wrapping around his chest again.

Dax lifted his head, eyes like saucers. "I seen—"

"I *saw*," corrected Elaine.

"The pictures in the bedroom. Was that really you riding a bucking bronco?"

He shot a look at Travis who stood pouring coffee. "You kept all those photos?"

"Why wouldn't I?"

"Because you disowned me?"

Travis arched a brow, as if to say, *so you want to dive in right now?*

Yeah, he did.

Travis let out a heavy sigh. "Why don't you come in, have a cup of coffee and slice up some of that pie Dottie sent over. Not the first time she's sent over pie," he answered before Colton could ask how Travis knew what was in the bag.

"Can I take your coat, Colton?" Elaine asked from where she was curled up on the couch.

"I got it, thanks." He shrugged out of his jacket, then exchanged the bag for a steaming mug of coffee.

"I never disowned you. I did tell you that you couldn't stay here until you'd cleaned up your act."

"Same difference," he said stubbornly, not quite ready to admit his version of events might be a little skewed.

Travis regarded him soberly. "I'll own that I was too high-handed and probably overbearing."

"Probably?"

Travis narrowed his eyes a fraction. "You were hell-bent on self-destructing, and I wasn't going to sit idly by and let you do it." His face softened. "You were my kid brother."

Colton's gut clenched, he'd been dreading this conversation for years. Part of why he'd avoided returning to Prairie for so long. But it needed to happen. Both of them had held onto old hurts, let them fester and the boil needed to be lanced in order to heal. "I hated you."

Travis flinched. "I know."

"I kept expecting you to follow me."

"I know."

"And when you didn't…" his voice trailed off. He'd never felt so alone as he had in those first few months. Nobody, not even Dottie, knew that he'd been kicked off the first two ranches he'd worked at. Let go for showing up stoned, doing shit work. He'd squatted in the woods, even woke up frost covered one morning. He'd have frozen to death that first winter if not for a crusty old hunter who made a deal with him after catching him trespassing. He'd worked his ass off for Thirsty Stevens. By spring he'd sobered up, and Thirsty had brought him along on a cattle drive. "I'd never felt so alone," Colton uttered thickly, not liking the ache in his belly.

"You make it seem like I enjoyed kicking you off the ranch."

"Didn't you?" he accused, failing to keep the resentment from his voice.

"Of course not. Dottie's never wasted an opportunity to let me know how disappointed she was in me. Who do you think pushed me to reach out?"

"So if not for Dottie we wouldn't be talking now?" Grief sliced through him, fresh and sharp. Maybe he'd been a fool to come home.

"No. I'd been thinking about it." Travis scraped a hand over his face. "Hell, Colt. I know I was an ass and I felt like shit about it. I kept tabs on you… after a while. I set up a Google alert with your name." He looked shamefaced.

"Stalking me?" Colton laughed bitterly.

"Honestly? I was afraid you'd end up dead in a ditch someplace, and I was still in and out of missions and dealing with my own shit." Travis grimaced. "But then you started winning, and I didn't want to fuck it up."

Colton speared a fork into the cream pie and took a bite,

not really tasting it. He'd nursed a grudge against his brother for so many years, he wasn't sure how to fill that void, now that they were attempting to patch things up. He felt like he was swinging in the wind, helpless.

Travis braced his hands on the counter and stared hard at him. "I'm not proud of how I behaved. All I can offer is that I didn't have the coping skills to manage myself, let alone parent you and try and run a ranch from the other side of the world when I was gone. I fucked up, and I'll always regret not being a better example to you."

"You think that would have made me a better man?"

Travis flashed him a wry grin. "You've always had a touch of the crazy in you. Still do, according to the rodeo blogs. I'm just glad you never got arrested."

Heat prickled up his neck. "What's wrong with wanting to have a little fun so long as no one gets hurt?"

Travis gave him a fatherly glower. "Fun is good. Lord knows, Elaine has helped me have more of it. But at some point, you have to grow up. Take responsibility. What have you done with all your endorsement money?"

Pissed more of it away than he should have. "I've saved some."

"How much?"

"I bought a small ranch outside of Steamboat Springs, Colorado."

Travis's eyes widened. "No joke?"

"I'm not a dumb-ass. And in case you were wondering, I was serious last night. About helping you."

He waved a hand. "Calm down, calm down. I never said you were stupid. Glad to hear someone's talked some sense into you."

Colton had gotten lucky. Rodeo champ Ty Sloane had

seen him lurking around the chutes when the rodeo had come to Steamboat, and had taken him under his wing. When he'd started winning, Ty hadn't been stingy with his advice. "This is a finite career, son. Your body can only take so much. Wooing the ladies is nice, but them that's got is them that gets. Put your money in land, and make sure you have plenty to pay the bills when you're too old or broken to work."

Colton had seen too many old cowboys barely making it and spending their entire earnings on booze. And now that he was looking at his winningest year ever, it was time to diversify. And beyond the money, if helping Travis would mend things between them, it was money well spent.

Travis crossed his arms and narrowed his gaze. "What I want to know though, is whether or not you're going to stick around, or if this is a one and done visit." He tilted his chin to where Elaine and Dax were sprawled on the couch reading. "I've got a family now. I'd love for you to be a part of it."

The air whooshed out of Colton's lungs and his stomach filled with unease. "I…" he took a deep breath. "I can't move back to Prairie, if that's what you're asking."

Travis rolled his eyes. "That's not what I'm asking, although I hope you come 'round more than once in a blue moon. What I mean is, there's a kid over there who's pretty interested in you, and maybe more someday soon, can you visit? Stay in touch?"

Colton let out the breath he'd been holding. "Of course. If you don't get sick of me. I-I'd like that." He smiled genuinely at his older brother, heart skipping erratically.

"I won't get sick of you, Uncle Colt," piped up Dax. "Will you teach me how to bust a bronc?"

Both men chuckled. "You've been watching too many old cowboy movies, kiddo. Learn how to ride a horse first."

"I'm gettin' good," Dax answered proudly. "Dad lets me go on rides with him."

Colton snuck a glance at his brother, marveling at how happy Travis looked.

Travis held his gaze, a teasing glint in his eye. "So. Were you planning on telling me about you and Lydia Grace?"

CHAPTER 7

S UNLIGHT STREAMED BRIGHTLY through the window as
Lydia's eyes fluttered open and a demon took an icepick
to her forehead. Groaning, she rolled to her side and pulled
the pillow over her head. The motion only increased the
relentless pounding.

The inside of her mouth felt like sawdust. Stomach? A
little queasy. All the reasons why Lydia rarely drank came
crashing back with vicious force. How much *had* she drunk
last night? She groaned as the throbbing in her head surged.
Even with the pillow covering her, it was too bright in here.
She slipped a hand underneath and covered her eyes, sighing
with relief.

The relief was short-lived, as someone began to knock
insistently on her bedroom door. "Lyds?"

Cassie.

"I'm still sleeping," she groaned, a new round of pounding right behind her eyeballs taking her breath away.

The door creaked. "It's eleven. Are you gonna sleep the
day away?"

Ugh. "Yes," she whined, rolling over and turning her back
to the door. She could do whatever she wanted. After all, she
was on vacation. Permanent vacation. "Go 'way."

Cassie's chuckles filled the room. "Somebody's
hungover," she called out in a sing-song voice, moving

through the room and yanking open the curtains.

Even through the pillow, Lydia could sense light flooding the room. "Hey, stop that."

Her sister laughed mercilessly. "Ohmygod. You really were drunk last night."

"I don't want to hear it." She just wanted her head to stop screaming at her.

Cassie yanked off the covers, still laughing. "Nope, nope, nope. You're gonna hear it. Sit up."

There was no winning this battle. Once Cassie got it in her head to do something, that was it. With a heavy sigh, she removed the pillow and sat up, squeezing her eyes against the blazing sunlight and the accompanying wave of nausea that roiled through her.

"Here. This will help." Cassie held out a glass of fizzy water and two pills.

Lydia accepted the offering, grimacing at the flavor, but grateful for the water. And the ibuprofen.

Cassie sat on the bed, smirking. "They'll kick in shortly. Chores are done, and Pops is checking on livestock. He said don't wait lunch for him."

"I never want to eat again."

"That bad, huh?" Cassie shook her head sympathetically, laughter sparkling in her eyes. "Why don't you take a hot shower, and I'll meet you downstairs with some strong coffee and pancakes. It won't be mama's breakfast, but it should help." She stood and paused at the door. "And then I want to hear about last night."

Shit.

She pressed her temples trying to piece together last night. Old Fashioneds. Bonfire. Colton. Kissing. Lots of kissing. Clothes off? Heat flooded her. *Oh no.* She hadn't... had she?

Maybe the shower would help. She dragged in a breath. "Sure. I'll be right down."

Once she heard her sister on the stairs, Lydia rose and stepped gingerly down the hall, only relaxing when she stepped into the hot water. She braced a hand on the wall, letting the hot jets sluice over her. They'd danced and kissed. Her body came alive thinking about the kiss they'd shared. He might be a devil, but lordy, could the man kiss. An ache bloomed between her thighs at the thought of his mouth on her. Sure. Strong. Possessive.

No wonder they'd ended up in the barn. But she couldn't remember what happened after she'd ripped her dress off. How had she gotten home? Had she slept with Colton? Panic momentarily sliced through her. What if? Her stomach dropped. No. She always carried condoms with her. Not that she'd ever relied on them once. But she'd been shameless about handing them out to her girlfriends. Surely, she would have...

She turned her face into the stream, breathing through her mouth as the water hit her face. No more red thongs for her. No more whiskey. Ever.

No more Colton.

How could she face him again after last night? How could she face anyone?

She sighed heavily. Hiding out in the shower wouldn't change last night's events, or the week leading up to last night. What did Cassie always say? Time to put on her big girl panties? Squaring her shoulders, she turned off the water and stepped out of the tub. At least she could arm herself with her favorite terrycloth robe and fuzzy slippers. She'd never have worn anything like this in New York, but here, she was in her comfort zone. And there was something so reassuring about being at home amongst family who loved her. Even when they discovered she'd made a real mess of her life.

She toweled her hair to damp and gave a last glance in the mirror. The shower hadn't done a thing for her bleary eyes, but at least she no longer felt like the bottom of a wastebasket. The heavenly aroma of coffee greeted her as she lightly stepped down the stairs. Her head still hurt, but now it was more of a persistent throb instead of the icepick brigade taking up residence behind her eyes. She could manage this. And after a cup of coffee, she could face what remained of the day.

Cassie turned as she rounded the corner into the kitchen, and waved her to the table. God bless her sister. Her favorite mug waited, already doctored with cream. With a grateful sigh, she slid into a chair and wrapped her hands around the steaming mug. Coffee always tasted better when someone else prepared it. Of course, she had been banned from making coffee at her office. But why learn the art of coffee making when there was always someone to hand her a cup like this? She took a sip. "You and mama always make the best coffee."

At the stove, Cassie barked out a laugh. "You're *such* a princess. That's just because we were always first up. You never did learn how, did you?" Her tone of voice implied she already knew the answer.

"No need to mess with perfection."

Cassie brought two plates piled with pancakes and covered in syrup and set one down in front of her before seating herself across the table. "So. How long do we get to enjoy you for this time? I feel so lucky I've seen you twice this year."

Cassie was right. It *was* unusual for her to be home, let alone twice. But there was no way she'd have missed Cassie's wedding the month before. Even if Christian LaSarte had thrown a manbaby tantrum over it. Come to think of it.

That's when her troubles with him had started. Egocentric prima donna. Women might wait hours in line for the chance to buy his shoes, but the man chewed people up and spit them out. Her mistake? She'd been arrogant enough to think it would never happen to her. She let out a bitter laugh and shook her head, spearing her pancakes with vehemence.

"Lyds? What's up?" Cassie's voice instantly grew concerned.

Lydia slowly chewed, drawing courage from the salty sweet of buttermilk pancakes cooked in salted butter and drenched in maple syrup. "Turns out you'll get to enjoy me indefinitely," she answered quietly, cheeks flaming at the admission.

"What? What do you mean?"

Lydia let out a ragged breath. "I mean I won't be going home to New York."

Cassie set down her mug with a bang. "*What?* What happened?"

Lydia winced at the sudden noise, but nodded. "The short story is that I fell out of Christian LaSarte's graces and somehow, my shoe designs ended up in the hands of another assistant, who he deemed more worthy."

Cassie's mouth dropped open, and her eyes grew as wide as the pancakes on her plate. "*Noo.* He can't do that. Surely you could take him to court. Have you called Lex? Lex'll know how to handle this."

Good old Cassie. Lydia'd chafed against her sister's protective streak when they'd been young. But now, she was touched. And grateful.

"Lex is an environmental lobbyist. She doesn't deal with intellectual property."

"But she's a lawyer." Cassie waved a hand. "She could

send a lawyerish letter, right?"

"And do what, Cass? Give me back my job? My designs?" Lydia shook her head. "Intellectual cases are hard to prove. It's not considered stealing. It's considered *inspired*." Lydia quoted the air. "I know that somehow, my colleague saw my designs, but she was clever enough to change them just enough that they were now hers." Lydia grimaced. All that hard work, all that passion, down the toilet. "If it makes you feel better, I *did* talk to Lex." In one of those typical twin moments, Lexi had called Lydia the afternoon she'd walked out of her job, and the whole story had come pouring out as she walked down 5th Avenue. "But to pursue a case like this would take years and tens of thousands of dollars I don't have. It was better to cut my losses."

Cassie's eyebrows drew together. "But your designs–"

"I have no shortage of ideas. I'll *always* have other designs. I just have to figure out what to do with them." That was the crux of it. She laughed, shaking her head. "What's an unemployed shoe designer going to do in Prairie?"

Cassidy smiled slyly and dug into her pocket. "So is that what this is about?" She pushed a piece of paper across the table. "Colton Kincaid, huh? I always thought he was too much cowboy for you, sis."

Lydia's face flamed as the memory of their kiss came roaring back, making her mouth tingle. She shrugged nonchalantly. "I don't know what you're talking about."

"Your blush says you do. Something happen between the two of you at the wedding?"

Could the floor swallow her up right now? Lydia stirred her pancake pieces in the syrup. If she even peeped at Cassie, her sister would put two and two together. She could never hide anything from her sisters. She scooped up a bite and popped it into her mouth, chewing slowly.

"Lyds?"

She glanced up. She couldn't help it. As soon as their eyes met, it was game over. Cassidy covered her mouth, laughing with glee. "*Ohmygod you DID.*"

Lydia shook her head furiously. "I didn't." Her chest burned.

"Don't deny. You were always the worst liar. Was it good?"

Lydia brought her hands to her cheeks. She would never live this down. These were the kinds of stories that got hauled out at future Christmases and weddings. "I can't remember," she wailed, shaking her head.

Cassie gaped at her. "*You can't remember?* As in you were too drunk?"

Lydia nodded furiously. "Please don't say anything. Not to Caro or Lex. I will never live this down."

"Damn straight you won't," Cassie answered with awe in her voice. "No wonder he told mama he wanted to talk to you about a pair of boots. He wants to talk you out of yours."

Lydia rolled her eyes. "You're such a knee slapper."

"Would you do it?"

"Do what?"

"Make him a pair of boots?"

"I don't know." She shrugged. "I guess I could. I've never made men's shoes, but it can't be that different."

"You already checked out his feet, didn't you? I bet they were the perfect size." Cassidy laughed and waggled her eyebrows.

"Oh *stop* already." She had, she always did. She couldn't help it. She could discern a person's shoe size in one glance.

Cassie's expression turned serious. "Have you thought

45

about it?"

"Thought about what?" Lydia's guard went up. The look in her sister's eye only meant one thing. Trouble.

"Opening your own shop. Doing custom-made? How many pairs of wedding shoes have you made for the ladies here? I bet they'd let you take pictures. You'd have a built-in catalog. Make a pair of men's boots, and folks would go crazy. You'd have tons of orders pouring in. I know it."

Cassie's enthusiasm was infectious, even though the thought of striking out on her own terrified her. Making bespoke shoes was vastly different from dabbling in her spare time. "I don't have the startup funds. Shoemaking equipment, and materials, are expensive. Like tens of thousands of dollars expensive."

Cassie speared her with a determined look. "So what if you started small? Took only enough orders to help you purchase the next piece of equipment, or the material for the next pair?" Cassie's expression turned sly. "What if you got your cowboy to wear your boots everywhere? Nothing like a little free advertising."

"He's not my cowboy."

Cassie waggled her eyebrows. "But he might be. And he wants some boots."

Lydia suppressed a giggle. The way Cassie's voice lingered on the word *boots* implied far more than boots. "Nothing's ever free. Even you know that."

"Well, he's already interested, so why not ask him?" Cassie leaned forward, an excited light in her eye. "The worst he can do is say no. If he's serious about having you make a pair of boots, why not trade him? I don't follow rodeo, but I'm sure he has corporate sponsors."

A knock at the door saved her from answering. Lydia

sprang up, ignoring the stab behind her eyes as she moved too quickly. "I'll grab it."

The knock sounded again. More insistent this time.

"Coming," she called, as she straightened her robe and tightened the belt. She flung open the door, smile freezing on her face as the air left her lungs.

Colton Kincaid, looking as delectable as one of her mother's desserts, stood with an arm braced on the door jamb, smiling down at her with an expression that could only be called wolfish. Out of the frying pan and into the fire.

CHAPTER 8

F OR A SECOND, he forgot to breathe. Lydia's hair, still damp at the ends, curled in tousled waves. Heaven help him if this was what she looked like first thing in the morning. Soft and touchable, ready to be tumbled. Her eyes widened, and pink stained her cheeks. Not for the first time, he wished he'd taken her up on her offer the night before.

"Hi," she said, a husky note to her voice.

It might be rude, but he couldn't stop staring. In the light of day, she looked even more beautiful. Plump lips that invited kisses, curves that cried out to be worshipped with fingers and mouth. "You feeling okay?" he asked when he finally found his voice.

Her cheeks flushed darker, and she cast her eyes down. "I'll live." She glanced up through her eyelashes and quickly looked away. "So... did we, did we... ah–"

His belly shook. He shouldn't laugh at her discomfort, but she looked damned adorable all flustered. More than anything, he wanted to take her into his arms. Feel her soft curves melt into him the way they had last night. "You don't remember?"

Her gaze flew up, tangled with his. For a split second, before her eyes narrowed suspiciously, she'd looked at him like she wanted him. The way she had last night. Only this time she was sober, and damn if that didn't send a bolt of lust shooting straight to his toes.

"Would you regret it if I said yes?"

She drew in a sharp breath, mouth parting, cheeks flushing full red. She held his gaze while the air left his lungs and his heart galloped off to the races. And when the corner of her mouth slowly tilted up, he was lost. "Would you?" she countered.

"Hell, no," he answered, his throat suddenly rough.

She raised an eyebrow, as if not believing him. "The bad boy bedding the good girl in the barn at his brother's wedding. That'd give tongues something to wag about."

"Let 'em wag."

"Wouldn't that ruin your bad boy reputation? Being linked to someone uptight like me?"

He doubted she was uptight. Not if last night was any indication. Underneath her proper exterior was a hot-blooded wanton woman. "Maybe I'm not that bad anymore."

She stared at him a long moment. Did she feel it too? The electricity arcing between them? Again, her mouth curled up. "Maybe I'm not that good."

Holy. Hell.

His eyebrows jumped up. "What are you sayin'?" He leaned in, so close, her scent enveloped him, as warm and welcoming as a kitchen full of fresh-baked cookies. "You sayin' you wanna start somethin'?"

Lydia's pulse thrummed wildly at the base of her throat, and her delicate hand gripped her robe more tightly. "No," she whispered with a tremor.

Liar.

Her voice betrayed her. More than that – it was her eyes. "Such an unconvincing liar," he murmured, stroking a thumb down her cheek, not missing how her body trembled at his touch. He tilted her chin, watching raptly at how her tongue flicked out to slick her lower lip. It would be so easy to take her mouth right now, pick up where they left off. Assert his claim. But this was Lydia. Sooner or later, she'd regret it. She'd look at him with the same mixture of frustration and disappointment she always did before he'd left town years ago. "I'd make it good for you. So good, you'd never look at another overdressed metrosexual again."

She pulled her head back, eyes snapping. "So you're saying we didn't?"

Damn. He'd overplayed his hand.

He took a step back, jamming his hands deep into his coat pockets. "You might think I'm all kinds of bad, but I'd never take advantage of an intoxicated woman," he said flatly. That she'd think that of him, burned. But he'd never given her any reason to think highly of him. No, he'd only let her see him at his worst. And maybe someday, he'd unpack why that was. But that time wasn't now.

Hell, why was he even here? What had he hoped for by coming over? The only reason she'd made a pass at him last night was because she'd been flat-out drunk. Disappointment crashed over him. He cleared his throat. "I'm glad you got home okay. See you 'round." He turned to step off the gracious front porch.

"Wait." Her hand snagged his coat.

Slowly, he met her gaze. "Change your mind?" He flashed her a cocky grin.

Her eyes lit with something he couldn't identify, but her mouth tightened into a familiar thin line. "Cass said you were interested in a pair of boots?"

Oh. *That.* Dammit, he wanted to kiss her, not discuss the finer points of hand tooled leather. "I heard you're pretty good." Let her make of that whatever she wanted.

Damn if she didn't give him a coy smile and lift a shoulder. "You'll never want another."

"Nope." He barely shook his head, not taking his eyes from her. "Don't suppose I will." The air hummed between them, and he leaned in to take another whiff of her intoxicating mix of sweet and sexy. "Want another pair of boots," he rasped into her ear before pressing his mouth to her temple.

"*You...*you devil," she huffed indignantly, giving him a push.

Laughing, he took a step back.

"Everything okay?" called a voice from inside the house.

They spoke at the same time.

"Colt was just leaving," Lydia said.

"I was asking about a pair of boots."

Cassie appeared behind Lydia, looking sharply back and forth between the two of them. "Forget your manners, sis? Mama'd tan your hide if she learned you kept a guest on the porch."

"Then don't tell her," Lydia sassed as she stepped aside, motioning for him to come inside.

Colt bit back a snicker. He always liked Cassidy. Tossing a wink at Lydia, he followed Cassidy into the kitchen.

"Coffee?" Cassidy held out a mug.

"Thanks." He accepted the steaming cup.

"Don't mind Lydia. She's, er..."

"A bit wrecked?" Colt supplied.

Cassie laughed. "Yeah. You could say that."

Lydia bustled in holding a pad of paper and a pencil. "Mama still have a tape measure in the drawer?"

"Yep," answered Cassidy. Smirking as she shot a look his direction, she made her exit. "I'm off. Don't get too crazy in here, kids."

Lydia snorted while rooting through a door below the coffee maker. With her back still to him, she raised a finger. "Sit. Take off your boots."

Colton sat slowly, mesmerized by her backside. The fluffy robe might be bulkier than he liked on a lady, but it clung to her ass, putting her firm round curves on full display. Hers was an ass he'd love to grip while he buried himself in her softness.

"Stop staring," she said crisply, turning and catching him in the act.

He smiled unapologetically. "Nothing wrong with appreciating the view."

Her cheeks pinked up again, and her mouth twitched. "Boots."

Still holding her gaze, he toed off his boots, letting them fall to the floor with a thud. "What now?"

She held up the paper. "First, I trace your feet."

"On the first date? I'm surprised at you, Lyds," he said, unable to keep himself from sliding into her nickname.

She muttered something as she crouched by his feet. It sounded an awful lot like "*You have no idea what I could do on a first date.*"

He bit back a groan as she lifted her head and trapped his gaze. Her eyes smoldered with heat and his body answered in response. "What do you want?" he asked with too much rasp in his voice. She had him off-kilter. Like he had a bad grip on the rigging in the chute. And that would only land him one place – on his ass.

Her mouth twitched again, and she shook her head, grabbing his ankle and signaling him to lift his foot. "You could charm the skin off a rattlesnake."

"I promise only to bite gently." The words flew from his mouth before he could stop them.

She snorted and tugged on his other ankle, then motioned for him to stand. Her touch was light as she adjusted his foot and then traced the outline on the paper.

"You're tickling me," he said gruffly. Not that he minded. Her touch was gentle. Intimate. And it did funny things to his insides.

"Sorry. You can sit again. This will only take a few minutes."

He sat and wiggled his toes, unsure of what to do next. Hell, if she were a buckle bunny and they were at a bar after a rodeo, he'd woo her with whiskey and dancing, whisper scandalous things in her ear, invite her back to his room. But he was pretty sure if he tried that with Lydia he'd end up with a slap across the cheek. Regret burned a pit in his stomach, but he quickly pushed away the feeling. He might not be proud of his past behavior, but there was nothing he could do about it now.

"You okay?" She tilted her head sideways, a curious light in her eyes.

"Of course. Why?"

Her smile looked bemused. "You look... nervous." A soft giggle filled the kitchen as she firmly grabbed his foot and wrapped the tape around the ball, pausing to write down the measurement.

"No one's ever touched my feet like this before."

Their gazes collided again, and the electricity snapped between them. The seductive smile that lit her face had him squirming in the chair, and a myriad of lascivious thoughts flying through his head in rapid succession. If he'd let things play out to their natural conclusion last night, where would they be now? Holed up in his hotel room in Manhattan with her naked and crying for his touch? His cock pressed painfully against his jeans, and puffing out his cheeks, he studied the ceiling. This would not do. She was measuring his feet for chrissakes.

"Why I do believe you're blushing, Colton Kincaid," she said with a husky laugh as she took his other foot and made the same several measurements.

Aww, hell. He could feel the heat racing up his neck, building from his balls.

She winked at him and stood. "Getting naughty inside that thick skull of yours?"

He stood too, towering over her, at odds with himself about how to answer. She was clearly flirting with him, and he liked it. If she were anyone else, his hands would be inside her robe faster than the first time he was thrown from a bronc, but her mother's warning echoed in his head. With a sigh, he dragged a thumb down her cheek. He'd allow himself that much, at least. One touch of her silky skin. "Always." He wouldn't deny it. But he took a step back, pushing the chair out of the way.

He could have sworn disappointment flashed in her eyes, but she turned away too fast for him to be sure. She cleared her throat, placing the papers on the counter. "When you in town again?"

"Christmas. I'm headed to Vegas for the NFRs."

She turned back to him, arms crossed, leaning against the counter, all business. "I don't know what Mama told you, but I have to be upfront. I've never made men's boots before."

Damn. It might be for the best, but his cock disagreed. "Is there a difference?"

She stuck out her foot. "You tell me."

Okay, so she had a point. Her foot was tiny. Dainty, with a high arch that he ached to cover with kisses. But he couldn't keep his eyes off the creamy expanse of thigh her movement exposed as her robe fell away. Even more delectable in the light of day. "I see your point," he choked out. Hell, he had to get out of here before he crossed a line. Boldly holding his gaze, she lowered her leg and readjusted her robe. What the hell? Had she done that on purpose? Was she trying to make his balls explode?

"As I was saying," she continued primly as if she hadn't flashed him an eyeful of leg. "I've never made men's boots before, and I've also never charged for anything I've made."

"I'm sure they'll fit fine."

"They'll fit more than fine," she said with confidence. "But I'd like to hold off on discussing payment until I'm satisfied with my results."

The businessman inside him took notice, and he stood a little straighter as admiration zinged through him. "Fair enough." He liked this cocksure side of her. "Anything else we need to discuss?" He could come up with a whole laundry list, but he'd be the farm all his topics of discussion were off limits. "Color? Style?"

She cocked her head giving him a little half smile, then shook it. "Nope. Black. No flash. Sexy, but durable."

His eyebrows jumped in surprise.

She raised her own in answer. "Snip toe, spur ridge, standard heel, premium leather." She flashed him a self-assured grin. "How'm I doing?"

Colt rested his hands on his hips and let his head fall back as he rumbled with laughter. "You're full of surprises, Lyd. Full of surprises."

"And?"

"And you've nailed my style." Of course, she had. She'd always been the quiet one whose eagle eyes never missed a thing. She had the uncanny ability to sum up someone's insides with a look. And right now, she looked like a cat who'd just discovered a bowl of cream as she met his gaze. Before he could move toward the door, his feet closed the distance between them. Damn feet, going in the wrong direction. He tucked a stray lock of hair behind her ear, amazed at its softness, wanting desperately to bury his hands in it. He should kiss her now. End the tension for both of them... but he couldn't. He settled for pressing his mouth to her temple, and breathing in her intoxicating feminine scent. "I'll see you 'round," he murmured huskily.

Before he did something he regretted, he spun, and this time his feet moved in the right direction. But his heart tripped a little when he heard her sigh in frustration as he walked away.

CHAPTER 9

Three weeks later

LYDIA FINGERED THE club floor pass while she waited for the bartender to pass over her Old Fashioned. For at least the fifteenth time in the last two hours, she looked longingly at the exit. What had she been thinking? Hopping on a plane, spur of the moment like this was *so* unlike her. So was asking Travis if she could make use of his unused NFR tickets and club pass. Her face still burned at the memory of Travis's knowing smirk when he handed over the envelope. Of course, everyone would read into it and jump to conclusions. It turned out more than a couple of folks had seen her plastered against Colton at the wedding.

It had been a mistake coming to Vegas.

She should have waited until Colton came home for Christmas, like she'd planned. But the hope that Colt might wear her boots when he claimed the title of best All-Around Cowboy tomorrow night, had been powerful. And something Colton had said about playing it safe floated back to her out of the fog of her disjointed Thanksgiving memories. She was tired of playing it safe. Where had that gotten her? A big fat nowhere.

In for a penny in for a pound. Her mother's voice echoed in her head.

Glancing down the bar filled with cowboys and glammed

up ladies, there was no doubt she was all in. She'd pulled out all her New York City fashion stops for tonight. She'd spent way too much money on a blowout and manicure, then donned a gray fringed leather skirt, a sheer black turtleneck, and topped it off with a short black leather jacket. Lastly, she'd pulled on her favorite pair of confidence-boosting booties – the first pair of shoes she'd ever made on her own. It didn't matter she wore twice as much as any of the bleach blonde buckle bunnies posted all over Colton's social media, she was here to make a business deal with one of the hottest cowboys in the rodeo world. She'd been stunned to see Colton's face, larger than life, on no less than three billboards around town. In rodeoland, Colton Kincaid was nothing short of a rock star. And she could see why. He'd been mouthwateringly good in the arena tonight, and when he'd jumped off the bull named Straight Shooter a full second after the buzzer had sounded, the crowd had gone wild. Same as her heart.

Where was her drink?

She'd sipped on club sodas all evening, but right now, she needed liquid courage as her thoughts turned again to the boot box propped against her barstool. Her blood, sweat, and tears were in that box. Hell, her entire future depended on that box. She'd worked night and day on the boots over the last two weeks, spending what little remained of her savings on a set of lasts that would match Colt's foot, and the best leather she could buy. Emmaline Andersson had saved her hide by letting her borrow the industrial sewing machine that had managed to come through the spring's tornado unscathed.

"Will that be all, miss?" The bartender pushed forward her drink.

She slapped a twenty on the counter and nodded.

"Thanks." She downed the beverage in one long gulp, then checked her lipstick. Rolling her shoulders back, she slipped off the stool, grabbed the box, and hugging it to her chest, made a beeline for the elevator. The lobby was crowded with cowboys and couples, but she kept her gaze firmly on the buttons above the doors, even as the crush of boisterous guests swept her into the elevator. With each stop, Lydia's heart pounded louder and louder.

At the club level, the elevator opened onto a large area, filled with high top tables, a band in the corner by the window, and a long buffet. Cowboys, sponsors, and fans mingled in clusters. It was crazy. The clock showed long after midnight, yet folks were dancing and laughing like it was dinnertime. The scene reminded her of any number of restaurants in Midtown that hosted the post-Broadway show acting crowd. Theater people lived by a different clock. Apparently rodeo people did too. But where was Colton?

Travis had mentioned he was staying on the club floor, but she'd naively assumed she'd find him here, at the party. Especially after his showing in tonight's events. Colton had been one of only a handful of cowboys to take his rides all the way to the buzzer, and was in first place going into tomorrow night's final rodeo.

Lydia looked longingly at the buffet, groaning under the weight of barbecue, prime rib, fruits, cheeses, and pastries. She was too nervous to eat. "Go big or go home," she chanted under her breath. "Go big or go home." Those had been the last words Cassie had said to her as she boarded the plane for Vegas.

She hadn't come this far to chicken out. Straightening her spine, she walked over to the closest cowboy and tapped him on the shoulder. He swung around, swaying a touch. "Excuse me. I'm looking for Colton Kincaid."

"I think you're a little overdressed for his party, darlin'," the young man drawled, eying her with bourbon glazed eyes.

Lydia fought back a sigh of exasperation. "Can you please tell me where to find him?"

The man leaned forward, his whiskey laced breath heating her cheek. "Only if you'll tell me what all you pretty ladies see in him. He doesn't know how to treat a lady."

Her eyes jumped skyward. "I bet he knows how to hold his liquor, for starters," she answered tartly. She had no idea if that was true. It hadn't been the case for the younger Colton, but surely as a rodeo star with a reputation to uphold, maybe he'd cleaned up his act a little? He'd told her outright he wasn't as bad as he'd been. Thanking the man, she headed for one of the halls leading off the lounge. The first open door wasn't Colton's room. It was a party hosted by Carhartt. All eyes turned to her when she entered. Face flaming, she pointed to the box. "I'm looking for Colton Kincaid?"

One of the older men made a face and shook his head. "Keep going, hon. You'll know it when you see it."

She left the room as fast as her booties could carry her, but not before she'd heard another young man complain. "Man, how come he gets all the pretty ones?"

The smile that had started froze on her face when the older man replied. "Kincaid might ride the shit out of rough stock, but he's a rake. Don't know how his sponsors stand it."

Lydia went cold, and her feet slowed. Stopping, she leaned back against the wall to catch her breath. What was she getting into? Had the Colton at home been an act? Was she stepping into a den of snakes? It wasn't too late. She could leave now, and no one would be the wiser. But this was her one chance. And if she was going to put everything on the line to take a chance making custom boots, she wanted to know right now how bad it was. What she was getting into. Steeling herself with a deep breath, she marched down the hall. She rounded one corner, then another. And then she heard it.

Giggling.

Lots of giggling.

Oh, God. He wasn't alone. Of *course* he wasn't alone. This was the same guy who'd bragged he'd had a girlfriend in every town between Prairie and Manhattan. *Duh.* Again, the urge to flee grabbed her. But like the girl in the horror movie who crept into the basement, even though everyone knew the axe murderer was waiting behind the furnace, against her better judgment, she wanted to see for herself.

She knocked.

"Come on in, the more, the merrier," Colton hollered from inside.

The sound of her heart slamming against her ribs filled the silence of the hall. If she left now, she could be around the corner before anyone came to the door. But her booties remained glued to the carpet.

"Coming," he called.

She should have called him and arranged a meeting like a normal person. Just like in the horror movie, this was a bad, bad idea. Her pulse raced with the same terror.

The door swung open, answered by Colton himself, dripping wet, wearing nothing but a towel.

Her heart stopped mid-beat.

Colton fully clothed was a fine, fine man. But Colton stripped down to his skin was a rodeo god. From his damp hair curling at his neck, to the water droplets slowly meandering down his chiseled torso, he was a sight to behold. He had a scar across his left ribcage, thick and silvery. His abs rippled and disappeared beneath the towel barely clinging to narrow hips. But it was the large, black, tribal tattoo over his right shoulder that sent heat rushing straight to her pussy. Colton Kincaid was bad to the bone. And shame on her, she wanted every inch of his badness.

Their gazes slammed together, and for an instant, neither spoke.

Colton's widened eyes acted like a switch and Lydia spoke. "I've come at a bad time."

"No. Wait."

She shook her head, mortification singeing her with the heat of a prairie fire. "No. Really. I should have called first. I thought, I thought." She caught her breath. "I'm sorry."

Her booties finally came unstuck, and she spun away, tucking the box under her arm.

"Don't go." His hand caught her wrist. "Please? Give me just a minute."

Something in his tone pulled at her and she paused, daring to meet his gaze again. There was a vulnerability in his eyes that arrowed straight to her soul. She couldn't walk away. At least not this second.

"Who is it?" Tittered a feminine voice.

Lydia's face flamed. She could absolutely walk away. What was she thinking? "Never mind. I'll catch up with you at home."

Colt ignored her and strolled into the room. "Party's over ladies. I've got important business to attend to."

She trailed after him, then stopped dead at the scene in front of her. Not one, but *three* bikini-clad women climbed out of the hot tub, each wearing too much makeup and a pout the size of Texas.

"Oh my lord. Colt, I didn't mean to–"

"Thanks for stopping by, ladies." Colt continued as if he hadn't heard her, topping off each lady's glass with champagne.

She did her best to ignore the grumbling from the other women, but couldn't help rolling her eyes when one of them shot her a scathing glare.

Silence engulfed them when the door clicked shut behind the last woman out. All Lydia's well-practiced speeches vanished from her brain as what she'd just witnessed sunk in. "You were... naked in there?" she choked out.

"I worked hard tonight. Needed to get the kinks out." Colton's mouth twitched.

Damn him, he was *laughing* at her. "I know. I saw," she said baldly.

His eyes registered surprise. "You saw me ride?"

"Yeah. You're really good." 'Really good' didn't begin to describe his talent. Granted, the last rodeo she'd attended was the county fair outside Prairie, years ago. Colton owned the animals he rode. He moved with a wild grace that captivated the viewer and demonstrated unequivocally that he was in control. She'd never seen anything like it.

He shot her a cocky grin. "Kinda makes you want me even more, huh?" His eyes dared her to disagree.

Fighting the heat racing up her spine, she gave him a slow perusal, bringing her gaze to rest right where his hand rested on the edge of the towel. He'd get no argument from her. *No, you don't, girl,* her brain scolded. *Do not give him the satisfaction.*

She lifted a shoulder nonchalantly forcing her eyes up to meet his molten gaze. "Nope." She wasn't sure how she managed to let out a whopper like that and still look him in the eye, but she did. "Not really. I find other things sexier than your six-pack."

Turning, he struck a pose. "Like my ass?"

The laugh escaped before she could rein it in. He did not need any encouragement. Least of all, from her. She shook her head. "Kindness. Compassion. Honesty."

Momentary guilt flashed in his eyes, but quick as a wink, his bravado returned. "You look good, Lyds. Damn good. That honest enough for you?"

Ignoring his taunt, she studied his tattoo. "When did you get that?"

"This?" He lifted his shoulder. "First year I made it to the finals. I was competing only in saddle bronc at the time, but I felt like I'd finally made something of myself. I wanted to remember what that felt like."

Lydia's heart softened. He tossed off the achievement like it was nothing, but his eyes told a different story. And she knew the pain there, had helplessly watched so much of it unfold before her eyes, unsure at the tender age of seventeen, how she could help. Her throat grew tight. "I hope you never forget that feeling," she said sincerely. "Not many people know how much you struggled."

His eyes grew hard. "And not many people will. I've made it this far by keeping the past in the past."

Colt's meaning was clear. "I didn't come here to dredge up the past," she snapped.

"Why are you here? Exactly?"

She stared at him a full minute before answering. "Some stupid crazy itch to see you again. And to give you these." She thrust out the box, pulse hammering.

His eyes lit devilishly. "Stupid crazy, huh?"

Okay, maybe not her best choice of words. Flames licked up to the roots of her hair. He stepped closer, one hand still on his towel. "Will you put some clothes on?" As curious as she was to see underneath the towel, his muscles were distracting her from her mission.

He smirked. "Seeing how one of us, namely *you*," he pointed out, "prefers a state of undress, I'm good with the towel." His eyes dared her to object.

She rolled her eyes. "That's going to be you on another billboard, isn't it?" She arced a hand. "Colton Kincaid for Grace boots. Boots so good, you only need a towel."

His laughter rang off the walls. "Good one, Lyds." Then he lasered in on her. "Grace boots?"

CHAPTER 10

S HE'D KNOCKED HIS socks off, showing up dressed to the nines, half uptown girl, half urban cowgirl. The effect was intoxicating, and he was a dirty dog bastard for wanting to get her out of that fringed skirt and discover if the sheer thing she wore was a shirt or a bodysuit. Heaven help him if it was a sheer bodysuit.

For half a minute, he'd been embarrassed she'd caught him with his friend Trevor's party girls. But he had nothing to be ashamed of. They'd just been hanging out, relaxing in the hot tub when she'd knocked. Although it pained him to admit it, his promiscuous days had ended months before he'd come home to Prairie. He might have rightly come by his bad boy reputation, but truth be told, he'd grown tired of it. Somewhere deep inside him, by little increments over the past year, a longing had erupted that couldn't be assuaged by the average buckle bunny. He couldn't put his finger on what it was exactly. He had everything he could possibly want – fame, wealth, a sweet ranch in the mountains. He'd chalked his discontent up to exhaustion, figuring he was just tired of living on the road most of the year. Not for the first time, he worried something was wrong with his equipment. But kissing Lydia in the barn at his brother's wedding, hell, seeing her rip off her dress, had put an entirely new twist on things. All he had to do was remember how glorious Lydia had looked in the moonlight, skin glowing in red lace, and he became hard as iron with no relief until he'd put himself out of his own misery.

But other women? Even half-naked ones? Nothing. Zero. Zilch. Nada.

So yeah, he was concerned.

Lydia's presence here put an end to his speculation. His equipment worked just fine. In fact, he was trying to do everything he could not to show her his equipment was ready and rarin' to go. A flimsy hotel towel didn't offer much protection from her sharp eyes.

"What's this about Grace boots?" he repeated.

She worried her lip and looked away.

Ah, so there *was* something to Grace boots. Had she returned to Prairie to start something? Suddenly, he was grateful he'd offered to help his brother with Resolution Ranch. "Lyds?" he pressed, stepping into her space and taking the box.

She took a deep breath, shoulders rising. "I have a proposal for you."

Awareness zinged through him, firing up all his nerve endings, and he tossed the box on the bed. "We finally gonna pick up where we left off?"

She shook her head once. "We both know I'm not one-night-stand material."

"Who says it has to be that?" One look at her face and he instantly regretted the words. He didn't even know where they came from. The flat-out disbelief etched on her face and the way she rolled her eyes, ate at him. He was capable of more than a one-night stand. He'd just never been interested before.

Her hand was warm on his face as she gave him a pat and a funny little smile. "I'm not your type."

It took everything to not encase her hand in his and keep it there. "Maybe you are."

A soft laugh escaped her, and she shook her head. "Maybe when hell freezes over. In the meantime, I have a business proposal for you."

A business proposal?

"Wait," he snapped, stung. "So your stupid crazy itch to see me again was because you have *a business proposal?*" He crossed the room in four steps, stopped, turned, and stalked back. "So I'm not good enough for a fuck, but I'm good enough to do *business* with?" He didn't care he was being crass. Her estimation of him hurt.

She seemed entirely unfazed by his outburst. "I've always thought there was plenty of good in you, Colton." She winked. *Winked.*

"But not good enough," he spat.

She lifted a shoulder, the sexy half-smile he liked so much returning. "You like being bad. Being shocking. It allows you to keep people at arm's length. In bed, I'm the kind of woman who will always want more than you're willing to give. But in business? I think we could be good for each other."

Her words hit him like a rampaging bull. "But *you* made a pass at *me.*" He crossed his arms over his chest.

Her face flushed pink. "I did," she answered in measured tones. "You're as handsome as they come, Colt. And I was intoxicated. And you're charming. Too charming. But that doesn't mean we should go there." For a split second, remorse covered her face. "Even you had the presence of mind to take a step back."

"Something I've regretted every day for the last three weeks." He captured her gaze, letting his words sink in. It might be unwise, admitting it. She could use it against him.

He'd met plenty of women who would. But Lydia the rule-follower seemed hell-bent on breaking all the rules where they were concerned. The scorching look she aimed at him went straight to his balls. Did she regret it too? Hope sparked in his chest.

Her tongue slipped out to wet her lower lip, and her voice wavered when she spoke. "Open the box." She jerked her head toward the bed.

With a frustrated sigh, he went to the box and opened it, giving a low whistle. They were incredible. A fucking work of art.

"Kangaroo tops and American alligator vamps."

He nodded, studying the craft. She'd gone with a tradi-tional embroidery design on the tops, but had used metallic threads alongside traditional thread, so that the pattern took on dimension. In the negative space, she'd inlayed more alligator. On the pulls, she'd inlayed his initials. They were the finest dress boots he'd seen. Subtle, yet oozing style. He glanced back over his shoulder. She stood eyes downcast, worrying her lip. Was she seriously concerned he wouldn't like them? "They're hot shit, Lyd."

The tension left her body. "Try them on?"

"Towel on or off?" He smirked, heat rising through him at the thought of getting naughty with Lydia in nothing but a pair of boots. *Her* boots.

Her mouth twitched. "I told you to get dressed."

"Best way to show off a pair of boots is in nothing else."

Shaking her head, she turned around. But not before he caught her smiling openly. Colt rolled up the socks she'd included in the box, then sat to pull on the boots. His foot slipped in like it was greased in butter. He stood and shut his eyes, reveling in the feel. The arch hit him perfectly, and there was plenty of room in the toe box. Damn if she hadn't ruined him for any other pair of boots. "They fit perfectly," he called over.

Slowly, she turned, her gaze dropping first to the boots, then crawling up his body. Her sexy smile returned, and he stood a little straighter under her scrutiny. "You look good. Real good."

He cocked an eyebrow. "I'll look better without the towel."

"Before you say that, read this." She dug into the small bag she carried and pulled out a bundle of folded papers, holding them out.

"What's this?" She shook the papers, and he took them. He scanned the papers, stiffening as anger and disbelief knotted in his chest. "No," he said, shaking his head. "No way."

Panic flashed across her pretty features. "What do you mean?"

"No one, and I mean *no one* offers fifty-one percent of their business to a potential investor," he growled. "You'll lose a lot more than your shirt that way."

She narrowed her eyes. "What if I said you're taking a chance on a no-good untalented designer who's a bad bet?"

Someone said that to her? Anger flashed in his gut, hot and sticky. He'd happily take aim at the asshole who'd told her that. "Whoever said that never put a foot in your boots." He raised a finger. "But that's not how you make an investment opportunity attractive. Besides, if you'd just asked, I'd have helped you out."

She scowled. "I don't want a favor. This is a business proposition."

"And clearly, you don't know the first thing about running a business."

"But I'm good." She gestured to the boots.

"Yes. You are. And you're smart. Too smart to make a rookie mistake like this. What gives?"

Her color heightened. "I was hoping it would incentivize you to be hands-off."

"That's not how you get me to be hands-off, darlin'." He shook his head with a laugh. "The more money I invest, the more hands-on I'm going to be."

"But Travis mentioned you were going to be a silent partner," she said in a small voice.

He puffed out his cheeks and stared at the ceiling, blowing out a long breath. "That's... different," he finished lamely. "And fundamentally more complicated."

"I see." Disappointment radiated from her.

He hated that. Hated to see her upset, knowing he might be the cause. But this wasn't the average endorsement deal he made, where he whored out space on his body for a fancy company logo. This was... personal. "What do you think your start-up costs will be?"

"I can bootstrap it for about twenty. I have some savings left–"

"But you don't wanna operate without a safety net. Believe me." He scrutinized her, in full business mode now. "Where you gonna get your clients?"

She met his gaze directly. "I was hoping you could help with that."

"How are you gonna compete with the likes of Paul Bond? Or Heritage?" He ran a hand over the back of his head. "Hell, what about Lucchese or Tony Lama?"

Fire snapped in her eyes. "While you were carousing and rodeoing all over the west, I worked with one of the finest shoe designers in the world. My designs are good, my fit is excellent, as you can attest to, and I understand *instinctively* how to make the perfect shoe or boot for the client."

He liked her all riled like this. Passionate and strong. Too many times in their youth, she'd let the others run roughshod over her. Hell, he'd been as bad, maybe worse than the others doing it too.

"You're an influencer," she continued. "You wear my boots tomorrow night, and people will take notice. I'm ready to take orders and work fast. A couple of years of hard work, and I can hire a team. Scale up."

"What happens when you can't keep up with orders?" Hell, a couple of Instagram posts from him, she'd probably have orders for six months, or more. And once that first wave of clients spread the word, she'd be inundated.

"I'll cross that bridge when I come to it. Besides," she added. "I don't need world domination. I just want to make a living doing something for myself."

That, he understood. The pride of accomplishment. Of being able to stand on your own two feet and look the world in the eye. "I know exactly what you mean."

Their gazes tangled and the air between them sparked with a moment of mutual respect and more. So much more. She was damned irresistible. Unable to stop himself, he closed the distance between them.

"One kiss. Just one kiss, Lyds. While we're both sober and in our right minds." He brushed her hair behind her ear, not missing the shiver that went through her.

"I don't think I can possibly be in my right mind when you touch me that way," she murmured, never taking her eyes from him.

It might only be a slight opening, but he'd take it. He

lowered his head, brushing his mouth against hers slowly. When she didn't pull away, or push him, he pressed more firmly, nearly dropping to his knees when she leaned in, opening her mouth. She tasted better than he remembered. He caught the faint taste of whiskey on her tongue, but heat enveloped him as they deepened the kiss and his mind reeled from the pleasure.

With a groan, he pulled her close, winding an arm around her. Her hands fluttered up his chest, touching, caressing, landing on his shoulders as she stood on tiptoe, pressing into him. "Ah, Lydia," he sighed as he peppered kisses along her jawline. "Let me make you feel good. Let me show you how good it can be."

She stiffened in his embrace and pushed on him.

Disappointment crashed through him as he dropped his hands and took a step back, hands raised in surrender. "What? What'd I do?"

With a heavy sigh, she pressed her hands to the bridge of her nose, shaking her head. Flashing her palms, she spoke. "Business. We can't—"

A ringtone sounded in her purse.

"Ignore it," he rumbled.

She shook her head as she rooted in her bag. "I can't. That's Lex. She only calls if it's super important." She glanced back with a guilty expression. "I'm sorry. It'll just be a second. Hey," she said into the phone.

He fisted his hands on his hips, letting out a ragged breath. Cockblocked by the sister. The Grace sisters had an uncanny ability to show up at the most inconvenient times.

Lydia's face paled, and she covered her mouth with a gasp. "Noo. Oh poor Caro."

"What?" he growled, protective instincts arising from

someplace deep within. "What is it?"

She looked at him wide-eyed, shaking her head. "When?" she asked her sister. Lydia's face crumpled at whatever Lexi told her.

Dread pooled in his stomach. Had something happened to Dottie? Whatever it was, by God, if he could, he'd help her.

"I'm on my way," she said quietly and disconnected. "Carolina's fiancé was killed a few hours ago. I have to go."

His feet were already moving to his suitcase. "I'll take you to the airport."

CHAPTER 11

COLT STOOD AND shook hands with the two ad-execs who'd flown in from L.A. with his boxer-brief sponsorship contract.

"We're looking forward to working with you Mr. Kincaid," the young woman Maria, obviously fresh out of college, said with a hint of star-struck awe. "C. Klein is thrilled to add a rodeo star to its athletic wear lineup."

"Please. Call me Colt. I'm not much for formality."

"Of course," her boss, Alan answered smoothly. "Anything you need before we schedule the shoot, you let us know."

He had half a mind to ask if they'd shoot him in Lydia's boots.

"Thanks for the rodeo tickets last night," Maria gushed. "I've never been to a rodeo before."

Colt smiled benignly. "Well, if you're gonna go to a rodeo, the National Western's one of the best around. I'm just sorry I didn't perform so well last night."

Alan clapped him on the back. "We were impressed, and our photographer got some great shots of you coming out of the chute."

He wasn't impressed with his performance last night. He'd drawn a bad horse and had a poor bareback ride. Then, adding insult to injury, he'd drawn the meanest bull of the lot, and had lasted only six seconds. But what he thought didn't matter so long as the sponsors were happy and the checks kept coming.

Again, his thoughts drifted to Lydia. He hadn't talked to her since Vegas. All the Graces, even Dottie, were in Chicago when he arrived home Christmas Eve, rallying around Carolina, the youngest of the Grace sisters. And Lydia had been so distraught as he drove her to the airport, his only thought had been helping her keep it together. Asking for her number had been the furthest thing from his mind. Something he kicked himself for, now.

Tipping his Stetson, he said goodbye and stepped outside the Cattlemen's Clubhouse into the bright January sun. Reaching for his aviators, he wove through the participant's lot on the backside of the National Western complex with a spring in his step. He might not have pocketed the prize money he'd hoped for during the National Western run, but he'd more than made up for it in endorsements. And every cowboy knew, there were ups and downs on the rodeo circuit. As long as he had more ups in the coming year, he'd finish out on top next December.

The truck rumbled to life, and he pulled out of the lot and onto I-70. But instead of heading west toward his ranch in Steamboat, he turned east. Toward Prairie. He questioned his motives for the next thirteen miles. Travis was due home any day now from a six-hundred-fifty-mile trek to Santa Fe along the historic trail of the same name. And he had souvenirs for Dax. He slid a glance over to the box that took up the passenger seat. Of course, if Lydia was home, he'd pay a visit to the Graces. Offer his condolences in person.

It still disturbed him she'd offered him fifty-one percent of her venture. It made no sense. And it raised his hackles that she thought to entice him into being a hands-off investor. Was he really so awful that she wanted nothing to do with him? That didn't reconcile with the mind-bending kisses they'd shared. He chewed on that thought for another seven miles.

Maybe he was looking at it all wrong. Maybe she'd offered so much because she wanted to get his attention? That would be exactly the kind of reckless action *he'd* take if not for his financial advisor. Lydia certainly had his attention. Although it didn't take offering up more than half her company to get it. Her plan was solid. Measured, and well thought-out. He'd looked it over so often since Vegas, he had most of the details memorized. Protectiveness for her surfaced again. What if she'd offered that to someone else? Someone more... nefarious? He clenched the wheel. If anyone dared take advantage of her...

He pressed the gas closer to the floor. If he pushed it, he could be in Prairie shortly after dinner. Maybe, just maybe, luck would be with him, and he'd find Lydia at the Trading Post. An ache settled low in his belly just thinking of her. Maybe this time the fates would conspire on their behalf instead of placing more obstacles between them. He'd give his left kidney to spend a day having slow, dirty sex with her. Someplace quiet with no phones, no interruptions. No dying in-laws or free booze. He fisted his hand against the steering wheel, punching out a rhythm in an effort to calm down his overeager cock. This was the longest dry spell he'd ever endured, his dick reminded him painfully. Nothing except a few stolen kisses with Lydia for more than six months. And the more he thought about those kisses, the more he wanted another.

His phone rang from its spot on the console. Activating the Bluetooth, he answered. "Colt, here."

"Colt, son. Glad we reached you," a booming voice spoke jovially.

Hal and Harrison Carter, and Colton could tell from Hal's tone of voice, something wasn't right with his largest sponsor. His pulse fluttered at the base of his neck. Carter Holdings owned half of his brand endorsements and accounted for two-thirds of his income last year. He couldn't afford to piss-off his bread and butter. At least not now, not with so much of his cash tied up in Travis's Resolution Ranch.

Colt smiled before he spoke, infusing his voice with an enthusiasm that felt far from genuine. "What can I do for you, Hal?"

Hal cleared his throat. "We've been fielding some complaints from our brands."

"Oh?" Colton's stomach dropped. This was not good. Hal only called and did things like clear his throat when his brother Harrison, forced him to have uncomfortable conversations. *Like dropping someone.* Colton had seen it play out a few years previously, and it hadn't been pretty. Hal cleared his throat again. "Some of the brand owners are disappointed in your performance recently."

What??!?

Colt's temper got the best of him. "Are you fucking kidding me?" he bellowed, foot jamming on the gas as he flew down the highway. "I just won second in the all-arounds at the NFR's, and you're disappointed? Did any of your other cowboys come close to that? Who's disappointed?" he demanded.

"We're a family company," Hal reminded Colt. "And a few of our brands are speculating that your love of the ladies is getting in the way of you taking top honors."

White hot anger zapped through him, fusing his hands to

the steering wheel. He knew *exactly* where this was coming from. And it wasn't some random brand exec. Nope. This was from Satan herself, Samantha Jo Carter, head of Vanguard Chaps and Leather, and one-thousand-percent daddy's little girl.

Taking a steadying breath, Colt tried to speak as evenly as possible. Hal and Harrison both had a blind spot where Sammy Jo was concerned. He'd give her credit, he'd never met a woman as fierce as her, but not in a way that garnered respect. Sammy Jo was a shark through and through, and only wanted a man she could boss the way she did her daddy and her uncle. Worst? She'd take you down with a smile on her face if she felt you'd crossed her. And evidently, he'd crossed her. It wouldn't take much. They'd tangoed off and on over the years, but they tended to mix like oil and water. And the last time, when she'd ended it, Colt had insisted it be for good.

"Maybe the ladies are my good luck charm," he countered. "I've made the NFR five years running, each year placing higher and higher."

Hal coughed. "And that's done a great deal to elevate our brand. But," he paused to clear his throat *again*. "We think it's time you settle down and become a family man."

Oh. Hell. No.

That was code for marry Sammy JO It wasn't the first time they'd hinted at that possibility. And each time, he'd firmly sidestepped them.

"Or what?" Colton asked tersely, mind spinning. Losing the Carters' endorsements would be catastrophic. For starters, a move like that would brand him as bad business, and the rest of his endorsements would follow suit like a stack of dominoes. He knew. He'd seen it happen before. If Carter

Holdings pulled, he'd be back to square one overnight. Not only would he have to liquidate, he'd have to go back on his word to Travis. The thought churned his stomach like a meat grinder.

Hal's voice became firm. "We're tired of the bad-boy image. Of all the party shots on your social media–"

"I can't help it if my name has become a hashtag," Colt snapped bitterly. "And I certainly can't help it if people wanna take their pictures with me."

"This isn't just about photos, son. And you know it. How many women were you with the night before the NFR finals? How much liquor did you pour down your gullet?"

Colton clenched his jaw, grinding his teeth together so hard that for a second, he missed his competition mouth guard.

"That's what I thought."

So Hal had assumed his silence was an admission of guilt? Fuck that. It wasn't the party ladies that had thrown him off his game the next day, it had been Lydia. And his concern for her and her family in the wake of her sister's heartbreak. He'd own he couldn't stop thinking about the way she kissed him, either. He'd been so distracted, he hadn't set his rope right when he'd been in the chute. His saddle bronc ride had been pathetic, he'd barely hung on, rode more like a rookie. The bull he'd drawn tossed him clean off less than three seconds into his ride. To be honest, he hadn't slept well since he'd taken Lydia to the airport. But he'd never admit any of that to the likes of Hal Carter. Or any other Carter.

Hal continued. "We want to be able to tell our brand managers that you're settling down. You know, polishing your image. Becoming more... er... respectable. You know... like Jude Lawson."

Colt rolled his eyes. Be like Jude Lawson who beat him out for best all-around cowboy by only ten grand, and who'd married his high school sweetheart several years ago. His wife had pretty much been pregnant the entire time. Hal's meaning was loud and clear.

"Let me get this straight," Colt ground out. "You're telling me I need to find a wife and start popping out babies or you're going to drop me?"

"Pretty much."

"Well lucky for you I'm halfway there. I got engaged over Christmas." The lie popped out before he could stop it. Screw Hal for trying to meddle this way.

"And you were going to tell us, when?"

"When I was good and ready. We're still working out the details."

"Hmmmph." Hal made a suspicious noise. "And when do we get to meet this lucky lady?"

"I'll bring her around this spring. No need to get your chaps in a twist."

"See that you do that, son." Hal's meaning was clear. He'd believe it when he saw it.

Colton disconnected and threw his phone across the cab. He was well and truly fucked. Where in the hell was he going to find a fiancée?

CHAPTER 12

COLT STEWED THE entire drive to Prairie. The sun hovered just above the horizon as he hit the familiar hills surrounding Prairie, casting the clouds in colors of gold and orange. Travis had insisted he was welcome at the ranch, but even after enjoying Christmas with his brother, Colt still felt like an interloper, so he'd called over to Brodie and Jamey Sinclaire's and reserved a room at their hunting lodge. He'd head over to the ranch first thing tomorrow to help Elaine with anything she needed.

Pausing at Prairie's lone stoplight, Colton debated his next steps. If Lydia was in town, she'd be one of three places. She'd be home at the Grace ranch or hanging out at her sister Cassie's. If he was really lucky, she'd be at the Trading Post. He weighed those options as he waited for the light to change. His safest bet was checking out the Trading Post first. For starters, it was less likely to raise eyebrows.

Gunning the truck a little too hard once the light changed, he made his way toward the outskirts of town where the Trading Post had been a landmark since before he'd been born. Typical for a Saturday night, the parking lot was full, and he had to content himself with creating his own space in the field behind the bar. He cut the engine and contemplated the boots still sitting on the passenger seat. It would be muddy outside the truck, and he hated the thought of Lydia's artwork getting dirty and scuffed. On the other hand, if she was inside, she'd assume he didn't like the boots if he wasn't wearing them. With a sigh, he pushed back his seat and tugged off his ropers, tossing them on the floor. He needed all the good will from Lydia he could get tonight, even if it meant dirtying up her boots. Once he'd pulled on the boots, he reached into the glove box and grabbed a couple of Altoids, then he checked his reflection in the rearview before jamming on his Stetson and hopping out.

Even from behind the lot, the jukebox music leaked out into the coming darkness. Colt shook his hands to dispel his excess energy as he trudged through the grass and gravel to the door. It felt more like a big ride and less like he was dropping into a familiar watering hole. With any luck, a familiar face would invite him to take a seat. Slowly, he was reconnecting with old faces. But it wasn't easy. Some still judged him through the same lens they had when he'd been an out of control teenager. Others viewed him with suspicion, but adopted a wait-and-see attitude. He'd place Lydia in that category. Still others, like Tony Cruz who waved at him from the bar, gave no shits. He gave an answering smile as he threaded his way through the crowd to where Tony stood sharing a pitcher with a couple other guys. No sign of Lydia yet, but it was early, and the place was already crowded.

Tony held out a hand. "Nice to see you, man. Heard you did well in Denver."

"Not according to my sponsors." Colt shook his hand. "They're only happy when I win."

Tony shook his head. "Everyone knows it's a statistical impossibility to win a hundred percent of the time in rodeo." He signaled the bartender for another glass, then poured a pint, handing it to Colt.

"Have you ever thought about sponsoring a rider?"

Tony's head fell back in a belly laugh. "Hey Parker," he called. "Kincaid thinks we should sponsor him."

Parker turned around and gave Colt a wave. "Sure thing, if you want to drive to the next rodeo in an ancient broke down firetruck. Be my guest."

Colt raised his glass, glad to see Parker. "Deal." If Parker was here, chances were his wife Cassidy was, too. And by extension, Lydia.

Colt braced an elbow on the bar and scanned the crowd. "Why so crowded tonight?"

"First warm day in a month. Makes everyone stir crazy."

Colt nodded in acknowledgment. January in the Flint Hills could be dreary. On days when the wind blew from the south, and the sun came out, even the cattle got frisky. His eyes lit on Lydia. Out on the dance floor, she stomped her way through the movements of the latest line dance to make its way through the clubs, happy and flushed from exertion. His breath stalled. Seeing her like that sent a shot of hot lust straight to his cock. And made him think of all the other ways he could make her happy and flushed. Hell, he hadn't been in town twenty minutes, and all he could think about was whether or not Lydia was wearing a red lace thong, and how much he'd like to remove it from her. Slowly. With his teeth.

Tearing his eyes from her, he turned toward the bar and signaled the bartender. "Whiskey. Neat. Two."

By the time the bartender had served up the drinks, Lydia was sitting with a group of ladies just off the dance floor. Leaving a ten on the bar, he snagged the drinks and made a beeline for the table. She was even prettier up close, her color high and a ready smile curving her full mouth. "Mind if I join you?" He asked when she looked up.

The right corner of her mouth pulled higher as she slowly looked him over. He stood proudly, warming under her perusal. Let her look. As far as he was concerned, she could undress him with her eyes all night. Her eyes settled on his boots before snapping back up to his face, a satisfied expression on her face. "Nice boots."

"My new favorites."

She gestured to an empty chair. "Have a seat. I think you know Emmaline Andersson, she made your sister-in-law's wedding dress. And I'm sure you know Luci, Tony's sister."

He nodded, and set the drinks down. "You ladies need anything? I'm happy to buy a round." He'd learned early in life that often the best way to a woman was by charming her friends. Lydia might try to friendzone him, but he'd bide his time.

Emmaline flashed him a smile of appreciation. "I'm fine, thanks."

"Me, too," echoed Luci.

"In fact," Emmaline said, reaching for Luci's arm. "We were just going to hit the dance floor again. C'mon, Luce," she said, giving Luci a significant look.

With a giggle, the women slipped out of the booth and disappeared into the crowd. Colton slid in, pushing the whiskey in front of Lydia.

Lydia looked from the glass to him, then back to the glass, then back at him.

"You taste like whiskey when I kiss you," he explained boldly.

Pink exploded across her cheeks, and raw lust flashed in her eyes. His body responded in kind. Had she lain awake at night thinking about their kisses too?

"Oh." She lifted the glass. "Thanks."

He clinked her glass, then took a sip, letting the burn flow down his throat, using it as a means to slake the fire building elsewhere. "How's your sister?"

Her face clouded. "Heartbroken, but she won't come home. And she sent us home after two weeks."

"Think you'll visit her?"

"Depends. She inherited mama's stubborn streak."

He nearly choked on his drink. They all did. The Grace sisters were a force unto themselves, and everyone in town knew it.

Lydia leaned in, eyes lit with curiosity. "How are the boots working out?"

"I meant it when I said they're my new favorites."

"Really?" she practically squealed.

He nodded, unable to stop from grinning. "For real. And they get good attention. You nailed the design."

She puffed up like a prairie hen at his compliment. He liked seeing her that way, in spite of the funny things it did to his insides. "And the fit is perfect. I don't know how you managed it right off. Sometimes it takes a couple of tries for a boot maker to get the vamp right."

"You have a high instep, so I bet most boots feel tight across the top, yes?"

He nodded. "How'd you know?"

She preened under his gaze, eyes twinkling. "I'm magic."

Right then, he'd believe it. The light in her eyes pulled at him like a magnet. He'd do anything for her to keep looking at him that way. "Care to dance?" he uttered, surprising himself. Anything to get close to her.

She cocked her head suspiciously.

He lifted his hands. "I swear, no funny business." At least not right now. He scooted out of the booth and extended his hand, lacing his fingers with hers as he led her to the crowded floor, thrilled for the perfect excuse to hold her close. She softened against him as his hand splayed across her lower back, and they moved to the strains of Brad Paisley. Colt loved dancing. Loved the way a woman felt in his arms, loved the physical communication. The body never lied. And Lydia's body was telling him a different story than her words. Paisley's voice wound around them like a lasso, tightening, and pulling them closer together. He shut his eyes and let the music direct his steps, trying his best to ignore the sudden ache in his chest. As the final strains of *Then* faded, and the cacophony of the bar came crashing into their little bubble, he stepped back, shocked at the emotion coursing through him. He didn't get emotional. He didn't do feelings. Ever.

The tension in his shoulders released in relief when Lydia tugged on his hand. "Can we find someplace to talk? Have you given more thought to my proposal?"

The short answer was yes, but after his conversation with Hal Carter this morning, he'd thought of nothing else the whole drive. "We can go sit in my truck where it's quiet, but someone's sure to see you leaving with me. You okay with that?"

She gave him a rueful smile. "Fine. You leave first. I'll follow."

"I'm parked out behind the lot." He tipped his hat and spun, hurrying to the exit. The cold evening air blasted his face as he stepped outside and an involuntary shiver ran down his spine. But not because he was nervous. He was entirely in control of this show.

Hot air blew from the vents in the cab by the time Lydia knocked on the window, and hopped inside, cheeks bright from the cold. "I forgot to ask you," she started as soon as she'd settled herself. "How was your first Christmas back in Prairie?"

"Dax is a trip."

"And what about Travis?"

Lydia never beat around the bush. He simultaneously loved and hated that about her. He shrugged, tense again. "We're... finding our way."

She reached for his arm, giving an encouraging pat. "That's a start." But as quick as she'd reached for him, she pulled back. "So..."

The word hung between them, full of expectation. Colt's heart tripped at the hope reflected in her eyes. There was no way she would agree to his proposition. He cleared his throat. "I have a counterproposal."

Instantly her guard was up. "Oh?" Suspicion laced her voice.

"For starters, the most interest I'll agree to is forty percent. It wouldn't be fair to take more. Your plan is solid, and I think you'll be solvent ahead of your timeline." His financial advisor had agreed with him on that.

With a squeal, she launched herself his direction, throwing her arms around him and kissing him on the cheek. "I promise, you won't regret it. I can start paying dividends when I get my first orders."

He had half a mind to return her kisses. If only his back weren't up against a wall.

"That's not all."

She pulled back, confusion flickering across her face. "What do you mean?"

He shifted uncomfortably. Ah, hell. It suddenly felt too warm in the cab, the space, too close.

"Colt? What is it?"

"So I have need of a wife." Subtlety had never been his strong suit. "And you were the first person I thought of."

"You have need of a wife." She repeated flatly, mouth turning down and eyes flashing.

Ooh, she was pissed.

"Mmm hmm."

"Are you kidding me?" she said, her voice going shrill at the end. "And I suppose if I tell you to go to hell that you won't invest?"

"No, no." He held up a placating hand. "Not at all. I don't want to sleep with you."

"You don't." Her voice dripped with incredulity. She reached for the door handle, shaking her head. "You're a special kind of Crazy, Colt. I'm outta here. I'll find another investor."

Damnshitmotherfucker. He was totally bungling this. Seeing the door crack spurred him to action. He captured her wrist as desperation filled him. "Wait, please? I'm doing a shit job of explaining. Of course, I want you. So bad, my balls ache. Any man would be lucky to spend the night with you. But that's not what this is about."

She glared at him. "You have exactly 27.6 seconds to explain yourself before I get out of this truck."

"One of my biggest sponsors is going to drop me if I don't settle down."

"So you're suggesting—"

"I haven't exactly, ah… been a model citizen." Heat raced up his spine.

"No foolin'," she scoffed. "Fifteen seconds, cowboy."

Oh shit. He had to explain himself. Never in his life had he wanted to run as badly as he did right now. Facing Lydia's wrath might possibly be worse than facing her mother. "I might have told them I'm already engaged."

"Colton Kincaid, you dirty-dog liar. *How could you?*"

She was pissed alright. Her voice gone dead quiet, just like Dottie's when she was about to unleash a can of whup-ass.

He laughed self-consciously. "It was pretty damn easy, actually. Just kind of popped out."

"Just popped out," she repeated incredulously.

"Would you help me? You're nice, Lyds. The nicest person I know."

She sighed heavily and stared out the window. "And you want me to clean up your image." The disdain dripped from her voice. But something else too. She sounded... disappointed.

He hated that. He didn't want her to be disappointed in him. Not anymore. "Okay, I haven't been able to stop thinking about you since Thanksgiving, but that's beside the point. I need help, you need help. Maybe we can help each other?"

CHAPTER 13

"SO YOU WANT me to be your fake wife." Lydia didn't know whether to feel flattered, disappointed that the only reason he asked her was because she was a 'nice-girl', or angry that Colton would think she'd ever go along with a scheme like this.

"At least fiancée. Only for a little while, until the sponsors cool down."

She crossed her arms. "How long is a little while?"

"I don't know."

He looked fit to be tied. Agitated and ill at ease. If she wasn't so discombobulated, she'd find his discomfort amusing. She'd never had the upper hand where Colt was concerned. Even as a teenager, he'd been cocky and confident, always in control. In fact, the only time she'd seen him scared and unsure of himself was the night he'd shown up on their front porch asking for help. And even though he made her crazy, her heart had gone out to him. She couldn't help it. But posing as his fiancée? That was asking a lot. And what would it mean for her boot company?

He scrubbed a hand across his jaw. "Look, can we go somewhere quiet and talk about this?"

She should hop out of the truck, go back inside and ask Luci Cruz or Emmaline to take her home. But her inner voice chided her. What would wild Lydia do? If she was truly done being Librarian Lydia, she should hear Colton out. Besides, there might be… perks to this arrangement.

"Fine. You know how to get to the fire station?"

He nodded and jammed the truck into gear.

Lydia pulled on her seatbelt. "Two blocks down and one block behind it.

"Got it."

Neither of them spoke on the short drive over. About seven minutes later, Colt pulled into the driveway of the bungalow she shared with Luci and Emmaline.

Colt let out a low whistle. "Nice place. How'd you score this with the housing shortage?"

"I didn't. I'm just renting a room. Luci's parents own it. The worst of the tornado went a few blocks north. It needed a new roof, but that was from the hail. Emmaline's staying here until Main Street reopens later this spring."

Colton set the brake. "Wait here." He hopped out and hurried around the front of the truck, reaching her door in time to offer his hand.

She took it, then instantly regretted it as a zap of awareness shot straight to her chest. Colt didn't let go once her feet touched the ground. She glanced up at him, heart kicking, but couldn't bring herself to remove her hand. Would he always have this effect on her? Lately, it felt like every touch was an effort in self-control. Against her better judgment, she held his hand up the walk and across the porch to the front door.

"My answer really has nothing to do with whether you'll invest in my boots?" she asked when they stepped inside.

"Scouts honor."

She waved him to the couch. "Coming from you, that's not much."

Colt removed his Stetson and sat at one end, hat in hand.

"I've changed Lydia. Give me some credit?"

She toed off her boots and sank into the opposite corner, tucking her feet underneath her. "Have you? Really? Then why ask me to be your pretend fiancée?"

She could see him struggling as he chewed on that. With a sigh, he set down his hat on the coffee table in front of them. Then he leaned back, throwing an arm across the back of the couch. "I would never lie to you Lyds. I might have been less than... honorable when we were young–"

She made a disbelieving sound in her throat.

"Okay, okay, I was a total jackass. I deserved everything Travis dished out. But I swear, I've changed."

She cocked an eyebrow. "There were three women in your hot tub in Vegas."

At least he looked discomfited. "Nothing happened."

"But would it have? If I hadn't interrupted?"

Two pink streaks erupted across his cheekbones as he shook his head. "Nope."

Lydia couldn't control the laugh that erupted from her throat. "I don't believe that."

He fixed her with a look so intense, she stilled. Was he telling the truth?

"I'll not deny I have a reputation."

"One that apparently your sponsors don't care for," she responded dryly.

"That appears so. But I also have a reputation to maintain in, er, other circles."

She rolled her eyes. "Oh for heaven's sake. That's horse-shit. Why not admit you like the attention? You always have."

"Of course I like the attention," he shot back, sitting forward. "Who wouldn't?"

"A normal person? Who values relationships?"

Her words hung suspended between them, and her heart sank at the stubborn set of his face. "Look, Colt, I'd love to help you–"

"Please," he rasped. "There's no one else I can ask. No one I'd want to ask," he amended, eyes darting to where she sat still curled up. "Name your terms. I'll even double my investment if you want."

"Oh for heaven's sake," she groaned, pushing off the couch and rounded the coffee table. She had way too much energy coursing through her to sit still. "You're not going to pay me to be your fake fiancée." She could feel his eyes tracking her as she paced back and forth across the room. "What about Millie Prescott?"

"The *hippie*?"

She'd laugh at his tone of voice if she wasn't so out of sorts. "Or-or Emmaline? Or Luci? You're friends with her brother." Surely, there was someone. And seeing him with another woman would be the perfect antidote to the late-night fantasies that had become a regular occurrence since Vegas.

He shook his head with a half-laugh. "Tony'd kick my ass if I looked sideways at his sister."

"Okay, good point." The way he was staring at her made her insides jump. Like he wanted to eat her up. And she liked that thought too much for comfort.

He stood, not taking his eyes from her. "Lydia."

"Emma Sinclaire?" she squeaked as he stepped around the coffee table. She stopped short, struck by the sheer magnetism of him. He moved with a lethal grace. To be sure, he had swagger, too much of it, but this was something else, born of confidence and trial by fire. "No go, huh?" she offered once her voice returned.

He shook his head, and caught her hands, bringing them

to his mouth. Her pulse ran out of control when his lips grazed the skin on the back of her hands, and a rush of exquisite heat settled between her legs. It was all she could do to not squirm from the sensation.

"Only you, Lyds."

She bit her top lip, hard. The pain didn't do anything to calm her breathing. But Colt seemed to like it, given his sharp inhale and the spark of desire that heated his eyes when she tongued the mark.

"You can't deny the chemistry between us," he murmured, grazing his mouth over her hands again. Her skin danced where he touched it. Fizzing like fresh champagne.

But no, she could, and she would. The second she gave into her baser feelings where Colt was concerned was the second things would spin out of control. "I-I don't want to talk about it," she said breathlessly.

His voice sounded like sin and smoke. "Darlin', you stripped down to your very sexy skivvies and propositioned me. We're absodamnlutely gonna talk about this. No going back."

The way he looked at her heated the room. Hell, it could set the whole town on fire. She could feel her resolve weakening. The curious, more reckless side of herself itching to take a walk on the wild side with Colt. "My mother will never buy this," she murmured faintly.

"She doesn't have to know."

"But she'll find out. Mama always finds out."

"Will that be the end of the world?"

His eyes were hypnotic, capturing her, melting her defenses one excuse, one kiss at a time. "She will tan your hide, Colton, if she finds out any way but from us." Her breath came in shallow puffs, dictated by the speed of her heart galloping in her chest. His hands were big and warm, and he had such a firm grip on her that for the first time ever, she wanted to lean into him, absorb some of his strength. His confidence.

She leaned forward. She couldn't help it. "You better keep your mouth shut about this."

"Anything else darlin'?" Colton gave her a saucy grin that reached all the way to his eyes.

"No other women. Not even in a hot tub."

"No problem," he agreed rapidly, without even a blink.

"No drugs."

"Been clean nine years."

"No booze, either."

"No booze?"

"Okay, no boozing when I'm not with you, and when I am with you, you better hold your liquor."

"Fair enough."

"Flowers occasionally."

He winked at her. "Happy to oblige, but don't you think that will make people suspicious?"

He had a point. "You're right. No flowers. What about church?"

"You might as well announce it with a neon sign."

"True. Okay, no church either."

"Business stays business."

"Of course."

Suspicion began to worm its way into her conscious. Was he so desperate to clean up his reputation that he was agreeing to everything? He was a businessman. He should at least want to negotiate something.

Alright then, she might as well push his buttons all the way. "And one last thing," she said primly, removing her hands from his, ignoring the hole the loss of his touch left inside her. "If we're keeping this strictly business – no sex."

CHAPTER 14

NO SEX?

She had to be kidding. She'd put the moves on him, and *now* she wanted no sex? When their chemistry was so explosive, it was a miracle the house was still standing? This woman would kill him. At the very least, give him a permanent case of blue balls.

But he was desperate, so he'd agree to anything she asked. "Sure you won't change your mind about the last one?"

She hesitated. "I think it would needlessly complicate things."

"Or it could be the perfect arrangement."

Her eyes grew hungry, and he took his opening, drawing a thumb down her cheek and sweeping it over her luscious lower lip. "I wanna see this mouth swollen from my kisses. I want to feel your gorgeous tits pucker in my hand and turn pink from my tongue. I want to feel your soft, sweet pussy wet for me, and I don't care if it complicates things. I want a long, good taste of you Lydia Grace, and I want to finish what you started in the barn. I'll jump through whatever hoops you toss up, but I dare you to deny what's between us."

Her eyes had gone hazy and unfocused. Fuck, she had no idea how magnificent she was. His cock did, and it strained against his pants.

"Say it," he rasped as he stepped closer, mouth watering to

kiss her again. He could see the answer in her eyes. The words were right there. His heart pounded with expectation, his reply ready on his tongue when she gave the word. "Say it, Lyds."

"You could charm the—"

"Pants off a rattlesnake," he filled in for her, stomach dropping in disappointment. "You've said that. And I pride myself on that skill."

"People will talk," she murmured.

"They always talk. Might as well give them something to talk about."

"Oh, they are definitely not finding out."

Her comment stung. In the back of his mind, all his old demons rose in a chorus of *you'll never be good enough.* Had he blown his chance with her in a fit of stupidity all those years ago? Because he couldn't stand even one person looking at him like they cared? Well, fuck him, if that's the way it went. Just another consequence in a long string of shitty consequences. Still, the overwhelming urge to prove himself to her, to show her that he could be worthy, hit him with the force of a charging bull.

With a sigh, he stepped away. "Fine. You're calling the shots, darlin'. But you know where to find me if you change your mind." He scooped up his hat, jamming it on his head as he made for the door.

He risked a look over his shoulder when he reached the door. His stomach twisted at the sight of her. Damn if she didn't look forlorn. Conflicted. It took everything he had not to close the distance and wrap her in a protective embrace. Instead, he tipped his hat and stepped out into the cold, letting the door snick shut behind him.

He counted the steps to the truck, hope rising in his chest

even though he knew better.

Two. He crossed the porch.

Five. His boots hit the bottom stair.

Nine. He reached the driveway.

Fourteen. His hand came to rest on the door handle. He paused, eyes drifting back to the door, willing it to open. Ten seconds. Twenty. "Ahh, hell." He shook his head and yanked open the door, hopping in with a swallowed curse. For a shining moment, an alternate future had rolled out before him. He'd been foolish to think he could win Lydia's trust. Or anyone's in Prairie, for that matter. He turned the ignition and gunned the gas, casting one final look at the door. As if in slow motion, the door swept open, golden light flooding out from behind Lydia's silhouette. His gut clenched as she bounded down the steps, flew around the front of the truck and knocked on the window.

Play it cool. He needed to play it cool. He jabbed the window button, and as the glass lowered, he was hit with the scent of her perfume.

"Don't go," she called softly, bouncing up and down.

"I'm not gonna play games, sweetheart."

"What if we started our agreement tomorrow? Got each other out of our systems tonight?"

His brows furrowed. "Are you sayin'–"

"One night. Full-on-sex. No regrets. Everything starts tomorrow."

She was still hopping. He craned his neck, trying to see down through the dark. "Where are your shoes, woman?"

She gave him a toothy smile, still bouncing. "You're right. Everything you said was right. I don't take risks. And-and, I've regretted that. At times," she added. "A-and..." she took a deep breath. "I can't stop thinking about you. And everything you said. And holy shit, it's freezing out here. Will you just come inside? Please? I promise I won't change my mind."

She didn't have to ask twice.

He cut the engine, not caring the window was still down. If some critter made itself at home, he'd deal with that later. She stepped back as he opened the door, and before she could turn, he scooped her up and stalked the fourteen steps to the still open door, kicking it shut behind him once he'd landed inside. "You sure 'bout this?" he asked gruffly. He didn't want this coming back to bite him in the ass.

She nodded, eyes wide. "My bedroom's down the hall."

He didn't stop until he reached her door. He hesitated, scanning the tiny space. One wall was covered with sketches of boots and shoes and a desk in the corner was covered with paper, pens, and samples. Aside from the chaos in the corner, the room was relatively sparse. His pulse threatened to race out of control as the realization hit him. He'd never once made love to a woman in her space. Always his – his terms, his space. Colt set Lydia down and moved to study the sketches, feeling like a bit of an intruder, yet savoring this tiny glimpse into Lydia's private domain. His eyes flicked from one paper to the next, amazed at how each design was unique, yet there was a gesture, a way she moved her pen that made them unmistakably hers. Kind of like the way a good rider threw his arm or marked his ride in a telltale manner. "These are good, Lyds. Real good."

The sound of material whispering to the floor had him turning. "I didn't invite you back to look at my pictures, cowboy," she said with a hungry look in her eye.

Oh hell, tonight her bra was blush pink. Barely there, and he could see her nipples, dark and dusky, pushing through the fabric. His hand went to his belt buckle as he moved a foot to toe off his boots.

Her eyes widened in shock. "Don't you dare toe off those boots." Moving with surprising speed, she dipped behind the bed, popped up and tossed him a boot jack.

He caught it with a grin and set it on the floor and set the heel in the groove, giving a little pull. "Yes, ma'am."

"Tell me you haven't toed them off."

"Never. Cross my heart."

She narrowed her eyes. "You just gave me an idea. I need to include a boot jack with each pair of boots I make."

He set the second boot next to the first and rose, hands on his hips. "I thought you didn't invite me here to talk business."

Her eyes lit as the slow sexy smile he loved curled up her mouth, and she sashayed to where he stood. He stilled as she placed a hand on his chest, right over his heart. Could she feel it kicking like a bronc just free of the chute?

"I wanna see your tattoo again," she said, her voice going husky and her eyes darkening to deep turquoise pools.

It took all of three seconds for him to loosen the buttons on his shirt and shrug it to the floor. He whipped off his tank top, deciding to give her the whole show. The appreciative rumble that came from her throat reverberated through his bones, settling in his balls with a tingle. "You have no idea how sexy those noises are."

"Hmm?" she answered as if she knew exactly.

She lightly traced the outline of his tattoo. The movement was so innocent, yet so erotic, a shudder rippled through him. Hell, he'd ink his entire body to have her touch him like that.

"Colt?"

"What is it, baby?"

"Take off your pants."

He eyed her jeans, perfectly molded to her curves, and slipped his fingers inside the waistband, tugging her closer. "You first."

Her eyes sparked with amusement. "On three."

"One, two... three." His fingers flew, loosening first his belt, then jerking down the zipper. Their pants hit the floor at the same time, the clatter of his belt buckle filling the space. Her eyes widened as she took in the bulge in his boxer briefs. "See the effect you have on me, sweetheart?"

Lydia's breath came out in a hiss, and she licked her lips. He was fucking lost. Stepping to her, he traced a line from the nape of her neck, across her collarbone, to the round of her shoulder. Then bent his head and followed the same path with his tongue, smiling against her skin at the ragged sigh that slipped through her lips.

Bands of desire tightened around his midsection, radiating out and pulling his muscles taut as he caught the faint floral scent of her perfume mixed with the slight musk of her skin. He was already worked up to the breaking point, but if this was his one shot with Lydia, by God, he was gonna make it damn good for both of them. He caught a finger under her bra strap and with a little tug, slipped it down her arm. "You're so beautiful." The words fell out of his mouth as he skimmed a finger over her creamy skin, over the luscious swell of her breast, stopping only when he came into contact with the lace top covering the best part. He grazed a thumb over her tight nipple, and again when she let out the sweetest moan. So alive, so responsive. The animal in him wanted to devour her, lose himself in her softness until he stopped thinking. "You have no idea what you do to me," he rasped.

She answered with a gritty laugh. "I know what you do to me."

Walking her back until the backs of her knees hit the bed, he tumbled them onto the sheets and rolled, positioning her above him. Pushing on his chest, she sat tall, arching her back while she reached behind to unclasp her bra. God, he loved a woman who gave as good as she got. A flash of hot jealousy stabbed through him at the thought that another man had enjoyed Lydia like this. The surprise of it knocked the air from his lungs. He wasn't a jealous type, at least he never had been. But everything where Lydia was concerned came as a surprise.

She tossed her bra aside, and his mind went blank. "Your tits are perfection," he whispered, awestruck. Heavy globes with dark pink centers that would fit perfectly in his palm. And sensitive too, as they puckered under his gaze.

"Take a taste, cowboy." She bent forward, offering herself.

For once in his life, he had no words. With a grunt, he clasped her waist and brought his mouth to her breast, first lapping the velvety underside before working his way around top, avoiding what they both wanted most. Saving it until neither of them could stand it anymore.

She rolled her hips against him with a groan. "Stop teasing."

He glanced up through hooded eyes. Her color was high, her lids half-closed, and that sexy smile pulled at the corners of her mouth. Fuck, if that didn't make him want to come instantly. His cock was hot and hard as a poker. With an answering groan, he sealed his mouth around her tight peak, lapping at it with his tongue until she cried out. Moving to her other breast, he repeated the same action, only taking her nipple into his mouth when she begged, and licking at it, sucking and grazing with his teeth until she bucked against his shaft with a cry. "I want you inside me, now," she growled with the ferocity of a baby kitten.

"Hold on, sunshine," he said with a chuckle. "We're gonna take our damned sweet time."

She raised her head and glared.

With a laugh, he rolled them over so she was caged between his arms. "You need some sweet relief, darlin'?" He hooked a finger through the side of her panties and pulled them down with a tug. She raised her hips to help. Sitting back on his heels, he gazed at her, mouth going dry at her beauty. Her pussy glistened pink and swollen, peeking out from a neatly trimmed thatch of dark curls. She was like one of those museum paintings, come to life, all curves and shades of pink. Her thighs were strong and muscled, and he began his upward perusal at her knees, drawing his hands slowly up and bringing them to rest on either side of those glorious shiny pussy lips. He looked up, catching her gaze, eyes coming to rest on her full lower lip, caught between teeth. His mouth pulled up, along with his eyebrows. "Should I stop?"

She half laughed, half growled. "I'll hurt you if you do."

"Ooh, such threats," he teased, half-curious to find out how far he could push her.

The teasing stopped when he touched her, reacquainting himself with her slick heat, only it was so much better this time because it wasn't the whiskey making these hot demands. For half a heartbeat jealousy overtook him again. It killed him to think she might have been this way with some dispassionate namby-pamby touchy-feely prep school type who couldn't possibly appreciate her depth of character or her passion. But as quick as it came, he pushed it away, refusing to let it get the best of him. Dropping to his elbows, he lowered his head to place a kiss on her thigh, nipping the soft flesh with his teeth, then smoothing it with the flat of his tongue. The scent of her buzzed through him like the finest bourbon. Her knee dropped open, inviting him in, and who was he to turn down a gift like that?

"You're fucking gorgeous," he spoke against her skin, a surge of desire pulling his muscles tight. "I wanna make you forget your name." He raised his head, gaze colliding with hers in a shower of sparks.

She let out a breathless giggle. "You're already halfway there."

"Then hang on tight, sweetheart. Things are gonna get wild."

The smile she gave him was so bright he forgot to breathe. "Promise?"

He answered by lowering his head and kissing the side of her pussy before acquainting himself with her taste. He lapped up her essence all the way to her clit. She tasted like spring and spice and summer heat. One taste, and he was love drunk, ruined for anyone else.

"Oh, more," she begged, lifting her hips.

He tasted again, filling his senses with the heart of her. Her thighs tensed as he lapped her up, and she clawed at his shoulders, writhing beneath his ministrations. He slipped a finger into her hot channel and twisted, searching for the bundle of nerves that would unleash her. Her breath came in harsh, sighing gasps, and as he tickled and tasted, she went rigid, letting out a loud keening cry that ended in a peal of laughter as her cream burst on his tongue.

An answering laugh of utter delight rose within him, along with gratitude that her roommates weren't home.

Lydia dissolved in a fit of giggles as he continued to touch and explore her, helping her ride to the very end of the sensations coursing through her. At last, he lifted his head.

This time, when their gazes locked, something deep in the recesses of his psyche pulled tight, and he braced himself against the distinct sensation of falling uncontrollably. His stomach lurched with the same realization he had the first time he was thrown off a bronc. One night would never be enough.

CHAPTER 15

LYDIA'S BREATH LODGED in her throat as Colton's dark, deliberate gaze pinned her to the bed. Her brain still swirled in the aftermath of the most intense orgasm she'd ever been given. Laughter bubbled up yet again from the wonder of it. Colton had played her body like a master. Drawing responses from her she'd never imagined. Ripping her gaze away, she dropped her head back to the bed and stared at the ceiling.

"You okay?" he asked softly, after a minute.

The concern in his voice made her chest ache. She was unsure how to respond to this tender, soft side of him. "Of course I'm okay." She rolled her eyes unable to keep the smile from her face. "You just took me to the freaking moon."

A low rumble vibrated through him. "You ain't seen nothin' yet."

She propped up on an elbow, eyeing him critically. "You mean, that wasn't your A-game?"

The look he gave her sent a rush of wet heat to where his mouth had been.

"But you're not cocky or anything," she snorted, still smiling. Who was she kidding? If he was promising more orgasms like the one she'd just experienced, there'd be no complaints from her. She ruffled her fingers through his dark hair. "Come up here."

Giving her a wolfish look, he complied, taking her into his arms and lying back, cradling her in the crook of his arm. She ran her palm over the ridge of his pec, and down his abdomen, sliding her fingers into the waistband of his shorts where hard muscle tensed under her. No denying his body was magnificent. Or that she'd itched to explore every inch of it since Vegas. She grazed his hip bone and down over his muscled ass and back across the top of his thigh, all hardened from years of riding. There wasn't an ounce of softness on him. Except apparently, in his heart, and she struggled to wrap her head around that. The Colton in front of her was not the heartless, selfish young man who'd left under cover of darkness years ago.

He rolled his hip into her palm as she continued her exploration. "You feel good," he said with a needy grunt.

Slipping her hand lower inside his shorts, she brushed the head of his cock, slicked with his arousal. Lydia's pulse took off to the races, as a soft giggle escaped. He was hot, hard, and huge.

He answered with a low chuckle. "Everything meet with your approval?"

She propped herself up on an elbow so she could stare into his eyes, hazed with desire. She dropped her hand down his rigid length, squeezing. Then she cupped his balls, giving a tiny tug. A groan ripped from his mouth. "Jesus, that's hot, Lyds," he rasped, bucking under her hand.

"You got that right," she answered on a sigh, dropping her head to place a kiss on his collarbone while she continued to stroke him, her own body responding to his. The salt from his skin acted like an aphrodisiac, and she nipped and sucked across his chest, lifting her head at intervals to make sure he liked it. His face looked tortured, and his hand gripped the sheets. But his mouth told a different story, and she pressed her lips to his. "Colt?"

"What is it, darlin'?" he said tightly.

She kissed the corner of his mouth, swept her tongue across his lower lip.

With a groan, his hand came to her back, holding her in place as he devoured her mouth with the same intensity he'd kissed her elsewhere. Her body responded in a rush of hot heat when she tasted herself on his tongue, mixed with his essence and the faint taste of whiskey. She continued to stroke his cock with the same rhythm their tongues took until he tore his mouth away with a noise that came from deep in his throat. "I'm on the verge, sweetheart. I'm gonna need that condom now if we're gonna make this good for you, too."

"You already made this good for me."

"Not by half," he bit out.

A thrill shivered down her spine as she rolled away, reaching for the drawer handle on the nightstand. When it opened enough for her to reach in, she grabbed a fistful and tossed them on the bed, coming to her knees. She yanked down his boxer briefs, and his cock sprang free, heavy and thick. She couldn't resist, she had to have a taste. She smacked her lips and bent over him, swiping her tongue up the length of him.

He let out a guttural moan and arched as she slowly explored him, swirling her tongue around the pre-come soaked head once, twice. "Lyds." His voice held a note of warning.

Her clit throbbed in answer and she straddled him, grinding her wet pussy up and down against him. The noises that came from her throat were not her own, they belonged to some wanton who'd taken over her body. But he felt so good, she couldn't help it. She wanted more, more, more.

"Condom, now," he rasped harshly.

She sat back, and grabbed a wrapper, tearing it open, then slowly rolled it over the swollen head and down his cock. Her heart beat wildly as she moved over him. He grabbed her hips and entered her with a heavy thrust. They both cried out.

"Damn, you feel good," he uttered, fingers splaying across her ass and digging into her flesh.

She liked that. A lot. "Do that again," she commanded as she rocked against him. He filled her completely, hit something deep inside her that sent her on an upward spiral back to the moon. She was a goner when he lifted his head and captured a nipple in his mouth, licking and sucking as he continued to thrust firmly. Her mind went white and blue as her vision blurred and she braced an arm on the headboard, completely lost in the sensations he was pulling from her. The tension built and spiraled, tighter and higher until she crested in a burst of sparks and she cried out long and loud from it.

Somewhere in the back of her mind, she recognized Colt's cries mingling with hers as she clamped around him, and he continued to thrust relentlessly until she collapsed on his chest, sweaty and spent. His heart pounded in her ear, a deep thrum that vibrated through her and acted as her guide back to earth. He stroked her back, still moving slowly, humming into her ear.

She lifted her head, giving him a crooked smile. "Are you singing?"

He raised his eyebrows with an answering grin and a shrug. "Maybe."

Reluctantly, she rolled off him, feeling a loss when his warmth was no longer a part of her. "Bathroom's down the hall."

He returned a few minutes later, washcloth in hand. "Here," he offered as he sat on the bed. "Let me." He cleaned her up, then tossed the cloth into her hamper, and pulled back the covers.

"What are you doing?"

"What does it look like?" He challenged, slipping under the covers and inviting her to do the same.

"You can't spend the night."

Lydia could have sworn she saw hurt flash in his eyes, but it was quickly covered by bravado. "Why the hell not?"

"Roommates?" She would never hear the end of it if Luci and Emmaline found out. Not to mention it would be all over town in a hot second. She was already a little concerned about the fact Colt's truck was parked in her driveway. But it was early yet, a few hours until last call. At least his presence here was plausible.

"Fair enough." The regret she detected in his voice, surprised her, but he opened his arm. "Lie with me for a bit, then?"

"I never took you for a cuddler," she teased.

"I'm not. Usually. But, if we're going to have an... er, arrangement, then we might want to talk about the details. You know, before you send me packing."

His voice stayed light, but something in his eyes tugged at her. Something that told her unequivocally that if she wasn't very careful, Colton Kincaid could smash her heart to smithereens. "Okay, what's next? I can't suddenly turn into a camp follower."

Colt gave her a reassuring pat. "It won't come to that. A few appearances with me on the circuit should be enough to satisfy my sponsors, and that should help your boots too."

"And you're sure no one here will find out?"

He shook his head dismissively. "Nah. This is only until things settle down."

"What do you tell them… later?"

"That it didn't work out. I can play the part of the broken-hearted cowboy for a few weeks, and no one will be the wiser."

Hearing him lay it out so matter-of-factly was unsettling. She shook her head. "I don't know."

"Don't tell me you're already getting cold feet?" He pushed her hair behind her ear, drawing his finger down her jaw in a way that sent shivers of awareness down to her fingertips. "That this was just a ploy to get me into bed?"

"You." She gently socked him in the shoulder. "Are incorrigible."

He flashed her a grin, waggling his eyebrows. "And proud of it." He grew serious. "When can you join me on the road?"

Her stomach yo-yoed at his words. She was really doing this. Starting a boot company and pretending to be engaged to Colt. If she was tired of living a boring, predictable, good-girl existence, she'd just jumped into the deep-end of the adventure pool. She shrugged. "I'm pretty flexible. But I think I should get a website up, maybe make you another pair of boots, and take some pictures of the wedding boots I made for Maddie Sinclaire. And Jamey Sinclaire's too. I'll get some sketches together and order some leather swatches."

He waved a hand at the wall. "What about these?"

"Those are just doodles."

"Pretty damned fancy doodles." Colton threw back the sheets and stood, apparently heedless to the fact he was beautifully, magnificently naked.

"Where are you going?"

"Nowhere. I just needed this." He bent, and stood a moment later, phone in hand, then crawled back into bed.

"First, I want your info in my phone. Second, we need to

take some pictures."

"Oh no." She shook her head vehemently, wrapping her arms around herself. "No nudie shots."

Colton's deep laugh filled the room. "You don't want a dick pic to remember me by?"

"Ewwww." But her own laugh joined his.

He leaned in, holding out his phone. "Smile."

She smiled at the camera.

"Again."

This time, when she smiled, he kissed her cheek. It was ridiculous that something as simple as a kiss on the cheek warmed her the way it did. She ducked her head, face flushing. "Give me your phone."

He handed it to her, and she typed in her information. "What do you want for a ringtone?"

"What do you mean, what do I want for a ringtone?" He asked suspiciously.

She made a face in exasperation. "All lovey-dovey couples have special ringtones."

"Since when?"

"Since always."

"No way," he scoffed, shaking his head. "That's for tennis players with sweaters over their shoulders and wives named Buffy."

She sighed dramatically. "Fine. Suit yourself." But she was determined to make sure Colt didn't forget her.

"Hey, what are you doing?" He craned his neck trying to peek over her shoulder, but she turned and kept punching into his phone.

"Nothing," she answered with a smirk, handing back his phone.

"Lydia?"

"Text me those pictures?"

"What did you do to my phone?"

She shrugged. "Nothing. Did you send the pictures?"

His eyebrows slashed together, but the corner of his mouth twitched. "I swear, if you put stripper music on my phone."

Her shoulders shook. "I swear. No stripper music." Then she turned serious. "It's almost eleven."

Colt's face fell. He flashed her a dazzling smile, but she could see his disappointment in the tightness of his jaw. He slid out of bed and jammed a leg into his pants, dressing quickly. "I'll be outta here in two shakes. Your girlfriends won't be the wiser."

Except for the overpowering scent of full-on sex that permeated the room. Her chest pinched. She hated to see him go. It was for the best, she reminded herself harshly, as she followed suit and grabbed a robe she'd left draped over a chair. Pulling it tight around her waist, she followed him down the hall.

At the door, he paused, leaning on it as he gazed down at her. "Any chance we can renegotiate our agreement?"

For a full second, she considered it. But she couldn't do this again, as much as her lady bits hollered for more. Rodeo life wasn't for her, and neither was Colton Kincaid. Someday, she'd meet a nice, stable man who was interested in settling down and starting a family, who wouldn't be threatened by her dreams. Colton was a wild adventurer, a risk-taker. The furthest thing from relationship material. Her stomach hollowed as she shook her head. "We're going to be business partners tomorrow. I'm sorry, I can't."

Or won't?

Her conscience pricked at her. She cupped his face and

popped up on tiptoe to drop a kiss at the corner of his mouth, savoring one last taste of him. "I-I don't regret this, though. Not for a second."

His face remained an impassive mask as he quietly stared back at her. Twice in the silence, she almost changed her mind. So when his cocky grin slid back into place, she nearly sagged with relief. "Me either, sweetheart." Tipping his Stetson, he opened the door. "I'll be in touch." Without a backward glance, he strode to his truck, all swagger, as if he knew her eyes stayed riveted on his ass.

CHAPTER 16

Three weeks later

L YDIA SAT AT a picnic table near her mother's food truck, leafing through a shoe equipment catalog with Emmaline and Luci. "You sure it would be okay to put another industrial machine in the dining room?" The first check from Colton had arrived by certified mail the day before and was currently burning a hole in her pocket. She was anxious to get the ball rolling.

Luci shrugged, giving Lydia a wry smile. "When my parents gave me the bungalow, I never imagined it becoming a sweatshop."

"I'll be moved back into my apartment over the dress-shop as soon as Main Street reopens," mentioned Emmaline. She turned to Lydia. "I have plenty of space in there. You're welcome to move your equipment in while you're in start-up."

Lydia pulled a sketchbook out of the bag she used as a catch-all for her wallet and everything else. "What do you think of this design?" She pointed to one of the Grace Boots logos she'd doodled. "And I've been thinking, Emmaline, what if we team up for bespoke western wedding wear?"

Emmaline's eyes grew wide. "You mean like trying to get customers?"

Lydia nodded eagerly. "Your dresses are gorgeous. And a bride would love nothing more than your special touches on a dress." She grinned across the table at her roommate. "And a custom-made pair of boots."

Emmaline shook her head. "Oh, wow. I don't know. I'm really just a tailor."

"Pfffft," Lydia scoffed. "You're brilliant. Can we at least team up for a photo shoot? Your dresses and the wedding boots I've made?"

"Morning, ladies." Jamey Sinclaire joined them.

"Just the person I was hoping to talk to," said Lydia, raising her cup of coffee. Post tornado, Jamey had teamed up with her mom to run the food truck while the diner was being rebuilt. It turned out that Jamey and Dottie made a great team in the kitchen, something that shocked and thrilled Lydia. She never thought she'd live to see the day her mother shared a kitchen with anyone, let alone a Cordon-Bleu trained chef. But stranger things had happened in the aftermath of the tornado that had nearly destroyed Prairie.

Jamey refilled everyone's cups, then straddled the bench. "What can I do ya for?"

"Emmaline and I were just talking about teaming up for western wedding attire–"

"I said I was *thinking* about it," Emmaline interjected.

"Give Lyds an inch and she'll blow a hole in the barn door," chimed in Luci.

Lydia raised her hands. "Okay, okay, we're thinking about it. And we wanted to know if you'd be willing to put on your wedding dress and boots again, for a photo shoot?"

"I'm sure Brodie would like that," Jamey said with a smirk. "Sure. You bet. Just tell me when and where." She waved at someone across the way. "You guys need to talk to my sister-in-law." She stood up, waving harder. A young, slim blonde woman, not more than twenty-three or four paused at the table. "Em, you know Lydia and Emmaline, right?"

Emma nodded, accepting a cup of coffee from Jamey. "Sure. What's up?"

"We've been catching up," Jamey said. "Emmaline and Lydia are thinking of teaming up to create a line of western wear." Jamey turned to them, brimming with pride. "You know my little 'sis, here is a crackshot marketing genius."

"Oh?" Emma perked up. "How can I help?"

"Branding for starters." Lydia pushed her sketchbook across the table. "I've got some ideas, and a template for a simple website sketched out, but my expertise is in footwear, not marketing."

Emma nodded. "I'd give anything for a pair of your boots."

Lydia blushed at the compliment. "I'd be happy to trade. My work in New York was haute couture, and with Emmaline's talent for dresses, the obvious starting place is bespoke wedding attire, but we need help."

"I can absolutely help," Emma enthused. "Have you thought about a photo shoot?"

"We were just discussing that before you arrived," affirmed Lydia.

"I'm going to rearrange my schedule next week and work from Prairie. Let me see what I can do. Have you thought of a name yet?"

Emmaline's eyes grew big, and she shook her head. "I only make clothing. Everything else is Lyd's thing."

Lydia took a big breath. This was it. The moment the dream came to life. "I always liked the sound of Grace Boots, but I'm not so sure if that works with the addition of apparel."

Emma nibbled on a pen, eyebrows pulled together, deep in thought. "I'll think on it. Maybe this needs to be a collaboration between two different brands."

Lydia took a big breath and glanced around the table, heat racing up her spine. "I should also tell you in the name of disclosure, that I made a deal with Colton Kincaid."

Emma's eyebrows flew skyward. "Colton? That's quite a coup. I think the man has more groupies in Vegas than Elvis."

"*What?*" Luci banged the table with the palm of her hand, practically shouting. "I *KNEW* there was something up between you two."

Lydia's face flamed. How Luci suspected anything was beyond her. She and Colton had been totally discreet when he'd briefly returned to town two weeks ago, and she hadn't seen him since. Of course, she hadn't been very discreet at Thanksgiving. But *still*. She glanced Emmaline's direction. Emmaline stared at her, slack-jawed. How in the heck was she going to pull off a fake engagement? Her roommates would smell a rat in a New York minute. "Umm, yeah. We... ah... have an understanding. But it's very confidential."

Luci stared at her speculatively. "Don't ever play poker, Lyds. You'll get your ass handed to you."

Truth. And exactly why she was so worried about this whole fake engagement business. She wasn't slick or sophisticated. If anyone was going to blow it, it was her.

"If you've managed to talk Colton into being a brand ambassador, you'll have orders in no time." Emma stood. "I've gotta run, but let's talk more next week. Jamey, would you be willing to make dinner? I'm certain there's a way I can help all three of you. I'm meeting my favorite print photographer over at Resolution Ranch shortly, so I'll talk to her too. She may have some ideas."

Jamey hopped up and gave Emma a hug. "I *knew* you'd be able to help."

Emma stood and topped off her coffee. "Figure out what night works for the three of you and send me a text. I'll bring my laptop and pens."

As soon as Emma had disappeared, Luci leaned forward. "An *understanding*? Between you and the hottest cowboy on the rodeo circuit? Spill."

Lydia tried not to squirm in her seat. "There's nothing to spill. I made Colton a pair of boots, he liked them, I asked him if he would invest in my crazy idea, he said yes. End of story."

"Girl." Luci shook her head. "That is *so* not the end of the story. There are always strings attached where Colton Kincaid is concerned. That boy doesn't have an altruistic bone in his body."

"Maybe he's changed," she snapped defensively. It had been on the tip of her tongue to confide everything in her roommates. But Luci's comment rankled her.

Luci's hands shot up. "Okay, okay, you're right. Maybe he's changed. I just don't want to see you get hurt."

"I'm a big girl, Luce. I can handle it." Lydia stood. "I'm going to go order my equipment, see you back at the house?"

Luci nodded. "I'll be over at my folks most of the day, let's meet for drinks at the Trading Post around six?"

"Great. Emmaline, you too?"

She nodded. "I'm in. I have to go visit mama today."

Lydia gave her roommate a sympathetic hug. "Let us know if you need anything." Not many people knew Emmaline's mother was in an Alzheimer's care unit up in Topeka. Lydia couldn't imagine what she'd do without her own mother, and unconsciously made her way to the food truck. "Have a good day, mama," she called once the line had cleared.

Dottie leaned out the window. "You too, sweetie-pie. I'll see you tomorrow for dinner?"

"Of course." All hell would break loose if she blew off her mother's Sunday dinner. Not that she'd miss it for anything. Sundays were the only day Dottie cooked for the family, and she held nothing back. Lydia could always count on roast chicken, mashed potatoes, fluffy biscuits, and most importantly, pie. She blew Dottie a kiss and hurried home to the bungalow, making lists of everything she needed to purchase to be 'official'.

She itched to call Colton. They'd texted back and forth over the last couple of weeks, but she wanted to hear his voice, share a couple of design ideas with him. She checked her watch. Eleven. If he'd had a rough night, surely he'd be up by now. Not bothering to wait until she reached the bungalow, she pulled him up and pressed 'call'.

The phone rang once, twice. On the third ring, his rich voice, still filled with the fog of sleep answered. "Circus music? You programmed circus music?"

Laughter pealed from her throat. "Like that?"

"I like pretty much anything coming from you."

Oh. Her stomach did a somersault. "I got your check yesterday. Thanks."

"Don't spend it all in one place."

"I aim to."

"Yeah? On what?"

"First major purchase is an industrial sewing and embroidery machine. I'll have some left over for website development. I'll need more lasts and samples, but I can purchase those with the first few deposits."

His voice filled with concern. "Do you need more? I can have my bank wire more if you need."

His concern shouldn't make her heart lurch the way it did. Any concerned business partner would ask the same question. Somehow, his tone of voice made everything more... personal. "I'm good, thanks. But I'll let you know."

"Do that. I want you to start off on the right foot. Have everything you need."

She couldn't help the smile that spread across her face. "Hey, can I tell you about the meeting I just had?"

"You bet, darlin'."

If anyone but Colton had called her that, it would have had her hackles rising. If a New York exec had 'little miss'd' her, she'd have hobbled out of the office on one stiletto, because the other would have been impaled in the wall behind his head. But coming from Colton, it felt sweet. "First off, Emmaline and Luce and I were down eating breakfast at mama's food truck, and Emmaline and I decided to team up for custom wedding attire. Emma Sinclaire is going to help us with marketing."

"Hey, that's great news." He meant it too, she could hear it in his voice. "But does that mean I don't get my custom ropers?"

She let out a little laugh as she turned the corner to make the final two-block walk to the bungalow. "For you, I'll make anything, but especially as a solo start-up, it makes sense to me to focus on high-end materials for special occasions. People will justify the cost of custom dress boots when they're walking down the aisle."

"Agreed."

As Lydia neared the house, a question that had been eating at her the last few weeks, surfaced again. Taking a breath, she dove in. "Do you ever think about getting married?" she ventured. "For real?"

"Me?"

"No. The man on the moon. Of *course*, you."

"Why you bringin' this up?"

She shrugged as she hopped up the steps to the front porch. "Curious. Probably a good thing to talk about if we're going to pull off being engaged."

Through the phone, she heard him sigh. "The short answer is no."

"What's the long answer?"

"You mean the complicated answer?"

"Sure. Go with that."

"Seeing Travis and Elaine together, being an uncle? Yeah. But I don't see it happening," he stated flatly.

"Oh." Her stomach hollowed at his denial. "Why not?"

"Rodeo life is hard. And not many women want to be, what'd you call it? Camp-followers?"

"Yeah, that."

"What about you? Do you see yourself married?"

"Someday, sure. I'd like kids. But most men want a homemaker. Someone to cook and clean and be mommy-taxi, but that's not me."

"Aww, c'mon," he chuckled. "I can see you wearing a frilly apron and prancing around in a pair of those girly shoes you made."

She laughed outright at the image. "With or without the cocktail dress on?"

"Definitely without."

"Oh, and I suppose you'd have me wearing one of those scandalous see-through crotchless bodysuits?"

His voice dropped an octave. "Would you wear one if I bought it for you?"

Her chest grew hot, and the inside of her mouth turned to

sandpaper. She moved her mouth, but no sound came out. She licked her lips, unable to stop the fantasy he'd painted from playing out in her head. Her eyes darted to the kitchen counter. She should hang up right now.

"I made you blush, didn't I?"

"I got the travel schedule you texted," she said quietly when her voice worked again.

His low laughter came through the phone. "Not gonna touch that one, huh?"

There was no way she was going to touch that one. "What if I joined you in San Antonio?"

"That'd be a good one not to miss."

"What are the chances I can get a last-minute booth at the exhibition hall?"

"If it comes down to money, don't hesitate. Book it."

Her stomach dropped. This was really happening. For a moment, paralyzing fear seized her. "Colt?"

"Yeah?"

"Do you think I can do this?"

When he answered, she was buoyed by the steel in his voice. "I don't make bad bets, darlin'."

CHAPTER 17

D AMN STUBBORN WOMAN. Why hadn't she let him pick her up at the airport? Colt checked his phone again as he paced outside the exhibition hall. She was late. Of *course*, she was late. She'd insisted on hauling all her gear by herself, and was probably trying to cram it all in the back of a tiny Uber car. He shook his head and continued pacing. He'd already taken a tour inside, found her booth and sized up the competition. Somehow, she'd managed to score a booth directly across from Stetson. Lucky draw. Vanguard Chaps & Leather was just around the corner, and Colt breathed a sigh of relief that Sammy Jo wouldn't be breathing down Lydia's neck the whole time.

Unease settled in his gut. Too much could go wrong this week. He and Lydia would have to play the couple in love in order convince Hal and Harrison Carter, and more importantly, Sammy Jo, that he had every intention of settling down. That wouldn't be too much of a stretch on his part. Not that he was in love, he wasn't, but he hadn't been able to stop thinking about Lydia the entire month they'd been separated. Sex with her had done the opposite of get her out of his system. He wanted more. So much more.

Where was she?

A mini SUV pulled up, and Lydia hopped out of the rear passenger door. His chest tightened in a painful rush of pleasure at the sight of her. He closed the distance between them in three steps and swept her into his arms, swinging her in a circle and surprising her with a kiss. Something pulled deep inside him when their lips locked, and he tightened his arms around her, savoring her sweetness. Her mouth was soft and pliant, welcoming. And in seconds, she was kissing him back. With a noise born of need, he slipped his tongue inside her lower lip, dying a little at the ache that erupted in his balls. She answered with a sigh of her own, tongue curling against his. He'd have stood there all afternoon, reacquainting himself with her mouth, her taste, but a series of catcalls registered in his ears, and he lifted his head, out of breath.

"You welcome all the ladies that way?" she teased, giving him a loopy grin.

For a moment he fell into her blue-green eyes, simply glad to see her again. But this was for show. Nothing more. "Just my fiancée."

Her eyes clouded, and she nodded. "Right." She gave him a bright smile that didn't quite ring true. "Sorry I'm late. I had to stop by the print shop to pick up my signs. It won't take me too long to get set up. If you have things to do, I can meet you back at the hotel."

He picked up both of the suitcases the driver had stacked on the sidewalk, and tucked a cardboard tube under his arm. "I'm not leaving you to set up by yourself."

"Don't be ridiculous, Colt," Lydia called after him, grabbing the remaining bag and following him into the building. "I've set up trade shows before. This is no different."

He ignored her, making his way to her booth. "What's different," he growled, setting the suitcases down in the center of her area, "is that you're my fiancée."

She dropped her bag and glared at him, hands on her

hips. "That may be, but I don't see other cowboys helping their sponsors set up. Don't you have things to do?"

Did she have to be so damned stubborn? He crossed his arms, widening his stance, and met her glare head-on. "The only thing I have to do is help your pretty little ass get this booth prepared. No gentleman would allow his *fiancée* to do that on her own." If she wanted to face off here, he had no problems staring her down.

After a long minute, she scowled and shook her head, the barest hint of a smile pulling on the corner of her mouth. "Fine. Suit yourself. Open that suitcase." She pointed to the one at his left. "Plastic container with the brochures gets set on the table."

He let out a low whistle once he opened the case. A pair of men's boots with shiny black lizard vamps and bluish-gold brushed leather tops with black lizard inlay, and shiny embroidery rested above the brochures. Next to them was a pair with pale gray vamps and slightly darker gray suede tops, embroidered with white flames. "Holy smokes." He whipped his head up to study her. "You've been busy." Her cheeks flushed pink, and she met his gaze. Only then did he see the lines of exhaustion around her eyes. She must have worked around the clock. Damn. He'd been so taken with her earlier, he'd failed to notice. "You sleep at all these last two weeks?"

Her cheeks darkened as she shrugged away his question and gestured toward the boots. "You like them?"

"'Course I do. You're gonna have orders out your ears."

"Maddie and Jamey Sinclaire lent me their wedding boots too, so I have four samples now."

"When do I get to wear these?" He stood, handing her the metallic pair.

She set the pair on a white pedestal at the center of the

space. "Not until the photo shoot."

"And when is that?"

"Next time you're in Prairie. We can set it up while I'm here." She held out her hand for the other pair. "Once you get the stand put together, the banner is in the cardboard tube. It's a pretty simple set-up."

Fifteen minutes later, Colton stepped back to take it in. He'd give her credit, she was good. Her booth oozed urban sophistication, but with enough softness in the colors, it felt warm and inviting. "This feels like you stepped into one of those fancy shops at the Bellagio, or Rodeo Drive."

Her eyes lit. "Yeah? That's exactly the vibe I was going for."

"You nailed it."

"Great, then I just need to lock up the boots, and we can be on our way."

Colton zipped the suitcases while she stowed the boots underneath one of the pedestals. "I tried to get us adjoining rooms, but you got one of the last rooms in the whole city."

"We'll make it work."

But as Colt stood at the check-in line with Lydia at the hotel, a hand clapped him on the shoulder. "I thought I might find you here, son," Hal Carter's booming voice made him freeze. "Is this the lady I've heard so much about?" He peered over Colt's shoulder to where Lydia stood.

Motherfucker.

Draping an arm across Lydia's shoulders, he hoped to heck he sounded happy to see Hal. "Sweetheart. Look who it is. You remember me telling you about Hal Carter?" He squeezed her shoulder, but he needn't have worried. Lydia was the epitome of gracious.

"Of course," she beamed up at him, then extended her

hand to Hal. "A pleasure to finally meet you, Mr. Carter. Colton's told me so much about you. You must be so proud of him."

"We are, we are," Hal boomed. "Harrison and I were stunned to learn someone finally caught this guy's attention. We're thrilled he's finally settling down." He gave Colton a meaningful look, but Lydia had jumped into her role with both feet.

"Believe me, I am, too," Lydia gushed with a big grin.

Hal zeroed in on her left hand, then shot a confused glance to Colt. *Shitdamnmotherfucker.* Colt braced for what was next.

"You mean to tell me you've been letting this pretty lady run around without your ring on her finger?"

Beside him, Lydia tensed. He hugged her to his side, placing a kiss on the top of her head. "You know, Lydia used to live in New York. She's, er, particular about things."

Lydia nodded vigorously. "Very. I flat-out told Colton if I wasn't there to approve the ring, that he shouldn't buy it. And this is the first time we've been together since he proposed." She batted her eyelashes up at him. "But we plan on going first thing tomorrow morning."

Okay, that was taking it a little far, but he went along with it. What else could he do under Hal's sharp eyes?

"Because as soon as we get married, we can't wait to settle down on his ranch."

What in the hell?!?

Colt tightened his grip on Lydia, silently trying to tell her to shut the hell up. "Don't worry," he assured Hal. "I have no plans to retire."

Lydia pursed her lips, eyes going wide. "Oh, dear." She looked from Colt to Hal and back. "I let the cat out of the bag, didn't I?" She leaned closer to Hal, and spoke in a loud whisper. "He promised we could start working on babies as soon as we get married."

Colt's mind went blank. She was fucking with him. She had to be fucking with him. If it was anyone but Hal Carter, he'd laugh his ass off at her shenanigans, but this? He had half a mind to turn her over his knee as soon as she was checked in.

Hal cleared his throat. "And when is that, exactly?"

They spoke at the same time.

"As soon as possible."

"We haven't discussed it yet." He tapped her nose. "Right, darlin'?"

Hal shifted nervously. "Looks like you've got yourself a live wire there, son." He cleared his throat again, a sign of his discomfort. "On another note, I came over to find out what floor you two are staying on. We've moved the sponsor floor to this hotel."

"Oh?" Colt fought for a semblance of calm. It seemed his plans were being messed with at every turn. "We have a suite on five."

"Good, good. Us, too. Sponsor floor is on six. Made sense to stay here this year."

Damn it all to hell. He risked a look down at Lydia, whose face was frozen in a smile. Yeah, she was going to *love* this. Although he'd be the first to admit he wouldn't mind sharing a room with her one bit. His cock sprang to attention at the thought of being alone with her for the next two and a half weeks.

Lydia spoke before he could, giving Hal a dazzling smile. "So we'll see you on the sixth floor in a little while? I can't wait to meet the rest of Colton's sponsors."

No. No, no, no. The Carters were ruining every single one of his plans. He'd already made reservations down on the Riverwalk to treat Lydia to a celebratory dinner tonight. Once the rodeo opened tomorrow, he'd have his game face on. He'd registered for all three rough stock events, which meant he wouldn't get as many rest days as his fellow competitors.

"You'll be watching him ride?" Hal asked.

"Of course," Lydia exclaimed, running her hand across his chest in a very possessive way. "Every night."

"Then you should join us in our box. Carter Holdings has the best seats in the arena. Right beside the chutes."

Oh hell to the no. Double, triple no. But before he could make an excuse, she gushed again. "I'd love to, thank you so much."

Thankfully, before Lydia could put the screws to him any further, the woman behind the counter motioned them over. He extended his hand, "Catch ya, Hal. I'll see you and Harrison later. Come on, *dear*." He pulled Lydia toward the counter and away from Hal. When he reached the woman, he bent his head and spoke low. "Already checked in, name's Kincaid. I just need another set of keys for my lady."

"Of course, Mr. Kincaid."

Colt braced an elbow on the counter and turned to Lydia. "So, *my dear*. You mind telling me what that load of horsepatooty back there was?"

Lydia rolled her lips together, eyebrows sky high, eyes sparkling. Damn if he didn't want to kiss her right now. For real, this time. Not for show. "Do you even have to ask?"

"I guess I do."

Her mouth curved up. "Let's just call it compensation for my trouble."

"What trouble?"

She gave him a look that said he should know. Then she winked at him. "I'll let you figure it out. In the meantime, I guess I'm glad I brought my flannel nightie."

Oh, hell. He wasn't used to a woman with a crack shot memory who gave as good as she got. It unsettled him. It aroused the shit out of him. He lowered his voice so only she could hear. "As long as you promise to wear nothing underneath it." Pink fired across her cheeks. He dipped his head closer. "So I can spank that pretty little ass of yours and turn it as pink as your sweet pussy."

She squeaked and kept staring straight ahead, cheeks darkening to red. He shook with suppressed laughter. Spending seventeen nights with Lydia was going to be entertaining as hell.

CHAPTER 18

"RISE AND SHINE, sweet thing. You're burnin' daylight." A mug of steaming coffee wafted under her nose.

Lydia fought opening her eyes. "It's still dark," she mumbled, turning toward the back of the couch and burrowing deeper into the comforter Colton insisted she take from the bed.

Colton's amused laugh washed over her. "You're on cowboy time, darlin'. We got a full day."

He was right, but she wasn't ready to face it just yet. She'd hoped now that she was in San Antonio, she'd be able to catch up on lost sleep, both from lying awake nights replaying being with Colton, and churning out two pairs of boots in record time.

"Suit yourself." The coffee table legs scraped against the thick carpet, and she registered the sound of the mug being placed on the glass top.

What peaked her curiosity was Colton's change in breathing, and what sounded an awful lot like moving. Holy shit, he wasn't? No. It didn't sound like what she imagined jacking off to be. Besides, Colt would never be that crass, would he? She pulled the comforter over her head and chased sleep. But when he grunted, she *had* to see what was going on behind her. With a yawn and a stretch, she rolled over, cracking an eyelid, then sat bolt upright. "*Yoga?*"

A chuckle rose from the floor as Colton moved from cobra into downward dog, shifting his gray boxer brief clad ass to eye level. Oh *hello*. She was barely awake, but her lady parts woke up with a rush of heat at the sight of his hard muscles moving through a sun salutation. "Gotta stay flexible," he grunted as he dropped into chaturanga, triceps bulging from the effort of holding himself inches from the floor. He stepped hopped to the edge of his map with the ease of a practiced yogi, then grinned down at her. "You might say it's my secret weapon."

Secret weapon indeed. She stared unabashedly at the bulge in his drawers. She swallowed, suddenly parched. "Coffee?" she managed to utter hoarsely.

"Ah, so you're one of those?"

She dragged her gaze up, locking eyes with him. He reached for her cup, clearly entertained, and offered it up. "What do you mean, I'm one of those?"

His dry laugh sent a shiver through her insides. She leaned her head back on the couch, eyes shut. It was too early to think straight, especially when seeing Colt in his glory had her regretting her hands-off policy.

"One of the first jobs I had the first winter I was in Steamboat Springs was to make sure the coffee was ready before morning chores. I had to get up before the ass-crack of dawn and make sure the coffee was hot and ready before the rest of the wranglers hit the barn. There were some that'd greet me with a smile, and others who grunted and stewed until they'd had a few cups."

She definitely fell into the latter category.

"Sleep all right?" He asked, returning to his sun salutations.

She grunted an affirmation, staring as he moved through

the series of poses, letting the coffee slowly bring her to life.

Colt moved into warrior two and slid her a look, mouth tipping up. "You could join me."

Her tired muscles ached to join him, but she needed at least another cup of coffee before she could even think about movement. "I'd rather stare at your fine ass," she retorted before she could stop herself. Her body flushed. Add verbal filter to the list of things that didn't function before coffee.

He dropped his head back with a laugh. "I like you first thing."

She snorted and took another gulp of the coffee, secretly pleased he'd added cream and sugar.

"This is good," he said from downward dog. "Now, when people ask, I can tell them how adorable you are first thing before the coffee's hit your system."

She saluted him with her mug. "Perks to sharing a room."

He stopped and stared down at her, cocking an eyebrow. "Always perks to sharing."

Somehow, she didn't think he meant it the same way she did. She fixated on his impressive bulge. Only looking away when he laughed at her again.

"Morning wood. Can't help it." He cupped himself loosely. "Of course," he started with a dramatic sigh. "If you hadn't insisted on sleeping on the couch, I could be waking you up to this every morning."

He was teasing her. Trying to get a rise out of her. His voice dripped with unexpressed laughter.

"Maybe I don't like morning sex," she said loftily.

He snorted. "Then you've never had it the right way. I promise you darlin', you'd fully enjoy morning sex on my watch."

"That's a pretty bold statement."

He turned back into downward dog. "I don't make claims I can't back up," he grunted. "Fully."

True. Colton might be cocky as all get out, but he wasn't a bullshitter. She respected that about him. She drained her cup. "I'm going to hit the shower."

"Want me to join you?" he called as she climbed over the couch.

"You wish," she shot back with a laugh. At least in the shower, she could hide from his glorious body and the memory of the kiss he'd greeted her with the previous afternoon. Or so she thought. As she stepped into the stream of hot water, her mind replayed every movement, every glance. The way his eyes had lit in appreciation at dinner the night before when she told him about her first runway show, the way he'd tucked her into his embrace as they'd strolled along the Riverwalk, taking in the lights and revelers. She knew it was for show, that they could run into the Carters at any moment, but on more than one occasion, she'd imagined what it would be like if there was really something between them. She rinsed those thoughts to the far recesses of her mind as she washed the conditioner from her hair. Colt might be entertaining and incredibly easy on the eyes, but he wasn't relationship material, let alone husband material. Soon enough they'd part ways, and better that happen with her heart intact.

She jumped as a knock sounded and the door creaked open. "You gonna stay in there all morning?" Colt called out.

"I'm not going anywhere as long as you're in here."

His voice sounded on the other side of the shower curtain. "I'd like that very much."

The innuendo set her stomach flip-flopping. The bad thing was, she would too. But if she engaged in a battle of wills, he'd sweet talk her right into bed. Best to ignore and divert. She turned off the water. "Hand me a robe, please? And no peeking."

His low rumble echoed off the walls. "Darlin', I've already seen you pink and wet. No need to hide it."

"Incorrigible."

His hand reached through the curtain, dangling the robe. "Appreciative is all."

She snatched the robe from his hand, slipping into it and wrapping it up to the neck. "Thank you." She pushed back the curtain, bracing herself for his nearness.

He stood with a hip braced against the counter, legs crossed, arms folded across his chest, as if he didn't have a care in the world. His eyes darkened, and she instinctively tightened the belt. "You're beautiful, you know." The husky burr in his voice sent a blaze of arousal through her, rooting her to the floor. "You don't have to dress all sexy, or wear make-up, or do your hair fancy. I like you best like this."

His frankness unnerved her, set her pulse hammering. Heat bloomed across her chest, creeping up her neck. Looking at him was too much, and she studied his feet. "I don't know what to say," she murmured, just above a whisper.

"Don't need to say anything," he said just as softly. "I just wanted you to know."

She looked up at him, genuine appreciation filling her. "I... that's sweet of you. No one's... no one's ever told me that before."

He shook his head. "Damned fools. All of 'em."

She waved toward the door. "I'm gonna get ready."

He lifted his chin in acknowledgment. "It won't take me too long." His mouth pulled up. "I'm not hiding."

She let out a huff as she slipped through the door. Incorrigible indeed. But she couldn't stop smiling as she got ready, opting for a pair of denim skinny jeans, a white blouse, and her favorite pair of heeled booties, the last pair she'd made while at Christian LaSarte. She loved them, and today she'd take all the confidence boosting she could get.

Ten minutes later, Colton strutted out of the bathroom, towel wrapped around his waist, hair damp. She held his gaze in the mirror, before breaking it to apply her lipstick. Ogling him would just wind her up and wouldn't change a thing.

"What time do you need to be to the exhibition hall?"

"Nine. What's your day look like?"

He gave her a crooked grin in the mirror before opening the closet where he'd stowed his suitcase. "Before or after watching you work?"

"You mean pestering me?"

"Call it what you like. You're watchin' me work tonight. Turnabout is fair play."

She scoffed. "Hardly. But I wouldn't mind the company," she admitted. "I'm a little nervous."

"People are gonna go crazy over those boots, hon." The sound of him shoving a leg in his jeans floated her way. "Don't worry about a thing. I can stay most of the day. I'll have to visit my other sponsors, and I do have to see a jeweler about a ring."

Her stomach fluttered, more from his words than her nerves. "Oh." She perched on a chair next to the dresser. She was ready to go, and there was nothing left to do but ogle him as he finished getting dressed.

"Tell me what you like." He pulled a blue plaid shirt off a hanger and slipped it on. A shame to cover up that six-pack.

She shrugged. "Nothing flashy. Something simple, understated. I never thought about it, really."

He folded his arms, shaking his head. "Uh-uh. I'm gonna get you the biggest, baddest-ass ring I can find. My reputation as a cowboy and a gentleman hinges on it."

Her chest tightened with laughter. "Because size matters?"

He hooked his thumbs through his belt. "Hell, yes. In buckles, boots, and babes."

She groaned, shaking her head. "Where do you come up with this?"

He shot her a grin. "You bring out the best in me, sweetheart."

She rolled her eyes. "Seriously. Nothing flashy. I prefer my flash to be on my feet." She pointed to her booties.

"I'll keep that in mind."

Several hours later a shiver raced down her spine, and she turned in time to see the crowd parting in the exhibition hall aisle. Colt carried himself with such easy power and purpose, people naturally stepped out of the way. She spied his Stetson a half-head above everyone else three booths down. What she wasn't prepared for was the jealous twinge that grabbed at her gut when three young women stopped him for a photo. She had half a mind to stalk over and shoo them along. Another jealous wave hit her. They were rubbing up against him like cats in heat. Who did that?

He means nothing to you she reminded herself harshly. Furthermore, she couldn't fault his behavior. He wasn't flirting with them, merely being polite. As much as she didn't like it, he wasn't dishonoring their agreement. Fangirling was bound to happen. He was too good-looking, his face too recognizable in rodeo circles. He caught her staring, and excused himself from the ladies, making a beeline for her while still holding her gaze. He stopped inches from her, eyes dancing. "Hi."

So much promise in a single word. It was a crime, the way it affected her. "Enjoy your fans?"

He raised his brows with a grin. "Not as much as I'm enjoying you."

Oh.

She should know better than to open herself up to comments like that. But she had to admit, she enjoyed his praise. She moved with a little more sass in her step when she knew he was watching, commenting.

"I have something for you."

"Yeah?" Butterflies launched in her chest.

He nodded, taking her left hand. "Shut your eyes."

The butterflies turned into kickboxing ninja grasshoppers, but she complied, biting her lower lip in a failed attempt to not grin like a kid who'd just been given the keys to the candy shop.

He slipped the ring on her finger, and she opened her eyes. "*Ohmygod it's enormous*" she squealed, as she stared at her finger, then Colt, then back at her finger.

"You might want to keep that information private, darlin'," he answered wryly.

The thing was huge. And heavy. The way it dwarfed her finger, the center stone had to be three carats, at least. The diamond was cut in a way that it flashed blue, green, and purple. It was surrounded by smaller diamonds, and even more around the band. The thing glittered like the Chrysler building in summer. She held out her hand, turning it in the light. "This is your idea of not flashy?"

His mouth twitched.

She tried not to smile back, but failed as she dissolved into giggles, shaking her head. "You did this on purpose, didn't you?"

He smirked and shrugged, studying the ceiling. "Pay-back," he mouthed.

"Oh, you devil." She covered her mouth, trying not to laugh. "Fine. I'll wear it. But you have to promise to take it back when this is all over."

Something fierce flashed in his eyes, and his face went taut. He shrugged. "We'll see."

"Colt," she insisted, glancing down at it again. "You can't keep this. I don't even want to know how much it cost." She shook her head. "Please tell me you insured it."

"Don't you worry about it. Just enjoy it."

"What happened to being discreet?"

"This is more fun."

Maybe. She felt like she'd borrowed a piece for the Met Gala. "I hope you know what you're doing. If mama finds out—"

"We'll handle it," he said, the cocky note returning to his voice. "Now give me a kiss. There's a crowd watching."

CHAPTER 19

H E COULD GET used to this, demanding kisses of her in public. She kissed him with the same intensity she had at Thanksgiving, and again the night they'd made love. He had to pinch himself to remind himself this was for show, and that if they'd been standing here in any other circumstances, her hands would not currently be twined around his neck. Nor would she be wearing that gaudy, God-awful ring. As soon as he'd laid eyes on it in the jewelry store, he'd had to have it, knowing it would provoke a response from Lydia. What surprised him, shocked him even, was the possessive instinct that rose up from a deep place inside him when he slipped the ring on her finger for the world to see. It might only be temporary, but for the time being, she belonged to him, and he liked it.

When they pulled apart, the cheers and whistles registered. Lydia looked around, wide-eyed at the crowd that had amassed, shooting him a fear-filled look when she saw the number of phones outstretched to take a picture. He pulled her close, ducking his head. "Don't worry sweetheart, they're just fans. No press. You don't have to worry about anyone at home finding out."

She nodded, sagging against him.

"Hey," he tipped her chin up, allowing himself another quick taste of her sweet mouth, to the delight of the crowd.

"Everything's gonna be fine. Think of your boots." He turned, keeping his arm around her, and raised an arm to the small group gathered. "Thanks, y'all. In case you haven't figured out here, this lovely lady has agreed to marry me. And she makes a mean pair of boots, too."

Lydia smiled, dipping her head bashfully, clearly unused to the attention.

"Took you long enough," a voice that grated on his very last nerve called out. "Daddy and I thought you were gonna keep your lady hidden until we flushed her out."

Beside him, Lydia stiffened. It took effort, but he kept his voice relaxed. "Nice to see you, Sammy Jo. I was just about to bring Lydia by to say hello."

The look on Sammy's face said she didn't believe him for a second. But she didn't have to, it was God's truth. He'd needed to pick up a ring before he showed up at Vanguard Chaps & Leather with Lydia in tow.

"Lyds, meet Samantha Jo Carter, Hal's niece. You'll meet her daddy, Harrison this evening at the rodeo. Sammy Jo is one of the smartest businesswomen I know, and head of Vanguard Chaps and Leather." Sammy Jo had an ego the size of Texas, and as long as she believed she was the best in the room, she'd be easier to handle. The second she felt threatened, the claws were likely to come out. The challenge over the next few weeks would be to keep Sammy from cornering Lydia. She didn't play by the same rules Lydia did, and even though he and Sammy Jo were old news, years-old news, he wouldn't put it past her to exact some kind of revenge if she thought she could get away with it. Hell, she'd once threatened to put cayenne in his briefs in a fit of rage, and he'd hidden his drawers for weeks because of it.

Instead of stepping out of his embrace and extending her

right hand, Lydia offered her left hand, angling her hand so Sammy couldn't help but see the ring. He suppressed a chuckle, entertained and pleasantly surprised by Lydia's claws coming out.

"So nice to finally meet you. Colt's told me so much about you. I'd love to take you to coffee and learn more about your experience running Vanguard. Colt speaks so highly of the job you've done, and since I'm just starting out," she gestured around the space, "I'd love any advice you could share."

Her brows slashed together as she frowned briefly. "Yeah, sure. I... yes. I'd be happy to."

It wasn't often Sammy Jo didn't know what to say. Pride surged through him. Lydia handled her like a pro. Maybe he'd underestimated her. A knot of tension across his shoulders began to release. This whole thing would go much more smoothly with Sammy Jo in check. Placing a kiss on the top of Lydia's head, he made their excuses. "If you'll excuse us, I wanna make sure Lydia gets some food. We'll catch you later." Before Sammy Jo could reply, he steered Lydia down the aisle and toward the food court at the center of the exhibition hall.

When they were out of earshot, Lydia glared up at him. "Why didn't you tell me your ex was a Carter?"

A twinge of guilt poked at Colt. "What do you mean?"

"I'm not a dummy, Colt. Anyone with half a brain could see she was fit to be tied. Only an ex would be that catty."

"You handled her perfectly."

She made a face. "I worked with a lot of temperamental types in New York. But that's beside the point. I would have appreciated some warning."

Colt rubbed his jaw. "Sammy and I were more off than on, and honestly, I figured I'd have more time."

She stopped in the middle of the aisle and turned to him, eyes flashing. "*Really?* Like before tonight? You've been leading the Carters on for what, four, six weeks? And I'm guessing you probably let it drop that I was coming to town... so you didn't think to lay all your cards on the table and give me fair warning?"

Shame licked at him, heating his neck. The way she framed it, ate at him. "All I'm doing is re-vamping my image to their liking. Which I was already planning on doing."

She cocked her head in disbelief. "Umm-hmm." She waggled her left hand at him. "And that's why you went to all this trouble?"

He flashed her a disarming smile. "Of course. And," he said stepping up to her and tilting her chin. "I get to spend more time with you. Which I like." He kissed the tip of her nose.

She shut her eyes briefly, shaking her head and screwing her mouth up into a little bow. "You are something else, Colton Kincaid. Something else."

He got the feeling she didn't mean that in a good way, which ate at him too. "What would you do if you were in my shoes?" he said low enough that only she could hear.

Her eyes narrowed, and she speared him with a look that arrowed into the deepest reaches of his heart. "I'd be honest."

That got his hackles up. "I may have been a lying, cheating sonofagun before Travis gave me the boot, but I learned." He grimaced as the memories flashed through his mind in picture form. "You have no idea how I learned. In fact, it was my very *honesty* about my life choices that got me into this mess in the first place."

He stared at the ceiling and counted to ten. Hell, he knew plenty of cowboys that had a woman at home and one on the road, and their sponsors knew it and looked the other way. He'd never been anything but up front that he wasn't looking for more than a good time from the women he was with.

"Listen up, sweetheart," he said tersely and bent close to her ear. "You like that nice sized investment check I sent you? I have the luxury of being able to do that because, in addition to my hard-won earnings, I have sponsors. So before you get all high and mighty over fifty shades of the truth, you'd best remember we're both in this together."

Lydia's face remained carefully neutral, but her eyes told him he'd hit his mark. She nodded once. "I see." She nodded again, staring at the ground. When she raised her eyes, her jaw was set. "Thank you for clearing that up."

Oh, hell. "Lydia, I–"

She held up a hand. "Save it for later. You're competing tonight, and I think I need to get back to my booth." She brushed past him, hurrying back the way they'd come.

Colt bit back a groan of frustration. Damn straight they'd talk about this later. Of course, it was his fault they were in this mess at all.

CHAPTER 20

COLTON HOPPED OFF the treadmill, winded, sweaty, and just as cranky as he'd been when he'd stepped on twenty minutes earlier. Screw him for ever thinking a pretend fiancée was a good idea. He guzzled the remainder of his sports drink and tossed it with extra force. It bounced off the rim of the trash can, landed and rolled halfway across the tiny hotel gym before coming to rest against the lat machine.

Nine days.

Nine days of 'don't even think of speaking to me until I've had a cup of coffee' Lydia. Nine days of her sweet ass in yoga pants joining him for sun salutations. Nine days of her perky tits taunting him through the tank top she slept in. Worst of all? Nine days of enjoying her kisses and public displays of affection, then lying awake sleepless as she snored quietly on the couch. He fucking loved those little snores, wanted to hear them in his ear as she lay nestled in his arms, not across the room.

He stalked across the room and snatched up the empty container, beating it against his palm as he returned to the trash can. She'd played her role to perfection after they'd ironed out their little disagreement the day he'd given her the ring. He'd laid everything on the table that night – his ups and downs with Sammy Jo until he'd called it quits, and the way she'd acted since then. The way Harrison had pressured him more than once to make an honest woman of Sammy Jo, all of it.

Surprisingly, it had felt good to get all that off his chest. Between his late father and his older brother, he'd learned at a young age to not talk about anything that bothered him, hence many of his poor choices as a young man. What surprised him the most, was how Lydia listened, really listened, to all of it.

Crushing the plastic, he jammed it in the trashcan and headed for the elevator mentally preparing himself for the vision of Lydia still damp from her shower. Maybe he should get out of town for a few days before the semi-finals. Take a breather. He had three days off after tonight's performance. There was a rodeo in Laredo he could hit, make some easy money, clear his head. But as soon as the thought entered his head, he discarded it. He'd never leave while Lydia was around. Who was he kidding? He'd take Lydia any way he could get her, platonic kisses, snoring and all. Even if it meant his balls would explode from frustration. He stepped out of the elevator and marched down the hall praying she was already dressed.

She stepped out of the bathroom, toweling her hair as he shut the door behind him. "Oh, you startled me," she squeaked, flashing him a smile as he stood staring unabashedly, heat lighting up her eyes. "You okay?" She cocked her head after a moment, sizing him up.

"Fine." He brushed past her. "Get dressed," he growled. "Gotta big day."

"The run didn't help your mood any."

Neither did her state of undress.

"Want to meet me for lunch today? I have a client coming at eleven to make a deposit and get his feet measured."

"Great news," he said, mentally rearranging his morning so he could stop by her booth around then. "How many is this?"

"Five."

"You gonna be able to keep up?"

"Of course. Why wouldn't I?" She caught his eye in the mirror.

"Because I know how tired you got making two pair in two weeks," he said gruffly.

"Worry about yourself, grumpy. I'll be fine."

Grumpy, indeed. How could he not be, when all he wanted was to pull her into his arms and kiss her senseless? Then treat her to a fancy dinner, maybe some dancing, and then make sweet love to her all night long? He should be a candidate for fucking sainthood. "I was thinking about heading down to Laredo tomorrow," he said as he dug into his suitcase. "There's a rodeo down there, and I could use a change of scenery for a few days."

She turned, eyes full of concern, clutching her clothing to her chest. "Don't you need to rest?"

"Time to rest when you're dead," he grumbled, pissed that he'd brought it up. Now he'd have to go to save face. "I'm not going to lose best All-Around cowboy by ten-thousand, this year, either."

"But you've ridden hard for nine straight days."

He shrugged, frowning. "That's the way of it. Hell, I know some guys who'll hit three performances in a day." God, he was an ass. She looked downright disappointed.

"Suit yourself," she said quietly. "But be careful, okay?" She retreated to the bathroom, returning two minutes later, fully dressed. "I'm gonna head over to the exhibition hall. Catch up with you later?"

"Yep," he said, staring out the window. Hell, maybe he needed another run. He needed to work this bad mood out of his system before the night's performance. He'd been in the money the previous two nights, but he'd drawn a good mount for tonight and was riding last. Tonight, he owned the arena.

RAZZLE DAZZLE BUCKED and kicked in the chute while the flankman struggled to secure the flank strap. The horse's mood matched his own. Difference was, he was gonna come out on top tonight. Colt had studied up on Razzle Dazzle, just like he did with all his draws. The horse would pull left as soon as he was out of the chute, and would give a first strong kick with his rear legs. Then, it was fifty-fifty whether or not the horse would twist. The 'twist and kick' as Colt referred to it, was the horse's signature move, and the reason not one cowboy had kept his seat this rodeo. Only three men this season had. Colt aimed to be the fourth. All he needed was a score of eighty-two to come out on top tonight.

After what seemed like an eternity, but in reality was probably only thirty seconds, the flankman gave him the signal, and he climbed over the rail. A guttural noise came from Razzle Dazzle as he jammed his gloved hand into the rigging and settled his grip. Warning bells sounded in Colt's head. The last time he'd drawn a horse this feisty, he'd ended up with three broken ribs. But not tonight. Adrenaline coursed through his veins, sharpening his focus to a laser point. Lydia was in the stands, and he wasn't some wet behind the ears greenhorn with more ego than sense. He'd studied the footage, gone over the ride in his mind and was ready.

"Tear it up, Kincaid," hollered one of his buddies.

"Show 'em who's boss," added another.

A chorus of encouragement rose up, and Colton smiled tightly. This was it. He set his spurs above the horse's shoulders, raised his arm, and nodded.

The chute swung open.

Razzle Dazzle shot out like a rocket, rebelling against the sensation of Colt's spurs. Colt's spine jerked at the impact of Razzle Dazzle's front hooves, and he braced his core, throwing his right arm back, ready for the rear kick. The kick came with a twist, but he was ready, countering the movement with his body, arm high, spurs marking across the shoulder break.

Another kick and twist, but to the inside.

This time Colt nearly lost his purchase. He struggled to right himself as he met the back kick, but he was losing ground with each buck. The horn sounded, and he dimly registered the cheers from the arena, but Razzle Dazzle wasn't done. He kicked and twisted, and Colt flipped ass over heels to the side. His training kicked in, and he went limp, consciously relaxing his muscles as he tried to pull his glove from the rigging. The horse bucked again, yanking him like a rag doll. Dammit, his glove was stuck. He caught the flash of a pickup man out of the corner of his eye, but he was in no position to get away, not with his shoulder being yanked out of its socket with each kick. One of the pickup men yelled something, but he couldn't hear it over the din.

The horse twisted and bucked into him, and Colt tripped, losing his footing as the horse dragged and bucked. His arm was on fire, and now he was completely at the mercy of the horse. With the next buck, he turned his body into the horse, praying he wouldn't earn a kick to his ribs. It was enough for him to pull out his hand and he crashed to the ground in a heap as Razzle Dazzle bucked away. He lay in the dirt, ears ringing loudly as he scanned his body. He wiggled his toes in his boots, tensed his leg muscles. His left hamstring answered back angrily. Slowly he drew in his belly and shifted his hips. No screaming pain there. He curled his spine as he came to his knees. Spine okay, shoulder not so much. He spread his fingers wide, then gingerly stretched his left arm. His left elbow popped loudly, shooting fiery barbs of electricity up to his shoulder. He clenched against the pain. It hurt like a motherfucker, but nothing felt broken.

"Can you stand up?" A pair of boots asked.

He shook his head, clearing his vision. "Just shook up."

A hand came to his elbow. "Let's go."

With the help of the judges, he got to his feet. A roar went up from the crowd. He gave a wave and a smile, and spotted his hat in the dirt. He walked over, grateful that his legs worked, and grabbed his hat, jamming it on his head before turning and heading out the gate to the cheers of the crowd. Seventy-nine point five. Disappointment crashed through him, but he couldn't argue with his score. Razzle Dazzle had won that round, he was grateful he'd stayed on long enough to earn a score. He'd finish in the money and move onto the semis, and that was good enough.

Lydia rushed up, eyes wide with fear. "Colt, are you okay? Are you hurt?"

Her concern triggered a sweet ache in his chest. So did the fact that she was wearing the shirt he'd purchased for her. He'd noticed her admiring it the other day and he'd given it to her in the morning. "Nothin' that some aspirin and an ice-pack won't fix." He'd be sore tomorrow, for sure. But he didn't feel like he'd seriously injured himself. "I'll schedule a couple of massages and take it easy. I'll be good as new by the semis."

He held out his good arm, and she stepped into his embrace, wrapping her arm around his waist. "I'm taking you to the doctor."

"Nope." He shook his head. "I'm fine."

She twisted, giving him an evil-eye that looked so much like her mother, he laughed outright. "This is not funny." Her scowl could have melted a glacier.

"Darlin', I'm sure you don't want to hear this, but just now, you were the spitting image of your mother."

She gasped, then turned bright pink. "You're right, I don't want to hear that."

He leaned in, catching a whiff of her floral perfume. A welcome sensation among the sweat, hay, and manure that permeated the arena. "It's okay, Lyds. I like it."

"I'm still taking you to the doctor," she said with a stubborn set to her jaw.

He had half a mind to let her. Not because he needed a doctor, but because her worry touched him. No one, not one person, had ever worried about him the way Lydia had. Even years ago, when he didn't deserve it, she'd been there to take his keys, or to try and convince him not to get stoned. He'd viewed it as judgment back then, meddlesome behavior from the class goody-two-shoes. But it hit him like he'd been slammed into the rails – all those times? She'd been worried about *him*. His throat choked tight at the realization. Not once in his career as a rodeo professional had anyone insisted he see the doctor. Not once.

"Colt?" She clucked at him like a mother hen, and again, his chest tingled at the sound.

"How 'bout this? There's a rodeo physician back here in the Justin Sportsmedicine Truck. I can have him take a look. Will that ease your mind?"

She looked dubious.

"I swear, he's a real doctor."

"Okay." She nodded. "Lead the way." They made their way back to where the enormous RV stood just outside the arena, and took a seat inside. Colt started to unbutton his vest, but Lydia pushed away his hands. "Here. Let me do that."

He gave her a crooked grin. "So this is all I needed to do to get you to undress me?"

Her eyes lit, even as she scolded him. "Stop. This is serious."

"Sweetheart, I promise you I'm fine."

She eased the leather vest off his shoulders, and he winced as he moved his left arm. "See? You're not fine."

"Just shook up is all."

Her hands pulled at the buttons of his shirt. And damn him for being a dirty dog bastard, but a lick of heat rolled through him. "Can you slip your arm out?" she asked, eyebrows pulled together so that two creases appeared above her nose.

At the moment, he didn't want to move. Her hands fluttering across his chest acted like more of a healing balm than any medicinal salve. But he'd learned through experience, that moving was the best thing he could do after a hard fall. Bracing himself for the flash of pain, he shrugged out of his shirt, hiding a grin as he caught Lydia's eyes going straight to his tattoo. He rolled his shoulders in a circle, ignoring the fire that shot across his shoulder. "See? I'm good."

The doctor walked in and pulled up a chair. "I'm Doctor Mike," he said with a slow Texas drawl. "Why don't you tell me what happened?"

"A horse named Razzle Dazzle tossed him around like a rag doll," Lydia interjected before he could open his mouth to speak. "His hand was stuck on the strap–"

"Rigging," Colt corrected.

Lydia glared at him. "Rigging." She turned to Dr. Mike. "The point is he got yanked around before he slammed into the ground, and I think he's hurt."

"I'm not."

Dr. Mike chuckled. "You've got a firecracker on your hands there, cowboy."

"She means well."

Dr. Mike smiled at him appreciatively. "You're a lucky man. Life is always better when you have someone in your corner. Now let's take a look. Left arm?"

Colt nodded, consciously trying to relax his body as Dr. Mike took his left arm and started moving it. First the wrist, then bending and straightening his elbow.

"Ouch." He winced as pain shot out of his elbow.

Dr. Mike squeezed around the joint. "Any pain here?"

Colt shook his head.

Cradling his elbow with one hand, Dr. Mike began to slowly move his arm in a big circle. As his elbow came level with his ear, Colt winced.

"Where does it hurt?"

"Front, just next to my armpit." For the first time, worry clutched at him. If he sustained a serious injury this early in the season, he was pretty much done for the year.

Dr. Mike dropped his arm. "You can get dressed. No broken bones, but you've got soft tissue damage at your elbow and shoulder." He reached for a notepad, scribbled something, then ripped off the paper, handing it to Lydia. "Call this guy in the morning. Tell him Doctor Mike recommended you get seen right away for an MRI."

"Are you kidding me?"

Dr. Mike swung his gaze around. "Absolutely not. If

you've torn your subscap, or your rotator cuff and don't have surgery, you could ruin your shoulder. At the very least, I recommend you start using an elbow brace and tape your arm. If you ride in this condition, you could tear something, even on a good ride."

Damn. He hated riding with tape on. He'd done it before, but had quickly abandoned it because he felt like it limited his movement and his ability to respond to the horse. But if it kept him in the game, he'd do it. Reluctantly.

CHAPTER 21

D R. MIKE'S DIAGNOSIS did nothing to put Lydia at ease. A shoulder injury could knock him out for the rest of the year, especially if surgery was involved. Worst? A severe shoulder injury could mean the end of his rodeo career. Brand ambassador for her boots be damned, after seeing him in his element – competing, interacting with the fans, giving interviews, she couldn't imagine Colt doing anything else. The angry, self-destructive teenager she'd lost sleep over had grown into a self-actualized, confident spokesman not just for the brands he represented, but for rodeo itself.

She pulled out her phone and started searching for rodeo braces, amazed at how many sites came up. Her heart sank as she realized all the sites were for custom braces. "Doctor Mike, do you have anything Colt could use in the short term while a brace is made?"

Colt scowled at her, but she didn't care. No way was she going to let him risk his career. Not when he had so much on the line.

"Let me go check our supplies. I'm sure we have something temporary." Dr. Mike hurried out of the trailer.

"What the heck did you do that for?" Colt sputtered.

"Because maybe I cringe at the idea of your arm pulling out of its socket the next time you ride," she spit back.

"I'm not gonna get hurt. I'm fine."

"And where's your medical degree from?"

Colt leveled his gaze at her. "I don't need a medical degree. I just need a few days to recover."

"Has anyone told you that you're the most obstinate, thick-headed, frustrating–"

Colt waived his good arm, voice rising. "Keep going. Please. You ladies all sound the same when it comes to rodeo."

Ooh, the nerve of him. Anger flashed through her so fast it felt like her hair was on fire. "Is that so?" Her hands flew to her hips. "And which ladies do you mean? The boob jobs who joined you in the hot tub? Sammy Jo? Someone else? Exactly how many *ladies* have expressed concern about your well-being?"

Gah.

She should walk out. Leave him to his hard-headed inflammatory statements. Let him wrap himself in the blanket of his over-inflated ego. But she couldn't. She never could, and that would be her downfall where he was concerned. She closed the distance between them. "Answer me. Because it seems like having someone worry about you is a good thing."

At least he had the grace to look shamefaced. For half a second. But then his bluster returned. "My sponsors worry about me all the time."

"Of course they do," she shot back, jealousy raging through her like a Flint Hills burn in March. "Sammy Jo informed me in great detail how she 'helped you recover' when you broke your hand a few years back." She air quoted with her fingers, still irritated at the woman's smug smile as she'd recounted helping Colt button his shirt.

Colt leaned back, eyes suddenly snapping with glee. "Why, I do believe you're jealous."

That may be, but admitting it would only complicate

everything. "Not." She'd regretted on no less than thirty-two occasions over the last week and a half, that she'd been the one to insist on a business only arrangement. And she couldn't change now. Not only would he never let her hear the end of it, but in the end, when he walked away in favor of the next flavor of the week, she'd be the one heartbroken and left to pick up the pieces in front of the whole town. Better to power through these pesky feelings and build a business.

Colt narrowed his eyes. "Liar." Jeez, why did he have to look so *damned* sexy without his shirt? His tattoo made her mouth water. "Lydia…" he drew her name out soft and slow, like he kissed. Her panties grew wet as she immediately envisioned the last kiss they'd shared. She swore, his public kisses were becoming hotter and hotter.

She reached for his shirt and held it out. She would not give in. "Here, slip your hurt arm in first."

The look he gave her melted her insides, made her heart careen wildly. She refused to be captivated by his muscled back as she pulled his shirt around to his good arm. Heaven help her, but she wanted to run her palms over every ridge and valley along his torso, ease his aching muscles. She could feel him smiling, as if he could read her mind. "Don't even start," she grumbled.

"I'm not saying a thing," he answered with a barely concealed laugh.

"I mean it," she warned, unable to keep her mouth from curling up, as he slipped his arm in the sleeve.

"Button me up?" he asked with a saucy grin.

"I'm pretty sure Dr. Mike said there was nothing wrong with your fingers," she answered tartly.

"Nope," he chuckled. "And I could show you exactly how healthy they are later." His gaze turned molten. "If you like."

The problem was, she did like. Too much. Her skin flushed under his gaze. "Stay here. I'll get your bag." She turned, but he caught her wrist.

"Lydia," he rasped. "Say the word, and we can renegotiate everything."

There was something so vulnerable, so honest, that flashed in his eyes, she stopped breathing. What power did he wield in the universe that he could pull at her this way? Say things that provoked her one moment, and the next speak from his heart? The change happened so fast, her head spun. "Can we? And which Colt would I get then? The cocky Colt, who hides behind a wall of bravado? Or the real Colt, who says things like "I like you," and "you're beautiful?"

About twenty-seven conflicting emotions passed through his eyes. He opened his mouth, then snapped it shut.

"I like you too, Colt. And God knows we have chemistry. But is that enough? What about when times get tough?" She waved at his shoulder. "What if you sustained a career-ending injury? What if my boot company never gets off the ground? Then what? Are you going to hide from reality in hot tubs with pretty ladies?"

"No," he rasped, his voice a husk. "Never."

She wanted to believe that with all her heart. She wanted to believe it so badly, she almost kissed him. "You have to show me, then."

His face fell. "You don't believe me."

A knot formed underneath her ribs, so intense she felt a little woozy. "Your track record shows me otherwise," she murmured, face overheating from the admission.

A muscle ticked above his jaw as he speared her with a look so intense, she might melt into the floor. "Then give me a chance, Lyds. Please. Just one chance."

The knot shot up her neck, lodging in her throat. Could she do it? Could she jump off the cliff and into Colt's arms? She reached for him, running her palm along the stubble of his jaw. "Colt, I—"

"Here we are," Dr. Mike called as he stepped back into the trailer holding a bulky package. "I grabbed the strongest one I could find." He handed another piece of paper to Lydia. "This is the name of an orthotist who can make you a custom brace. It will take a few weeks, so in the meantime, if you haven't been sidelined, tape underneath this."

Lydia bit back a sigh of frustration. Had the good doctor just cockblocked her? Or saved her from herself?

LYDIA SHIFTED UNCOMFORTABLY in her chair as she stared at the clock next to the bed. Four a.m. Colton lay sprawled across the mattress, face turned toward the window. In the dim, his face looked soft. Childlike. Free from the cocky persona he wrapped tightly around him like a blanket.

At least he was sleeping.

In addition to the brace, the doctor had prescribed a strong anti-inflammatory and a muscle relaxer. "Even with these, he'll be sore tomorrow," he'd said.

She'd been surprised when Colton didn't argue with her suggestion that she drive back to the hotel. Doubly surprised when he'd let her wrap his shoulder in ice. He hadn't even made a smart remark when she'd removed his shirt. Only looked at her with something akin to gratitude. All that did was ratchet up the confusion roiling inside her.

She'd thought her heart was going to beat out of her throat when he'd gotten hung up in his rigging. And when he collapsed in the arena, her body had gone hot then cold with dread. She'd dropped her soda in her haste to scramble out of the boxes and get down to him, angered that the Carters had sat there like what they'd witnessed wasn't that big of a deal. Sammy Jo snickered as she passed, but she didn't care. A hang-up like that might be all in a day's work for them, but Colton was hurt and she refused to sit back and wring her hands when she could *do* something about it.

At least the Carters had been waiting for them in the hotel lobby when they returned. That redeemed them a little in her eyes. But once they'd satisfied themselves he wasn't seriously injured, they'd headed for the sponsor's floor, only mildly disappointed that Colton turned down their invitation to join them.

Colton let out a deep sigh and shifted on the bed. The covers moved with him, slipping further down his torso to reveal the corded muscles across his back, tapering down to his hips. She marveled at his strength. The same muscles that dominated unruly animals held her with such tenderness. She ached to be in his arms again. For more than a public display of affection. It had been on the tip of her tongue to cave this evening, before the doctor had interrupted them, but the moment had passed, and they'd both retreated.

She replayed the moment for the hundredth time in the last four hours. *Just one chance.* The look in his eye when he said those words had pierced her straight to her soul. She didn't doubt his sincerity for a second. She doubted his ability to stay sincere, and that was her hang-up. Yet, since they'd reconnected he'd given her no reason to doubt him. Not one.

But what about the hot tub ladies?

She'd had no claim on him then, given him no reason to expect that she'd show up in Las Vegas. It wouldn't be fair to hold that against him. She twisted the enormous diamond on her finger.

What if?

Was she willing to renegotiate? It would make their fake engagement that much more believable. But what about when it ended? Colt wasn't the marrying kind, and neither was she, at least not right now. They didn't have to renegotiate for a happily ever after, simply a just for now. That seemed like a win-win.

Who's living and who's playing it safe?

Again, Colt's words from Thanksgiving rattled in her mind. She was tired of playing it safe. She'd played it safe her whole life and *still* had things crumble around her ears. Heart pounding in the silence, she stood and shimmied out of her yoga pants, then stripped off her tee-shirt, the cool air puckering her nipples. Holding her breath, she crawled into bed next to Colton, settling in the crook of his uninjured arm.

Her heartbeat slowed as she inhaled the masculine scent of him. He shifted again, and she shifted with him, twining her leg with his, and adjusting so she rested her head on his pec. Surrounded by him, she shut her eyes and drifted into blissful sleep.

CHAPTER 22

COLT DIDN'T WANT to wake up, the dream was too good. He'd dreamed about Lydia before, hell, nearly every night. But not like this. She felt so *real*. She sighed, a sound like music, and stretched her legs against his. With a groan, he tried to move his arm, surfacing from the dream as the realization hit him that his arm was pinned to the bed.

Holy shit.

He struggled to sit, chasing the cobwebs from his brain. There was a woman in his bed. *Lydia* was in his bed. His pulse roared in his ears. Was he hallucinating? He hated muscle relaxers, hated the way they made him foggy. "Lyds?" he asked thickly.

"Mmm hmm," she answered sleepily and stretched against him.

He definitely wasn't dreaming. She was next to him, very much flesh and blood. *Naked* flesh and blood. "What happened to your pajamas?" His voice wavered like a teenager's.

She turned her face to him, giving him a coy, albeit sleepy, smile. She pointed behind him. "Floor."

His blood pounded through his veins. He had to be imagining this. "I don't understand."

"Renegotiating," she answered burying her head into his arm. "Can we go back to sleep?"

"Sure thing, sweetheart." He didn't want to move anyway. He adjusted his arm to better cradle her, and dropped his injured arm to her hip. He only winced a little. So she wasn't completely naked. She wore some lacy thing he'd enjoy removing from her at a later time. Sleep pulled at him, and with a happy sigh, he gave in. If the angels claimed him right now, he'd die a happy man.

SUNLIGHT FLOODED THROUGH the windows. Lydia was still there, curled up against him, silky dark hair spread in short waves across his chest. Wonder filled him. He didn't know what had brought about her change of heart, but he wouldn't question it. Craning his neck, he tried to see the bedside clock without moving Lydia. It had to be past eight. His chest felt like lead. As much as he wanted to avoid the doctor, Lydia would insist he keep his appointment. Giving her a squeeze and placing a kiss on her head, he spoke. "Lyds, hon, wake-up. We've gotta get going."

She let out a sigh that sounded more like the coo of a dove, and stretched against him.

He bit back a groan as his balls tightened with need. "Come on, sweetheart. Time to rise and shine." He should be a candidate for sainthood. He wanted nothing more than to devour every inch of her.

She shook her head against him with a growl.

Of course. Coffee. She never moved without coffee. With heroic effort, he gingerly slipped from the bed, reminding his swollen dick that it wouldn't be much longer, and pressed the start button on the coffee machine. The machine gurgled to life, and he tentatively rolled his shoulders as he waited. A sharp pain shot down his arm.

Unease settled in his gut. Sharp pain didn't necessarily mean a tear. He'd learned from the hours of massage therapy he'd received over the years, it could just as easily mean a knot of fascia. Given his ride yesterday, he'd at least sustained some whiplash.

The coffee machine let out a final gasp, and he pulled the paper cup from the dispenser, added both the creams, and walked back to the bed. Slipping back under the covers, he nudged Lydia. "I've brought your caffeine hit," he teased.

The aroma must have registered in her sleepy brain, because she cracked open an eye. "You brought me coffee?"

"Just like every morning." She gave him a pleased little smile that shot straight to his cock. He'd bring her coffee every day just to be on the receiving end of that look.

"Thank you." She tucked the sheets under her armpits and sat primly, hand extended to receive her cup.

There was nothing prim about her like this. She was more like a 1960's pinup girl and the urge to tumble her pulled at him fiercely. But she had to get to the exhibition hall, and he needed to call the doctor.

As if reading his mind, she cocked her head. "How do you feel this morning?"

"Sore. Foggy from the pills."

"Do you want me to go with you?"

He shook his head, secretly thrilled she'd offered. "Nah. I know you need to get to your booth. I'll come by when it's over."

Her face clouded. "Are you sure? I have a nice stack of orders already. Shutting down for half a day isn't going to hurt."

"Drink your coffee," he ordered gruffly, not wanting to let on how much her offer meant to him. "When I get back, we can talk about this new development in our agreement." He cocked an eyebrow as he let his gaze run over her.

Her skin turned pink, moving up her chest, and brightening her cheeks. "There's nothing to talk about," she answered, chest rising and falling rapidly. "I-I thought about what you said last night."

"I said a lot last night."

"About the renegotiating everything."

So, they were talking about this now? "Okay…" he drew the word out, unsure of what to expect.

She held up a hand. "I'm not looking for marriage, in case you were worried about that." Her color deepened. "But the other stuff…"

"The other stuff?" Okay, he was fucking with her a bit. But only a bit. He needed to hear from her exactly what she wanted. "What other stuff?" he prodded.

"You're gonna make me say it?"

"Umm hmm." He nodded. "I want to know exactly what is going on inside that pretty little head of yours."

She took a deep breath and stared into her coffee, before raising her head with a determined glint in her eye. "Fiancée with benefits?"

He nearly choked on his tongue, and the laugh that bubbled up from his chest came out strangled. "I'll give you all the benefits you want, darlin'." He leaned over and landed a kiss on her temple. "I'll stop and get a box of condoms after I see the doctor."

Her answering squeak did something to his insides.

"Does that mean I should get two?" He dropped another kiss at her ear, awareness zinging through him.

She answered, voice breathy with anticipation. "What size box are you talking about?"

A laugh rumbled around in his chest. "Forty, if I get the variety pack."

She squeaked again. "One's probably fine. For now."

"For now," he echoed, tracing her jawline with his mouth. Waiting today might possibly kill him.

CHAPTER 23

NORMALLY, LYDIA KEPT her phone on vibrate while she was in the booth. She hated the way phones interrupted conversations, and she always wanted potential clients to feel like they were the most important person in the booth.

But not today.

Not when she was waiting on pins and needles to find out if Colt would need surgery. It bothered her that he wouldn't let her accompany him. But he was right, her presence wouldn't change the outcome, and she'd secured five more boot orders this morning. That put her total up to twenty orders. Exhilarating, affirming, and also terrifying. She'd already ordered leather and lasts so she could hit the ground running once she returned to Prairie, but doubt chased her. Working around the clock, she'd made a pair a week, but that pace wasn't sustainable.

In the back of her head, she could hear Emma Sinclaire reminding her that scarcity was a good thing. But not when a potential client could walk two aisles over and procure a pair of boots for the same price in half the time. With her heart in her throat, she'd quoted a bride a three-month wait on a pair of rhinestone embellished boots.

It could be worse.

She could have spent all this time making a portfolio and leave San Antonio with no orders. She'd known aspiring shoe designers in New York that had gone broke before they got off the ground. Custom-made cowboy boots held a mystique that the average stiletto couldn't match. And the two-page spread the local paper had printed on her, hadn't hurt either. The writer found a female boot designer a bit of a novelty and had angled the article to highlight the scarcity of women in rodeo, both in the arena and in the exhibition hall. Colt had been so proud, he bought twenty copies of the paper and insisted on mailing one home to her mother, which meant everyone in Prairie had read it by now.

Her phone vibrated and started playing Supertramp's *Give a Little Bit*. It had to be Colt. He must have figured out how to mess with her ringtones. "Nice song choice," she said wryly as she smiled into the phone.

His low laugh tickled her ear. "Paybacks, darlin'."

"Careful what you start, cowboy. I've got more songs up my sleeve."

"Bring it."

She turned serious. "Well? What's the news?" Her heart beat erratically, and she squeezed shut her eyes, bracing for the worst.

"I'm clean. Doc said all that yoga probably saved me from a tear."

Hot relief swept through her and her knees wobbled so hard, she dropped into a chair. "Oh, I'm so glad."

"Not half as glad as me." His voice lowered. "But as long as you don't tie me to the bedpost, I should be okay."

Wet heat burst between her legs, and she let out a nervous giggle. "No tying you up. At least not tonight," she added impishly. Let him stew on that for a while. "Where are you?"

"Look behind you."

She swiveled the chair around, to see him strolling down

the aisle holding the phone to his hear and holding a bag. Condoms? No, there was more in the bag than a box of condoms. It looked more like take-out. She disconnected and tossed the phone into her bag, walking to meet him halfway. Even from a distance, she could see the relief on his face and a lightness in his step. "What's in the bag?" She wrapped her arms around his waist, standing on tiptoe to feather a kiss across his jaw.

He turned his head and caught her mouth with his. The kiss turned hot and forgetting herself, she pressed against him, running her hand up his arm. She didn't know what it was about the way his rock-hard triceps fit against her palm, but the sensation acted like a match, igniting a fire inside her. He pulled back, gazing down at her through heavy-lidded eyes that spoke volumes. "Sustenance."

"I can close up early," she offered, heart kicking erratically.

"I don't mind waiting."

"I do." She stepped out of his embrace and took his hand, leading him back to her booth, where she hurried to put things away, profoundly aware of Colt's eyes tracking her like a wolf ready to pounce.

He wasn't the only one ready to pounce.

Her body hummed with anticipation as she locked her boots away and refilled the brochure dispenser. Turning back to him with an impish smile, she held out her hand. "Ready?"

"More than you know." His eyes lit with hunger.

Twining her fingers with his, she pulled him in for another slow kiss. "Let's get out of here."

He walked so fast toward the exit, she skipped to keep up with his long strides, pulse thrumming, propelling her forward. Without saying a word, Colt wove through the crowd, pushed open the door, and doubled his pace through the parking lot. When he reached the truck, he spun, pushing her against the cab and bracing an arm above her. Before she could speak, his mouth crashed down, tongue sweeping into her mouth with a possessiveness that stole her breath. Melting into him, she responded in kind, threading her fingers through his hair and knocking his Stetson to the ground.

"I want you so bad, I could take you right here," he rasped when they pulled apart.

"Really? Do you think anyone would notice?" She'd never done anything as scandalous as have sex in public, but Colt brought out her reckless side, and the thought of dropping his jeans for a wild ride in broad daylight made her clit throb with want. And *oh*, how she wanted him. Shocking and delighting her with his hands, his tongue.

His low laugh tickled her ear, sending jolts of anticipation through her, tightening her nipples and soaking her panties. She was so ready, it wouldn't take long. "I have a condom in my bag."

Again, his laugh danced over her skin like a sparkler. "Always prepared."

"Always." Her fingers played with the buttons on his shirt. She cocked an eyebrow as she pulled the top button free.

He momentarily looked discomfited, but then his cocky smile returned. "Far be it from me to say no to a lady in need. But then we're going straight back to the room and not leaving the bed until I've properly loved you up. Multiple times."

Her pussy throbbed eagerly. "Promise?" At this rate all he'd need to do was brush her clit, and she'd come on his hand.

He opened the door, then lifted her up on the running

board, eyes blazing hotter than the afternoon sun. "You sure about this?"

"If you're worried I won't come, don't." She pulled off a boot, tossing it to the mat. Next, she unzipped her pants, shimmied them down and pulled out a leg.

Colt tilted his head, amusement flickering in his eyes. "You look like you've done this before."

Her cheeks flushed as she shook her head. "Just have an imagination," she said as she let her knees fall open.

His breath halted. "I like your imagination," he said with a rough edge to his voice as he reached to touch her.

She dropped her head at his feather-light caress. "I swear, Colt. I'm ready."

He let out a dry laugh, shaking his head, and dug into her purse, rooting until he lifted out the sole condom left over from her stash. She'd removed them from her purse before coming to San Antonio, but had found a stray one earlier while she'd been reapplying her lipstick.

His belt buckle jingled as he loosened it and dropped his pants.

"Oh," Lydia gasped as she laid eyes on his heavy, hard erection.

His eyebrows jumped with pleasure at her gasp, as he rolled on the condom. "All for you, babe. Now lift your hips."

Hooking her leg around his hips, she pushed back on the side of the seat and angled her hips to receive him. He pushed into her with a grunt, and she swore she could feel him at the deepest part of herself. Clasping her neck, he pulled her mouth to his, as he thrust again. The friction acted like a match on a trail of gunpowder, sending heat racing through her. And maybe it was the danger of being discovered, but every nerve ending was firing, acting in concert to barrel her toward an explosive orgasm.

Colt's mouth landed on her neck, his breath coming in ragged pulses. But it was his teeth scraping her skin that sent her over the edge in a whoosh of white light. He followed her, ass clenching and hips thrusting so powerfully she thought she might split.

Hours later, as they lay spent on the bed back in the hotel room, limbs entwined, she traced a finger along the curve of his tattoo. "Don't you think you need to rest now?"

"Hmm." His thumb made lazy circles on her hip. "I've got four days to recover. Another day or two of this and I'll be in good shape for the semis and the finals." He spoke with the confidence of a man who knew he was on top of the world.

But Lydia's stomach clenched at the thought of returning to Prairie alone in eight days' time. Pushing the thought from her mind, she continued to trace the intricate design, fascinated with how his muscle rippled under her touch. Here and now was what mattered. Not the heartbreak that would come when their wild ride inevitably came to a screeching halt.

CHAPTER 24

COLT'S HANDS TAPPED an erratic rhythm on the steering wheel, his foot itching to press the gas pedal to the floor. The closer he drew to Prairie, the slower the time passed. But he knew better than to push eighty in a thirty-five. Weston Tucker, Prairie's new police chief, would happily write him a big old ticket with a smile on his face.

When they'd talked on the phone the night before, he'd informed Lydia he'd be stopping by Resolution Ranch first, before coming to see her. She'd agreed that was a good idea, but he could hear the disappointment in her voice. He'd be the first to admit, he liked it. More than a part of him had worried that she'd changed her mind after not seeing him in person for a month. They'd FaceTimed nearly every day for the duration, but that wasn't the same. Something his body could attest to. He'd been sporting a semi the last hundred miles as he imagined reacquainting himself with all of Lydia's sensitive spots. His mind began to race as he hit the outskirts of town. By the time he hit Prairie's only stoplight, his mind was made up. Instead of going straight and heading out to his brother's, he turned left down Main and drove the six blocks to Lydia's. Travis and Elaine could wait.

Lydia came bounding out of the house as he cut the engine. His throat tightened at the sweetness of her. How could she have grown prettier in the month? Somehow, she had. He hopped out of the truck, catching her in an embrace and swinging her around, not caring if the neighbors saw. He was home.

The comprehension stopped him mid-circle, and he pushed it out of his mind as quickly as it entered. He had a ranch in Steamboat. Prairie was no longer his home. He was just glad to see Lydia, missed the sweet taste of her. That was all. He took her mouth to prove the point to himself.

She twined her arms around his neck, kissing him back enthusiastically. Their breathing was ragged when they separated. "I missed you too." She grinned up at him.

The tenderness in her eyes made his stomach lurch. "Let's get you inside," he urged, ignoring the sensation in his belly. "Don't want those neighbors to get any ideas."

She made a noise that sounded a lot like frustration. "Right."

He followed her inside, stopping short at the overwhelming scent of leather. The living room had been transformed into a factory. Leather and lace strewn over every surface, a dress form in the corner, two industrial machines, one with a partially completed pair of boots next to it. He let out a low whistle, eyes widening. "You've been busy."

"Yeah. You have no idea. We just have to get through the boot shoot, day after tomorrow." She let out a sigh, body sagging in exhaustion. Colton kicked himself for not noticing sooner. He'd been too happy to see her to look closely. He narrowed his gaze, scanning her from top to bottom. Tension pulled at her shoulders, but it was her hands that alarmed him. They were red and swollen, curled in from too many hours of using scissors and needles. "What happened?" he barked, reaching for her and taking her hand, turning it palm up. The tips of her fingers were torn up. "You've been working too hard," he stated flatly, challenging her to deny it. Let her try, he was having none of it.

She shrugged. "Maybe. Gotta get these orders filled."

"Not by ruining your body. How many hours are you bent over that machine?" He tipped his head toward the one with the boot next to it.

"I don't know. Twelve, maybe fourteen hours?"

He let out a fierce growl, pulling her to the couch. "Sit."

She collapsed into the pillows with a reluctant sigh. "I wasn't expecting you until later."

"Good thing I showed up now. You need a rest."

She pulled her hand, but not very forcefully. "I need to finish this order before we do the boot shoot."

"Not until you've had a rest." He took her hand in both of his, working his thumbs across the palm of her hand, pressing firmly into her thumb pad.

"Ow," she yelped.

"Relax your arm. Hell, shut your eyes. Let me work on this." He attacked the tight muscles with all the techniques he'd learned. "You really need a professional to work on you, but hopefully this will give you some relief."

"We don't have a masseuse here."

He made a disapproving noise. "Then while I'm home, I'll drive you up to see someone in Manhattan."

Her head dropped back to the top of the couch, and she shut her eyes. "When I catch up with the orders."

He had half a mind to throw her over his shoulder and drive her to Manhattan right now. "You won't be able to finish your orders if you let this go any longer. How bad does it hurt?"

A tear leaked out and slowly rolled down her cheek as he pressed and prodded. "A lot," she said, voice wavering.

His chest went all achy at her teary reply. She was work-ing too damned hard, and he hated seeing her in this condition. "Can you hire some help?"

She shook her head, not opening her eyes.

"Why not?"

"No one here locally. Emmaline helps when she can, but her dress orders are cranking up. Don't worry. I'll get through this. Growing pains."

Growing pains, his ass. He'd have to figure out how to get her some help. He'd be damned if he stood by quietly while she worked herself to death. He reached for her other hand, repeating his ministrations. She groaned loudly. "Ohmygod, you have no idea how good that feels." Another tear rolled down her cheek.

That was it. This called for drastic measures. Scooping her into his arms, he stood and marched down the hall toward the bathroom. "Have you been eating?" He swore she felt ten pounds lighter.

"Yes," she mumbled into his neck.

"Not enough." He shouldered open the door, depositing her on the toilet and bending to turn on the hot water.

"What are you doing?"

"What does it look like?" He pulled up her shirt, startled she lifted her arms without protest. The ache in his chest grabbed at him. He'd been crisscrossing Texas, sleeping in comfy beds, signing autographs, and racking up the wins while she toiled at home, not caring for herself and doing a mighty fine job of keeping up appearances during their FaceTime chats. "You need some TLC," he said gruffly, whipping off his tee-shirt and tossing it to the floor next to hers. He toed off his boots, not caring that she'd scold. He was in a hurry, dammit. He dropped his jeans and briefs with a clatter, and helped her to stand, pulling off her yoga pants with an easy tug. He pulled back the shower curtain. "Ladies first."

She gave him a tired smile, but didn't argue.

He took her in his arms, angling their bodies so the hot water hit between her shoulder blades. A shudder wracked her body as she softened into him. "Just stay here, sweetheart. Let the water do its thing," he murmured, losing his fingers in her silky hair, breathing her in.

"I'm so tired," she admitted with a catch in her voice.

"I know. It's okay. Just rest a bit okay?" She nodded against his chest. He wasn't sure how long they stood like that, but with a start, he realized the hot water would run out if he wasn't careful. "Where's the soap?"

"Corner."

Reluctantly, he let go of her and turned, momentarily startled at the sheer volume of product in the corners.

Her quiet laugh echoed off the tile. "Three women, one bathroom."

"Does it matter which one?"

"Nah."

He grabbed the first bottle his hands touched, squirting flowery smelling shampoo into his palm. "Come here," he said rubbing his hands together and turning. He ran his hands through her hair, pressing his fingers into her scalp as he worked up a lather. She sighed appreciatively as he worked down the back of her head to her neck. "Your neck is like a rock."

"I know," she answered in a small voice.

"Let's get you rinsed off, and I'll work on it." He gently pushed her back into the water, wiping the soap from her forehead, and lifting her hair so it washed clean. Then he stepped back, reaching for the conditioner, repeating his motions and scalp massaging. Only then, was it time for the soap. "Turn around, brace against the wall if you need." Foregoing a washcloth, he lathered up his hands and started working the knots in her shoulders. "Take a deep breath, exhale the tension." He repeated all the phrases he'd ever heard from the massage therapists he'd used over the years. Slowly, the tension began to drain from her shoulders. She'd need hours of work, but at least this was a start, and hopefully gave her some relief.

"Colt?" She looked back at him over her shoulder, her gaze dark and hot. "Touch me."

Lust shot through him springing his cock to life. He stepped closer, bringing his hands to her front, cradling her breasts and gently tugging on her nipples. He bent his head, placing a kiss on her neck and murmuring into her ear. "You mean like this?"

"Yesss," she hissed, rolling her hips back against him, pressing her sweet ass against his cock.

Oh hell, yes. She was slippery with soap and arousal, and *fuck*. No condoms. He clenched his jaw as she slid along his cock. "Fuck you feel good," he groaned, body tensing as heat built to blinding proportions. "But we have no protection in here."

She fisted her hand against the tile. "We'll have to get creative, then, because you feel too damn good to stop."

He thrust his hips again, mind spinning with possibilities. "Turn around," he ordered. With a sexy little moan, she complied and arched her back against the wall, thrusting her gorgeous tits his direction. "I like how you think," he murmured, shooting her a naughty grin.

He dropped his head, blazing a trail with his tongue from

her collarbone down the swell of her breast, pink from the hot water, to her nipple, rosy and hard. She tasted of flowery soap, warm skin, and essence of Lydia. A combination that both aroused and settled into his bones. He flicked her nipple over and over until she cried out, and in a move that surprised and electrified him, her hand enclosed around his cock. With a groan, mouth still covering her, he thrust into her hand. It might not be her sweet, hot pussy, but he had no complaints. She stroked up his shaft, thumb sweeping back and forth across the head until he saw stars.

He teetered on the edge, burning with the desire to bury himself balls-deep in her heaven, but knowing he couldn't risk it. Even with her. Bracing a forearm on the tile, he traced a trail across her hip until he found her pussy lips engorged and slick. "That's it, babe," he murmured, finding her clit and teasing it with his thumb. "Touch me however you like. I love what you do to me." Understatement. She touched off a wildfire in him.

Her eyes became dark pools as a slow sexy smile tilted her mouth. Her tongue slowly swept across her lower lip. "Kiss me, cowboy."

He thrust a hand into her hair and pulled, tilting her mouth and claiming it with a fervor that left them both shaking. With a grunt, she squeezed his cock harder, spurring him on as he licked into her mouth, losing himself in her. His moan of ecstasy quickly turned to a cry of surprise as the water turned to ice.

Lydia's eyes flew wide as she squealed trying to dodge the spray.

Colt flung back the shower curtain, not even bothering to turn off the water. Wrapping an arm around Lydia, he scooped her up and stalked down the hall. Her gasps of breathless laughter echoed down the hall. He burst into her room, kicking the door shut behind him and collapsing on the bed with her. His heart stumbled at the sight of her, eyes bright, cheeks flushed. But as he stared, she bit down on that full lower lip he loved to taste, pupils dilating as her breath hitched. Holding her gaze, he stretched for the drawer at her bedside table and with his fingers, captured a condom.

He ripped it open with his teeth before handing her the package, blood rushing to his balls in anticipation of her touch. Still looking nowhere but at him, she rolled it down his length with sure, firm, strokes. "Lie back," he rasped, the room suddenly hot.

She rolled to her back, dropping her knees, baring herself to him. Then in an act of the sweetest submission, she raised her hands above her, stretching like a cat begging for a tummy scratch. Moving over her, he laced his fingers with hers, settling at her entrance, wanting to sheath himself in her warmth, but hesitating.

With a little cry, Lydia lifted her hips, stroking against him. "Please, Colt."

He couldn't resist her. With a grumble of pure pleasure, he drove home into her tight heat, seeking her mouth, needing to touch, stroke, lick. She answered with a moan of her own, deep in her throat as she canted her hips against his, and undulated under him as their kisses became deeper, more desperate. As they climbed higher and teetered on the precipice, fire raced up the back of his legs culminating in a laser point of white-hot heat that burst through him like a star shooting across the night sky. He was dimly aware of her cries joining his, but he could barely hear over the buzzing in his ears.

As she came slowly back into focus, he squeezed her

hands, marveling at how her eyes looked more green than blue after they made love. How she had faint freckles scattered across her nose and cheeks, a product of a childhood spent outside. Sex looked good on her, and for an alarming second, words shot up his throat, ready to tumble from his mouth. Big words he had no business thinking or saying. He clamped down on his tongue and kissed her instead, tenderly. "Let me go take care of this before someone surprises us."

"Don't worry, we won't be interrupted." Her voice called after him as he hurried down the hall to the bathroom.

"We're really all alone?" He asked when he returned, washcloth in hand.

"Luci's helping her folks make tamales today, and Emma-line left just before you got here to go visit her mother in Topeka."

He tossed the washcloth into the hamper, and crawled up next to her, settling her in the curve of his arm. "So no one will hear you scream my name when I make you come again?"

She cupped his face, giving him a relaxed smile. He liked seeing her like this, relaxed and sated from their lovemaking. "Who says I'm going to scream?"

He gave her ass a gentle pinch. "I'm going to make you scream so loud, they'll hear you the next block over."

Her eyes lit. "Promise?"

He nodded. "You need at least five more orgasms to work the knots from your shoulders."

"I like the sound of that," she purred, dropping a kiss on his collarbone and slipping a leg between his. "When are we going to get started?"

He pushed her onto her back, the first stirrings of desire sparking to life in his belly. "I'm not busy." He trailed a finger from the hollow at her neck between her breasts. "I think I should start here." He lowered his head to the swell, lapping at her skin.

"*LYDIA MARGUERITE GRACE!! I KNOW YOU ARE HOME.*" Dottie's voice boomed from the front room.

Lydia Marguerite? Colt covered a laugh as Lydia squeaked beneath him and with a superhuman heave, rolled, pushing him off the bed. He landed with a thunk.

"*Ohmygodit'smymother*," she hissed, wide-eyed, as she scrambled off the bed, searching for something to wear.

"*LYDIA??*" Dottie's voice sounded closer this time, and fit to be tied.

Lydia shoved a hand into her robe. "Don't move a muscle," she hissed as she shoved the other arm into the sleeve. "Coming, mama," she called loudly.

Giving Colton a last look, she slipped out the door, shutting it quietly behind her.

Holy. Hell. Shit was about to hit the fan.

CHAPTER 25

L YDIA FOUGHT TO keep a clear head. Her mother was on a rampage, and that could only mean one thing. She'd somehow discovered their engagement. Dottie rarely got angry, but when she blew her stack, she was known to make grown men cry.

"*Lydia,*" her mother bellowed a third time. "*Do not make me wait another second.*"

"Mama, I'm right here," she answered calmly, padding down the hall to where her mother stood blocking her path to the living room. "I was taking a nap."

Dottie gave her a look so frosty, Lydia's toes grew cold. "You were no more taking a nap than I was when I conceived each of you girls."

Lydia's stomach dropped like a stone. Her mother knew, and now there was nothing to do but take her lumps and try and work a little damage control.

"Okay," she answered levelly. She knew better than to try and engage her mother in conversation when she was this worked up. Eventually, it would blow over.

Dottie waved a magazine at her. "Do you know what this is?"

She shook her head. "I can't see it, mama."

"Here." Dottie opened the magazine to a dog-eared page and folded the paper back on itself, thrusting it at her. "Maybe you can see a little better."

Lydia took the magazine, half-sick. Before looking at the open page, she glanced at the cover. *Rodeo Today* covered the top third in big white letters. Just below was a picture of Colton with the byline "Is Rodeo's Casanova taking the plunge?"

She'd bet money the Carters were behind this juicy nugget of publicity. Flipping back to the page her mother had turned to, a picture of Colt dipping her in a hot embrace, glared up at her. The gaudy engagement ring circled in red. She handed back the magazine with a sigh. "I was afraid something like this would happen," she admitted.

Her comment lit her mother up like a sparkler. "Do you have *any* idea how mortifying it was to learn that *my daughter* is engaged to *Colton Kincaid* from *Diana Appleberry?*"

"I have no idea who that is."

"Exactly," said Dottie emphatically, crossing her arms and looking ready to cry. "Diana Appleberry is the librarian at the Marion Public Library. She saw fit to drive all the way over from Marion this morning to show me the latest edition of her favorite rodeo gossip magazine." Dottie fixed her with a glare. "I might as well have read it in People Magazine."

Ouch.

"Oh, Mama, I'm sorry."

Dottie held up a hand. "Save your breath. Where's Colton? I have a few things to say to that young man."

This was going from bad to worse. She prayed he'd had the presence of mind to wrap a sheet around himself. "Mama, I don't think–"

Dottie pushed past her. "I will discuss this with you later, young lady. *COLTON?*" She stalked down the hall to her bedroom and pushed it open. "You can't hide from me. I know you're in there."

Lydia flushed to her toes. She would never live this down with her sisters. She rushed after her mother. "Mama, please." She crossed the threshold in time to see Colt standing up on the other side of the bed, naked as the day he was born. "Oh, lordy," she gasped.

Dottie's hands went to her hips, unfazed by his lack of attire. "*What* do you have to say for yourself, young man?"

Colt flashed her a smile that could melt the coldest ice. "I intend to marry your daughter, Mrs. Grace."

What?

Lydia's heart stopped beating for a second, before kicking erratically. She must have heard wrong. This was not part of their agreement. She shook her head wildly, trying to get his attention, but Colt refused to look her direction, although she was sure he could see her, she was right behind her mother, hopping up and down like a crazy woman.

Dottie stepped aside, looking back and forth between the two of them, a look of horror on her face. "You mean to tell me you got engaged and *hid it from your mother?*"

When she put it that way, Lydia sounded like the worst child ever. She wilted under her mother's fierce expression. "I'm sorry, mama. I-I—"

Colt cleared his throat. "Mrs. Grace, it's my fault. Things moved pretty quickly between us."

"I'll say," Dottie huffed.

Colt continued as if she hadn't interrupted. "Lydia wanted to tell you right away, but I was worried about upstaging the fundraising efforts for Resolution Ranch. You know how people talk, and we didn't want to steal their thunder. We figured we'd wait until after, since the wedding's still aways off."

"And when were you planning to be married?"

Lydia couldn't hear for the buzzing in her ears. She tried to talk, but her tongue wouldn't move. Colt's voice hit her as if she was underwater. *August twenty-eighth.* Everything popped back to normal speed as her mother harrumphed. "At least that's a decent amount of time to prepare. Not like the others."

Colt nodded, looking cool as a cucumber. "Exactly."

Lydia shook her head at him again, but he wouldn't look at her. What did he think he was doing? Didn't he know he'd break her mother's heart if a wedding didn't take place? She couldn't be responsible for that. No, the charade had to be up now.

She stepped forward. "Mama, I don't think—"

Colt gave her a sharp look. "Dottie I'm sorry you didn't hear the good news from us first. Please don't be mad at Lydia. It was all my fault."

She'd think it was sweet he was throwing himself under the bus where her mother was concerned, if not for the fact that he'd committed her to a wedding in August.

"Oh, you kids." Dottie's voice softened and she wiped her eye. "You know I just want the best for all of you."

"I know, and I promise I'll do right by Lydia. I'll always make sure she's provided for."

"I can provide for myself just fine, thank you," Lydia shot back tartly, skin growing hot. He was acting like she wasn't even there. "And for heaven's sake, Colt. Put on some pants."

Dottie waved her off. "Oh pish. I changed his diapers when he was a little thing."

"*Mama!*" Lydia slapped her hand to her forehead, shaking her head. Could the floor swallow her up now?

"I'll leave you two. It's obvious I interrupted something.

Colton, I expect you for Sunday dinner."

"Yes, ma'am." He saluted her. "Wouldn't miss it for the world."

His mouth quirked as he said it. Lydia didn't think her mother noticed, but she did, and she would have a thing or two to say to him once her mother removed herself from her bedroom. She should feel relieved that her mother hadn't grilled her. If her mother had asked her if they loved each other, or anything else direct, she'd have caved on the spot. She was a shitty liar, not to mention her mother could sniff out a liar faster than a German shepherd hunting for narcotics.

Dottie pulled Colton into a fierce hug, naked ass and all. "I always thought the two of you might find each other someday," she said with a quiver.

"And you too, sweetie." Her mother reached for her.

Lydia shut her eyes as guilt washed over her. "Thank you, mama," she murmured, unable to trust herself to say more. Dottie would be devastated when the truth came to light. She'd cried for days over Carolina at Christmas. Her mother's heart was so big and so sensitive. Most people never saw it, but it was part of what made her mother beloved to the residents of Prairie. And she was the worst child ever. Giving her a final pat on the cheek, Dottie excused herself, eyes bright with future wedding plans.

As soon as the front door shut, Lydia closed the distance between them. "Are you insane?" She jabbed a finger at his chest. "Standing here buck naked, *lying to my mother*?"

"I wasn't lying."

"In what plane of reality was that *not* lying? You told her we're getting married on August twenty-eighth."

"And we might. We were going to have to set a date

anyway."

"So you decided now was the time? Without consulting me?" His mouth twitched again. Damn him, he found this amusing. "When this plays out, not only will my mother be heartbroken, she'll disown me."

"Why not get married?" He asked it like he was asking about the weather.

"You're kidding, right?"

He shrugged. "We make a pretty good team."

"That may be, but we don't love each other. Marriage isn't a business transaction."

The muscles in Colt's face pulled tight. "Maybe it should be. Maybe more of them would survive."

"How can you say that? I want more from a marriage than a business partner."

His eyes narrowed. "Seems like it's working well for you so far."

"*Because we're not married.*"

He widened his stance, which only served to accentuate his magnificence. "We may as well be. We've done everything else but blend our finances."

"Is that so?"

"I know plenty of married couples who don't talk as much as we do."

"Put some clothes on." And stop being so reasonable.

He gave her a saucy smile. "Why? Am I distracting you?"

She refused to answer. Turning her back to him, she sat on the edge of the bed. "My parents have been married over thirty years. Been together since junior high. They've been through hard times, awful times. And the only reason they survived was because they love each other."

"Disagree," Colt said flatly. "They're still together because they're partners. My parents said they loved each other and acted like they hated each other." He practically spit out the words.

Lydia could hear the pain in them. She swiveled to look at him, anger dissipating at the despair etched on his face. His gaze locked with hers. "Dad was never the same after mom left." He grimaced, lost in a memory. "I barely remember her. I remember the shouting, the dishes being thrown, the ugliness. Worst? I thought it was my fault she left us. So don't talk to me about love being the most important thing in a marriage."

Tears jabbed her eyelids at the hopelessness in his voice. She couldn't imagine living in a house like that. The love in her house was palpable. It held them together stronger than glue. And the fact that he'd grown up thinking the demise of his parents' marriage was his fault? Punched her in the gut. "I'm so sorry, Colt," she whispered.

He continued as if he hadn't heard her. "Love makes you stupid. Weak. You accept shit from people you love that you'd never accept from anyone else. I'm living proof of that."

Truth. No wonder he'd ended up a delinquent.

"I'd take a business contract for a lifelong partnership over marriage any day of the week."

"But you're giving up so much if that's all you want."

"Am I?" His eyes were bleak.

"Yes," she whispered fiercely, tears threatening to spill over, as countless holidays flashed in her memory, laughter ringing off the walls, eyes bright with joy, love shared generously. "I could never marry someone I didn't love. Someone who made me laugh, who held me when I cried." Oh drat, the tears started to spill. She brushed her eyes hurriedly, hoping he didn't notice. "Someone who was there to encourage me in my darkest hour or celebrate my greatest triumph with me." Her voice grew stronger as she laid out her vision of what she knew could make a marriage. "Someone I could dream with, and even if those dreams went bust, we'd build new ones, better ones. You can't have that without love."

His eyes bored into her, the pain in them cutting her to the quick. "That's a pretty picture you've painted, sweetheart. But that's all it is. A fantasy. Real life don't work that way." He stood rigid, muscles hard, as if he were ready to spring into a fight at any second.

Lydia's heart broke a little at the realization that Colton had probably never experienced true happiness, the love of family. She swallowed back a sob, heart sinking to her toes. "Whatever happens, however we deal with this," she said quietly, with conviction, "You better not break mama's heart." Or hers.

CHAPTER 26

"I HAVE TO go," Colt said, tensing his legs so he didn't run out of Lydia's bedroom. Fight or flight instinct raged through him. This conversation felt too personal, too uncomfortable, too... everything. He was good in bed, not good with feelings. "I'll figure it out, and I promise, I won't break your mama's heart."

She nodded silently, and looked away. He'd seen her brush her eyes, and he felt like the world's biggest ass for dumping his shit on her like that. Best to let things simmer down for a while.

"I'm going to go check in with Travis and Elaine, but I'll be back tonight. Take it easy, okay? No work?" He waited until she nodded. "I'll help you with anything I can. I'm decent enough with a pair of scissors."

She gave him a watery smile. "That's sweet of you. I'll manage."

That was code for 'I can do it myself.' Stubborn woman. Just like her mother. In spite of himself, his chest filled with pride. Her boot company would be a success, no doubt about it. Marriage business aside, he was happy to help her. He'd handle her mother. And the Carters. Planting a kiss on her head as he passed, he walked down the hall to retrieve his clothes, grateful that Luci hadn't shown up to add fuel to the fire. Dottie might spill to the whole town that he and Lydia were engaged, but she'd never let on they'd had an entire conversation without his pants.

He dressed hurriedly. By his reckoning, it would take Dottie all of twenty minutes to spread the word. Within the hour, the whole town would know about him and Lydia. By the end of the weekend, anyone who was anyone in Prairie would have seen the Rodeo Today spread pinned up at Dottie's food truck. Colton was pretty sure that before Dottie hit the front porch, she was already on the phone to his brother. And knowing Travis, there would be words. At the very least, criticism that he hadn't followed proper protocol by talking to Lydia's parents first. Nothing to do but to suck it up and plow ahead, just like he always did. Folks might get bent out of shape, but it would blow over. It always did.

The rhythmic sounds of the industrial sewing machine carried down the hall as he headed for the door. Colt shook his head, chagrined, and stopped behind her. "You have my permission to take a break."

"I don't need your permission."

"Fine. Then give yourself permission. You're no good to anyone if you work yourself to the bone."

"I'll stop as soon as I finish these tops."

"Promise?"

She stopped and turned, staring up at him through weary eyes. "Yes."

Her answer held weight, and an unspoken challenge. *Keep your promise and I'll keep mine.* "Be back in time for dinner. I'll cook." It was the least he could do.

Surprise flickered across her face. "You cook?"

"Hell, yes. Any cowboy worth his weight can make a few good meals. No one can beat my spaghetti and meatballs."

"Seriously?" Hunger flashed in her eyes. So she hadn't

been eating well, either. He'd see to all of that tonight.

"Finish up, then take a nap. I'll take care of the rest as soon as I get back." *Home.* For the second time, the word home had popped into his mind. Leaving a kiss on her forehead, he hurried out. Fifteen minutes later he shifted the truck into park in the wide dirt area in front of his childhood home. Travis sat on the porch, heels propped on the rail.

Of course, Travis was waiting. He'd already spoken to Dottie.

Raising his hand in greeting, Colt steeled himself and sauntered over. He'd play it cool. Let Travis do the talking. That was more his style anyway where the two of them were concerned. Travis railed, he pretended to listen, and then went about his business. As soon as Colt's boot hit the step, Travis cut to the chase. "Had a mighty interesting phone call from Dottie Grace, just now."

"Oh?"

Travis motioned to the empty chair next to him. "Why don't you have a seat, and we can talk about it?"

"I prefer to stand, thanks."

"Suit yourself." Travis's face remained neutral, except for a tick below his left temple. Colt knew what that meant. He'd seen it, all to regularly as a kid. "According to Dottie, you and Lydia have decided to 'up and marry'." He used finger quotes. "But instead of going through proper channels, it somehow leaked out in a rodeo magazine."

At least she hadn't thought to embellish the truth. "That about sums it up."

Travis's feet came off the rail and landed on the porch with a heavy *thunk*. "That's it? That's all you have to say?" Travis cocked his head, as if waiting for Colton to say something.

But why should he? Travis had already passed judgment. Just like he always did. The scabs began to peel off the old hurts, one by one.

"You've decided to marry the daughter of our neighbors, and someone who's arguably our oldest family friend, and the best you can come up with is *that about sums it up?*"

Colton shrugged. "Yep." No use explaining, Travis would jump to his own conclusions. Hell, he already had.

Travis stood and braced his arms on the railing, shaking his head. "I'm sorry. I know we're just getting to know each other again after ten years, but there's no way in hell that you're ready to settle down and marry someone like Lydia Grace."

Colt crossed his arms, heat spreading across his neck. "Why the fuck not?"

Travis stared at him hard. "You don't have the first idea about what it takes to make a good marriage."

"And you do?" Colt shot back. "You've been married less than six months, and suddenly you're the expert? Give me a fucking break."

"I do know that Lydia Grace is one of the kindest souls around, and—"

"And I'm not near good enough for her," Colt finished flatly, bile rising in his throat. Some things would never change. His teenage reputation being one of them. And people wondered why he'd never bothered to come home once he'd cleaned up his act. Why he'd stayed in Steamboat where people judged him on who he was now, not who he used to be as a screwed-up, scared teenager.

"Do you love her?"

Goddammit. Why did it always have to come back to love? First Lydia, now Travis. He could lie. Lord knew, it would be easy enough, and he'd done it often enough in years past. But he'd turned over a new leaf when he'd gotten a second chance. He might stretch things, manipulate the truth in such a way as it helped him out of a sticky situation, but he wouldn't flat-out lie. Not to a lady, not to his brother.

Travis crossed his arms, taking a very police chief-like stance. "If you break her heart, there's gonna be a whole long line of folks ready to kick your ass."

"Of course," Colt answered, more in response to the second statement, not the question. But let Travis interpret it however he wanted. Colt couldn't control that. Travis didn't understand what was at stake here. Besides, the agreement was between him and Lydia. It wasn't anyone else's business. Their families might be well-meaning meddlers, but what mattered was that he and Lydia were happy with the arrangement. And they were... mostly. A voice of doubt buzzed in his ear.

CHAPTER 27

E MMALINE LOOKED UP from her sewing machine across the room. "That's like the fourth heavy sigh you've let out in the last ten minutes. What gives?"

Lydia waved her off. "Oh, it's nothing."

"She's just missing her man," Luci hollered from the kitchen.

"Do you have bionic ears, or something?" Lydia hollered back.

"Nope. I just recognize a lovesick sigh when I hear it. Even from the kitchen."

"I–" The denial was on her lips, but Lydia caught a flash of the giant diamond out of the corner of her eye and stopped her protest mid-word. "I wouldn't call it lovesick," she amended, twisting her ring. "But I do miss him." That at least, was truth. She didn't want to miss him, she didn't want to think about him nonstop, or look forward to their nightly FaceTime calls, but she did.

"Understatement," snickered Emmaline, returning to her work at the sewing machine. "You've been moping around ever since Colt left after the boot shoot. Complete with sad puppy eyes."

"I do *not* have sad puppy eyes."

"You do," called Luci from the kitchen.

Emmaline raised her head, swiveling around. "If you miss

him that much, why not join him on the road again?"

"Are the shoemaker's elves gonna rip through that stack of leather while I'm away?" Lydia waved at her side of the living room, chaotic with leather, drawings, boots in various stages of completion.

Emmaline gave her a sympathetic look. "You know I'd help."

"But you've got your own orders piling up," Lydia finished for her. "I didn't expect success to be quite so exhausting."

"I know what you mean. And it's not like I can ask anyone in town to help."

"Right?" Lydia nodded vigorously. "We're so specialized, it would take weeks to train someone."

"And I can't bring in anyone from Kansas City because we still have a housing shortage from the tornado."

Luci came in from the kitchen with a bottle of wine and three glasses. "Let's toast Emma Sinclaire. It's her fault our businesses have exploded. If only she wasn't so good at marketing."

"At least your family can help you, Luci," said Emmaline with a note of envy.

"Yes, but they don't want to. They didn't plan on spending their free time helping me pack tamales." Luci poured out the bottle and lifted her glass. "To our success. And to Emma."

Lydia clinked her glass against her roommates'. "There has to be a way we can help each other through this. We're smart, we can figure out something."

Across the room, a phone began to blare out a bluesy saxophone melody that belonged in a strip club. Luci covered her mouth, eyes laughing as Lydia lunged for her phone.

"Sorry. I think Colt's been having fun with my ringtones again."

"You guys are too cute," Luci gushed, shoulders shaking.

Guilt slammed through Lydia. Would her friends disown her too, when the sham came to light? At the same time, butterflies launched in her chest as she grabbed her phone. "Colt?" Her voice was a little too breathless, a little too excited.

"Hey there, sweetness. How's your day been?" Colt's rich baritone shivered through her, lighting all her nerve endings.

"Just having a glass of wine with the gals, toasting our success. And our exhaustion," she admitted, hurrying down the hall to her room and shutting the door behind her.

"Tell me more."

With a voice like that, she'd confess anything. She flopped back on her bed, staring at the ceiling. "Thanks to Emma Sinclaire's brilliant marketing, Emmaline and Luci are in the same boat I am."

"And all this time, I thought it was me."

"It is. But Emma's amplified what you've done, and now the boot shoot has gone viral."

"That's fantastic."

Lydia warmed at the pride in his voice. "It is, but we're both in the weeds."

"Anything I can do to help?"

"Stop looking so sexy in my boots," she said with a smile.

His low laugh rumbled through the phone, lodging in the space below her throat.

In her mind's eye, she could see him stretched out on his hotel room bed, ankles crossed, shirt unbuttoned. Her voice dropped. "Tell me what you're wearing."

"You gettin' naughty on me, Lyds?"

"Maybe just a little." Colt loved to tease her when they talked on the phone. Only recently had she started dishing out the same heat. There was something exhilarating about saying the first thing that popped into her head where Colt was concerned. Something liberating. After their conversations, she walked with a little more sass in her step.

"I wore a blue paisley shirt today," he started.

"Wait. Stop. I totally forgot to ask, how was your event?"

"Ninety-two on a horse named Rizzo."

"Bareback?"

"Saddle bronc."

"That's amazing. That's your best ride this year, isn't it?"

"You know it. And I'm wishin' you were here to celebrate with me."

"I wish that too," she admitted with a little flutter.

Colt paused. "I miss you Lyds." His voice sounded rough with emotion, and the flutter in her chest grew stronger.

"I miss you, too. Now tell me what you're wearing… or not," she let the innuendo sink in.

"I love your dirty mind," he said with a chuckle.

"That's not all you love," she blurted out, then instantly regretted the words. *Shitshitshit.* The last thing she wanted was to bring up the L-word. Not after their conversation the last time he'd been in town. And she certainly didn't want him to think that she thought he loved her. Oh, crap. Why did she have to open her big mouth?

But he continued as if she hadn't said anything out of the ordinary. "Damn straight, darlin'. I love that pretty little ass of yours when you prance around in your favorite boots. And I love the way you clutch my head when you come on my tongue." His voice had gone deep and gravelly. And his words sent a shot of wet, hot lust straight to her panties.

Her mouth went dry as she imagined his mouth on her. "Damn you," she muttered. "Now you got me all worked up."

"You're not alone, sweet thing."

"Yeah?" She'd lost all control of her voice, the ache between her legs throbbed insistently, taking all her attention. "Is your shirt unbuttoned?"

She could hear the smile in his voice. "You know it."

"What about your pants?"

"Workin' on it."

Her heart sprang into a gallop. "Are you going to touch yourself?" She salivated at the thought, but she didn't care. Her mother would have washed her dirty mouth out with soap if she'd been in earshot. A giggle erupted at the thought of her mother overhearing.

"What was that for, babe?"

"Just thinking that mama would be horrified at my mouth."

"I love your mouth. Don't change a thing."

His words set every cell in her body tingling. "Are you touching yourself?" she whispered, body heating at her words.

"Are you?"

"My roommates are down the hall."

"Then you better not scream when you come." Oh hell, this was the sexiest, naughtiest thing she'd ever done. She wasn't even touching herself yet, and she was ready to burst. "On three?"

Flames heated her face as she slid her hand inside her yoga pants, letting out a sigh when her fingers hit her slick heat. "Yeah." She licked her lips, unable to fill her lungs with enough air. All her energy was wrapped up in relieving the ache between her legs.

"You find your clit, baby?"

Judging from his voice, he was just as overcome as she was. "Uh-huh," she panted, rolling her hips into her fingers.

"Is it swollen and slick?"

He was going to kill her. Was it possible to die from an orgasm? "Yeah," she said on a high sigh.

"Are you rubbing it back and forth like it was my fingers?"

Her insides flamed to ash, his words the fuel to her fire. There would be nothing left of her when he finished. "Just tell me you're doing the same," she gasped. "That your cock is slick and you're rubbing it all over."

"Oh hell, yes, baby. Keep going."

As her words grew more creative, her clit throbbed to the point she grew incoherent. Her legs shook from the strain. "Colt, I-I'm… *Oh Colt*,"

"Me too, baby, me too," he said with a groan.

Her orgasm burned through her, momentarily spotting her vision and making her brain go blank. "I don't think I can talk." Even her tongue felt numb.

"Then just be with me." His voice sounded slow and languid.

She shut her eyes with a sigh, imagining they were lying on the same bed, that she was curled into his side, listening to his heart thump rhythmically under her ear. How long they lay like that, phones to their ear, not talking, she had no idea. "I think I dozed off."

"Yeah. Me, too."

Her body grew heavy. "I should go."

"Me, too." Colt's voice suddenly sounded weary.

"Talk soon?" She hated the idea of getting off the phone.

"You know I'll be your wake-up call."

She could hear him smiling, and her heart twisted painfully. *I love you.* She sucked in a ragged breath. She'd been avoiding the admission for days, but she couldn't help it. The understanding that she was stupidly, desperately in love with Colton Kincaid had embedded itself in her skin, in every breath she took. She blinked back the tears that sprouted, pushed down the ache that closed off her throat. "Sweet dreams, then." She forced a smile to her face, hoping it translated over the phone.

"Sweet dreams, babe."

Lydia lay staring at the ceiling, feelings swirling around her like a spring storm. This was what she got for not playing it safe, and there was nothing to do but cowgirl up and push through it. Propping herself up on an elbow, she wiped the back of her hand across her eyes. It wouldn't do to have her roommates think she'd been fighting with Colt. Puffing her cheeks and blowing out a slow yoga breath, she sat up, stretched and made her way to the living room. Emmaline and Luci both turned as she paused in the entryway.

"You look so happy when you're talking to him," Emmaline said, envy flickering in her eyes. "I never would have imagined Colton Kincaid turning out nice."

Lydia smiled through the pain that arrowed straight to her heart. "Yeah, me either."

CHAPTER 28

COLTON FINALLY RELAXED when the captain's voice came over the intercom. "Flight attendants, take your seats."

His pulse drummed in anticipation as the plane banked, circling Manhattan's Regional Airport, squaring up to land on the tiny runway. Two and a half weeks. That's all it had been since he'd last held Lydia, smelled her perfume. Brought her coffee as she struggled to wake up at the crack of dawn.

It felt more like a lifetime. A lifetime of falling asleep without Lydia tucked under his arm. A lifetime of not seeing her happy smile after a good ride. A lifetime of watching her unawares, the way she moved in a room, or cocked her head while listening to a client.

A guilty twinge ate at him as he thought about all the time he was taking from her boot making today, but she'd insisted when he'd told her he'd managed to grab a last-minute flight back to meet his new niece. He never flew. Hated it. But he only had three days between rodeos and Ponoka, Alberta, was too far to drive. And if he could steal three days with Lydia, even if he had to sit around and watch her work on her boot orders, he'd do it. That decision was a total no-brainer. Ribs protesting, he bent to look out the window as the tiny plane taxied to its gate. There was no way he'd see Lydia from this distance, but it didn't stop him from trying.

Colt shot out of his seat the second the seatbelt sign turned off, careful not to knock his head. Grabbing his carryon and Stetson from the overhead, he shuffled out, mentally prodding his fellow passengers along. The early summer humidity hit him as he made his way down the roll-up steps. It was probably thirty degrees warmer here in Kansas than when he'd left Canada, and if his nose didn't mislead him, they'd have thunderstorms tonight. As soon as his boots hit the tarmac, he began to scan for Lydia.

"Colt," she called jumping up and down, waving from the unsecured part of the airport.

His mouth turned up as he picked up his pace. That was his girl, sweet as ever, and looking at no one but *him*. His chest expanded with warmth and something else. Something deeper.

She launched herself into his arms as soon as he cleared the gate. "Gently," he reminded her as he swung her around.

"Oh, right. Your ribs. Should you be lifting me?"

"Absolutely. It was only a small tumble. Just a little tape."

Her brows knit together. "I hate knowing you got hurt."

"Comes with the territory."

"And how's your shoulder?"

"Better with the brace." He'd been surprised what a difference the brace made this time around. He could see now, how over time, his shoulder had been growing weaker. With the added support of tape and a custom fit brace, he'd turned in his strongest rides of the season. "Stop talking and kiss me." He bent and took her mouth, something inside him sliding home as her lips surrendered to his. "I missed you," he murmured through a tight throat when they broke apart.

She tipped her head back, eyes dancing. "Yeah? How

much?"

So much, it hurt to breathe. The realization shook him to his bones, as if he'd been thrown by the meanest, nastiest bull, even as he recognized the truth of it. His buddies had razzed him for days about his surly demeanor, how he was no fun anymore, always turning down their invitations to hit the honky-tonks after a performance, but he didn't even care. He was hooked, and he wasn't the same without her. "I'll show you just how much, later."

Her eyes grew hungry. "Promise?"

"I do." Promising to make Lydia fly came as easy as breathing. He took her hands, pressing a kiss to the tops, using the gesture to study her hands. Her fingers smelled faintly of leather, but it was her swollen knuckles and red, ragged fingertips that sent concern ricocheting through him. "I thought you said you were going to rest."

Guilt colored her expression. "I'd planned on it."

"But?"

"But the orders keep coming."

He squeezed her hands, but not too hard, for fear of hurting her more. "You have to say no, hon. You'll burn yourself out. Worse, you'll end up with a repetitive stress injury. Hell, sweetheart, look at your hands." He shook them gently. "You're well on your way. Then what?"

"But a friend of mine who's a dresser for an up-and-coming New York designer just ordered six pairs for her models for a trunk show in August."

"When did this happen?" Excitement for her warred with hurt that she hadn't mentioned anything.

"I just received the deposit this morning. I thought there was a chance it would happen a few days ago, but I didn't want to jinx it by saying anything."

"You'd never jinx anything by telling me."

"Because you're my good-luck charm?"

"Something like that." He kissed her again, relaxing into his bones as their mouths met briefly. "Let's go. I want to meet this niece of mine."

"She's adorable, Colt." Lydia gushed excitedly, eyes lighting up. "She's got the cutest little face, and Emmaline made her a pair of booties that look like cowboy boots."

"This I gotta see."

"I'll warn you," Lydia stopped when they reached her SUV. "The ranch house looks like a pink bomb went off."

He laughed as he dropped his bag into the back and slid into the passenger seat. "Still like the new wheels?" he asked as she pulled out of the parking lot.

"Are you kidding? It's amazing. But you still shouldn't have. I'd never have purchased a new vehicle."

"Do you honestly think I'd let my fiancée drive a 1978 Dodge Dart? That old thing was a firetrap. Ask your sister, she'd know."

"Believe me, I appreciate it, but it's still too much. You have to let me pay you back."

He scowled out the window. "It was a gift, Lydia. Why can't you just accept that it was a gift?"

"Because I'm not really your fiancée," she finally said after a spell.

The pain in her voice gnawed at him. Unsettled him. "I don't care about that. You needed a car, and I wanted to give you one. Don't overthink it," he said tightly, ignoring the longing tightening his belly into a fist. He'd give her a million gifts to see her light up the way she had when he'd dropped the keys into her unsuspecting hand.

Ninety lively minutes later, Lydia turned under the arch

that now proudly displayed the Resolution Ranch logo. The rundown ranch of his childhood now completely transformed into a working ranch for veterans, thanks to Travis and the support of Prairie's tight-knit community. Lydia set the brake, turning to him with an excited smile. "Ready to meet your niece?"

He was. No joke. Eager anticipation rolled through him. This little person shared his DNA, the good, the bad. And with Travis guiding her, who knew what mountains she'd conquer in her lifetime? "Stay put." He hopped down and hurried around the front of the SUV, extending his hand to help Lydia down once he opened the door. He shut it behind her, then remembered. "Wait a sec. Can't show up empty-handed." He jogged around to the trunk and grabbed his carry-on. Lydia would be proud of him, he'd wandered the exhibition hall in Augusta, Montana, for a full hour before deciding on the stuffed pony and onesie, which he'd then wrapped – badly – on his own. He held up the gift bag as he shut the trunk. "Now I'm ready."

Travis opened the door as they hit the steps, little Avery Allison nestled asleep in the crook of his arm, and the biggest, goofiest grin on his face. "So this is little Avery."

Colt couldn't breathe, couldn't speak. He'd never describe his brother as a happy man. Yet, the man before him was fucking giddy. Glowing like the goddamned sun. Colt needed to sit. Or a drink. He couldn't process what his eyes were telling him. It made no sense. This was Travis. Happy. A rush of longing poured over Colton. He wanted *that*. He didn't have a clue how to go about getting *that*, whatever it was that Travis oozed. He stared at the scrunched up little person in Travis's arms, then back at his brother, then back to his niece. She was responsible for *that*?

Travis had looked happy at his wedding. Peaceful and calm. But this? This was something entirely different. Colt glanced sideways at Lydia who caught his gaze, eyes shining with the same light as Travis's. *What was it?* The longing nearly brought him to his knees. Swallowing and clearing his throat, he held out the gift bag. "Congratulations."

"Come in. Elaine's on the couch." Travis stood aside and let them pass, then handed the gift bag to Elaine. "Let's see what Uncle Colt brought."

Uncle Colt. The more he heard it, the more he liked it. "Where's Dax?"

"He's off at a friend's, but he'll be back for dinner. I hope you stay?"

"You better," Travis ordered. "We've got casseroles in the kitchen. Dottie brought enough food for a month."

Colton raised his brow in question to Lydia, who nodded. "The only plans we have involve cooing over that beautiful baby."

"Let's see what's inside." Elaine pulled out the horse with a grin. "This is perfect, Colt. We'll stick it in her crib." She pulled out the poorly wrapped package.

Lydia's eyes went wide, but she shot him a smile of approval. Elaine carefully unwrapped the package, then held up the outfit for everyone to see.

Lydia clapped a hand over her mouth as she let out a squeal.

"So I did okay?" Butterflies launched in Colt's stomach.

She nodded, hand still covering her mouth.

Elaine held up the pink onesie with the words "Future Rodeo Queen" embroidered in a rope font. "I love it, Colt," she said, giving him a grateful smile. The kicker, and what had sold him on the outfit was the sparkly pink tulle skirt sewn to the onesie. Who could resist that? Clearly, he was a sucker for little girls.

He planted a kiss on Elaine's cheek. "Congratulations. She's beautiful."

"How can you say that when you haven't even held her yet?" she teased. "Have a seat. Travis will hand her over. She just ate, so her tummy's full and she'll nap for a while now."

Colt's fingers buzzed with energy. He'd never held a baby. A human baby, at least. And they seemed much more fragile.

"Don't be nervous," Elaine assured him. "Holding her is easier than riding broncs."

He chuckled. "If you say so."

Travis closed the distance, and suddenly little Avery was nestled in the crook of his elbow. "She hardly weighs a thing," he said, awe filling his voice. Wonder filled him, choking off his air, and poking at his eyelids. He inhaled sharply. He didn't cry. Ever. But the sensation bubbled up again. He studied her tiny face, the barely-there eyebrows, the dark eyelashes sweeping her cheeks, the button nose, the rosebud mouth. He'd never seen anything like it. "She's perfect," he said thickly, voice cracking.

"Looks just like her mama," Travis said proudly.

"I think she looks like you," Elaine corrected.

After a few minutes, once he realized tiny Avery Allison wouldn't break, he settled back into the chair.

"See?" Elaine pointed out. "He's a natural."

"I don't know about that." He shot a look at his brother. "But I promise I'll do my best to be a good uncle. To give her what we never had." Again, his eyes prickled. Jesus, he was turning into a fucking water fountain.

Travis held his gaze, years of unspoken words passing between them. It didn't matter anymore. None of it. Sure, it would come up, but the old hurts needed to be released so this perfect little thing could grow up happy and supported. Colt resolved to do better, to be better. To be worthy of little Avery. To be someone she could be proud of when she was older.

Lydia grabbed his free hand, giving it a squeeze. He squeezed back like she was his lifeline. He couldn't let go. Not just of her hand, but of *her*. This? This was so much richer because he could share it with her. *She* was what was missing from his life.

And the way she stared with such love in her eyes at little Avery, punched him in the gut. Never in a million years, in a million plans for his life, had he envisioned settling down.

Until now.

The realization hit him with the momentum of a runaway truck on Rabbit Ears Pass. He was in love with Lydia. He wanted her – not just as his fake fiancée, but the whole hog. Picket fence, dogs and kids. For the first time in his life, she made him want a future, and it scared the shit out of him. More than anything, he wanted to see Lydia gaze at their baby like she gazed at Avery. And he wanted the perma-grin Travis wore, with a desperation that stopped his heart.

Someway, somehow, he had to convince Lydia to marry him for real.

CHAPTER 29

L YDIA DIDN'T TALK the fifteen-minute drive back to the bungalow.

Colt reached out, tucking an errant curl behind her ear. "You've been awful quiet. Everything okay?"

She blinked slowly, taking her eyes off the road for the barest of seconds as she looked heavenward for help she was certain wouldn't come from the ceiling. "Just tired." Lame excuse, and he'd probably see right through it, but she refused to open a can of worms, and talking about feelings with Colt would only do that, and worse.

"You're never 'just tired', Lyds," he admonished gently. "What gives?"

She blew out a long breath.

What gives?

How could she tell him how profoundly moved she'd been, seeing him hold his niece? The wonder on his face, the gentleness. The way he'd looked at Travis with new understanding. The ache in her heart had been so intense, she thought she might faint. He didn't want the same things from his life that she wanted, and she had to accept that. Brace herself for their inevitable parting, because when their show ended, when Colton's reputation was in the clear, her heart would disintegrate.

Just this morning, she'd started looking at cheap warehouse space in several cities across the country, because once Colton walked away, she couldn't stay in Prairie. Seeing him but not being with him would be more than she could take. She'd have to leave.

She pulled into the drive and cut the engine.

"Talk to me, Lydia," he murmured with that sweet seductive tone that always made her sing like a canary. He stroked a finger down her jawline.

The words jammed up in her throat. God forgive her for being a coward. She couldn't put herself on the line for him again. When he heard the words *I Love You*, his rejection would be swifter than the last time she'd showed her true feelings all those years ago. Colt might come to love someone someday, but it wouldn't be her, and it would be long after she'd figured out how to move on with her life. A sob threatened to replace the words stuck at the back of her mouth.

The porch light flashed, signaling that Luci knew she was in the driveway. Saved by the bell. Flashing him a smile, she unbuckled her seatbelt. "They're waiting for us inside."

"Who's waiting for us inside?" Colt muttered, obviously irritated.

"Luci's family. She has them for dinner once a week. Hope you saved room after mama's pie."

"You didn't tell me there was going to be a second dinner," he groused.

"Sorry. Forgot." She hopped out of the SUV before she said more. In truth, it had slipped her mind. She'd been too wrapped up in Colton for any other part of her brain to work, and at least now, the Cruz family would give her cover. Lydia put on her game face and pushed open the front door.

"We're out back tonight," Luci hollered from the kitchen.

"And don't worry, no one touched the projects."

The aromas coming from the kitchen were mouthwatering. "Is that posole?" Colton asked.

"Good nose," Luci sang as she handed over a bowl. "Condiments are outside. Green and red chile sauce, sour cream, cilantro, lime, avocado, and cheese."

"What about you, Lydia?" Luci asked. "Mama made it special tonight."

"What's the occasion?" Luci's mother rarely cooked anymore, having handed the primary duties to the younger members of the Cruz family. But she always cooked for special occasions.

"A perfect summer night." Luci leaned in. "I think she misses cooking for a group every now and then."

Lydia accepted a bowl only because if she refused, Luci would start grilling her, and Lydia didn't want to make a scene in front of her family. Her life felt dramatic enough at the moment. She followed Colt to the back deck, unable to hide a grin at the white lights someone had strung up. One of Luci's cousins played guitar in the corner. Someone had started a bonfire in the middle of the backyard. Clearly, they were here for the duration. Lydia fought a sigh. More than anything, she wanted quiet, space to think, to sort out her feelings where Colt was concerned, and to figure out a plan of action in the wake of a broken engagement that never had been in the first place.

Colt pulled out a chair for her, then sat next to her. "I know you're putting on a good face, but something is going on. What's it gonna take for you to fess up, sweetheart?"

Again, the words bubbled up, ready to be heard. She wavered. He'd never been anything but honest with her from the get-go. He'd let her call the shots every step of the way.

What were the chances that he'd turn her down? Significant, given their one and only conversation about love and marriage. He'd been honest about those feelings, too. Putting her posole down on an upside-down crate someone had turned into a table, she stood. "I'm sorry," she choked out. "I think I need some air." Never mind that she was already outside. She rushed back into the house, through the kitchen, and out to the front porch.

Fireflies winked on the front lawn, and she sank onto the porch swing with a relieved sigh. There, in the dark, she could gather her thoughts, and if the tears came, so be it. At least out front, no one would bother her. The swing creaked as she pushed it back and forth, joining the night chorus of tree frogs, crickets, and toads. She extended her arm across the back of the swing and dropped her head, letting the sounds wash over her. She'd always enjoyed summer nights in the Flint Hills, the sounds soothed her, grounded her, and tonight was no different.

The front door creaked. She ignored it, still pushing the swing.

"Penny for your thoughts," Colt offered quietly.

She'd give him props for persistence. "The night has me melancholy. I'm sorry." She scooted over on the swing. "Join me?" She patted the empty spot next to her.

He sat down and stretched out his arm, silently inviting her to come close. And like a starved puppy, she'd take whatever crumbs he offered. She scooted over, curling into him, and laying her head on his chest, pulse slowing to sync with the heartbeat under her ear. This would be enough, it had to. It was the best she could expect from him, and right now, fool that she was, she'd take it without question. With a sigh, she shut her eyes, and let the motion of the swing lull her. She caught a whiff of his cologne, spicy and warm underneath his natural masculine scent. She counted to one-hundred squeaks from the hooks.

At one-hundred-thirty-two, he spoke. "Why don't we take a drive? I know someplace quiet."

She nodded against his chest, unable to speak. She could sense the tension coiled in his body, his muscles wound tight beneath her hand. This was it – time to lay their cards on the table.

CHAPTER 30

COLT'S STOMACH JUMPED, refusing to settle. With every groan of the porch swing, his anxiety grew. Lydia was about to bail. That had to be why she was pulling back all of a sudden. Withdrawing. She couldn't even look at him, and that only meant one thing. She was done with him. With them. Fear spread through his veins like ice as he cast about for a place to take her, away from the well-meaning but prying eyes of their families and friends. "Why don't we take a drive? I know someplace quiet."

She nodded against his chest and pushed off the swing. "I'll grab some blankets."

Once she'd disappeared inside, Colt sprang to this feet, shaking his sweat covered palms. His breath came in short gasps as he chased after his scattered thoughts. Every self-preservation alarm in his body sounded in a deafening chorus. He'd carefully orchestrated his life to avoid this very situation. The Colt of six or eight months ago would have politely said goodbye and exited the arena as fast as his boots could carry him. But he was all-in for Lydia. Even though riding the orneriest bull on the rodeo circuit, followed by the meanest bronc, held significantly more appeal than opening his soft underbelly to her, he'd do it. Hell, he'd rather walk barefoot across a Texas parking lot in summer, but he'd man up for even the smallest taste of what he'd witnessed at Travis's.

His boots carried him back and forth across the porch. He might have been a failure in his young life, but he was different now. Had he shown her enough of that to convince her? Doubt assailed him as he replayed comments from his brother, from Dottie. Was he worthy of someone as special as Lydia? Probably not, but he sure as hell was gonna try.

The screen door creaked, and Lydia stepped out, a large quilt tucked under her arm.

Colt held out his hand. "Why don't you let me drive?"

She didn't make a sound, but fished out the fob from her jeans pocket and handed it over. Taking the steps by two, Colt bounded toward the SUV parked at the end of the driveway and held open the door for her before rounding the vehicle and climbing in.

"I snagged a few beers. They're in my purse," she offered quietly, clutching the blankets to her like armor.

"Good call." He shifted into gear and pulled out of the driveway.

Thirty-three minutes later, he pulled onto the access road that led to Marion Reservoir.

"I haven't been here in years." Surprise colored Lydia's voice.

"I used to come here all the time."

"To drink?" she asked wryly.

Heat prickled across the back of his neck and he kept his eyes on the dirt road. "Yeah. And… other stuff."

She snorted.

"Don't judge. It was the first place I thought of that was out of the way."

"I'm totally judging."

"You know I'm not like that anymore."

She nodded. "I know," she answered in a small voice.

"Can we go someplace you've never been?"

A chance to make new memories, unsullied by the past. He liked that. "Of course." He passed the first turnoff, heading into unfamiliar territory. They drove another mile, silence filling the cab. Glimpses of the moonlight reflecting on the water teased his peripheral vision. The lake would be glorious tonight. He turned onto the next road and wound through the trees, slowing to a stop at an old abandoned camp site. "I should have brought firewood, it might be buggy."

"It's okay. I have bug spray in my purse."

Always prepared, his Lydia. He kicked himself for not planning ahead. A fire would have been much more romantic. At least no storms were on the horizon. She hopped out of the SUV before he could make it around the front to open the door. An old cottonwood log lay a short distance from the shore. Lydia spread a blanket on the gravel and draped the other over the back of the log. He sank to the ground, butterflies launching in his stomach.

Lydia joined him, angling her body toward his.

He took her hand. They spoke at the same time.

"I need to tell you some things."

"I need to tell you something."

Lydia's mouth turned up for the first time since they'd left Resolution Ranch, melting his fear with its brilliance. "You, first."

He laced his fingers with hers. "You sure? I have a lot to get off my chest."

She nodded, giving his fingers a squeeze.

Taking a big breath, he started. "I was five the night my mom left. I don't remember much about her, but I remember that night like it was yesterday." His gut churned, and he was back at the ranch, a scared kid in the midst of chaos. "She'd been drinking. But this time I remembered my dad begging her not to go. I'll never forget the desperation in his voice. She said she didn't know why she'd agreed to live in this godforsaken town, that he'd lied to her. Sold her a bill of goods."

Lydia gasped, covering her mouth with her free hand.

"It gets worse. Trav stepped in and pleaded with her on my behalf, and she looked at me like I was nothing. Worse than a pig in mud."

"Oh, Colt."

For years the memory had torn him up, made him want to toss the contents of his belly, and the only thing that numbed the grief was booze, or pot, or women. It still hurt, probably always would, but not in the same way. Now, he could take out the memory and turn it in his hand. Examine it like he would a flank strap, or a new belt.

"What broke me? Broke dad too, for all I know, was when she told dad it was my fault I was born. That she never wanted me and that she was going home to Florida."

Lydia let out a sob, squeezing his hand tight and wrapping herself around him. "I'm so sorry. I can't even begin to imagine how that devastated you."

"I was too young to process it, all I knew was that my mom didn't love us and that was why she left. My dad was never the same. I-I think that's why he got sick and died."

She shook her head. "You must know better, now."

Colt scrubbed a hand across his jaw with a sigh. "Yeah. But sometimes..." A shudder wracked him. He'd never told anyone his deepest, darkest fear. He swallowed down the dread that gripped him. A bead of sweat trickled down the back of his neck. "Sometimes, I think my dad blamed me for her leaving." It sounded awful, giving voice to the thoughts he'd kept locked tight for decades. "Sometimes, I'd catch him staring at me when he thought I wasn't looking. And-and I could tell."

Lydia lifted her head, and forced his gaze up. "*It wasn't your fault,*" she declared with conviction. "You were a kid. A *baby.*"

He forced himself to keep going, to hold the emotions threatening to railroad him at bay. "I'm not proud of the choices I've made. How I handled things." He stared out at the water, drowning in its darkness.

"That's all in the past, Colt. It's not who you are now."

Unable to look at her for fear of what he'd see, he focused on the tree-line on the far shore. "And who am I, Lyds? Who do you see?"

"I see a man who uses bravado like armor, but his loyalty is fierce if he considers you a friend. I see a man who takes his responsibilities seriously, who is as good as his word, who is generous and encouraging." She hesitated.

"And?"

"Who's cocky, and funny." Her breath hitched, as if she was struggling to say something. "And who is very, very lovable," she finished in a rush.

Well, knock him over with a feather.

She climbed onto his lap and dropped her head, laying kisses along his neck. "I can't erase the past, but I can give you this right now." She brought his hand to her heart.

What was she saying? Longing surged through him as her heart thumped beneath his fingers, steady and strong. This. This heart, this woman anchored him. Gave his life purpose. If there was even the slightest chance she felt the same way, he'd charge through that opening with everything he had. Skating his fingers over her collarbone, sliding up her neck, he tipped up her chin. "Say the word," he urged, not even sure he knew what he was asking for.

She answered with a kiss, her mouth opening, tongue darting along his lip. With a groan, he responded, giving her access to his mouth, to any part of him she wanted. It was like kissing her for the first time again, the way their tongues slid and curled in a conversation that went straight to his soul.

Her hands pulled at the buttons on his shirt. In a flurry of fingers, they disrobed, mouths still drinking each other in like water in the desert. They broke apart only to shimmy out of their jeans, tossing them on the growing heap of clothing.

Gently pushing her back, he drew a hand down her torso, reveling in the way she glowed in the moonlight. "So perfect, so sweet," he murmured, circling a finger around one taut nipple. Goosebumps erupted on her skin as she arched into his touch.

Her hand fluttered from his shoulder over his pecs, coming to rest where his ribs were taped, her touch like the kiss of butterfly wings. "Does it hurt?"

"Only in the sweetest way possible."

She reached lower, thumb pressing up along the ridge of his rigid cock, fingers encircling its slick head.

He followed suit, sweeping his fingers through her wet curls and parting her slick seam with his thumb, stroking up to find her clit, swollen and ready for his touch. With a gasp, she bucked her hips, bowing into him and pulling him in for another kiss. His will frayed.

"Sweetheart." He wanted so badly to feel her slick heat encasing him. To lose himself in her softness.

"Condoms are in my purse," she murmured between kisses.

"What if we..." He let the words dangle between them.

She'd never hidden that she was on the pill, but since it had never come up, he'd always assumed she wanted the condoms as much as he did. But maybe they'd crossed into new territory?

She pushed up to an elbow. "Are you sure?"

He nodded, not trusting his voice.

Her eyes were dark pools in the moonlight, as deep and fathomless as the water behind them. They held him captive as he shifted over her, rubbing the head of his cock along her slick entrance, coating himself in her essence.

Time slowed. The only thing between them, their ragged breathing, and his hope.

"I... want you." She reached up and cupped his face, eyes luminous, the movement heartbreakingly tender but at odds with her words.

An ache lodged in his chest as he slid home into her, refusing to release her gaze as he thrust slowly, her tight heat encasing him. Surely she must feel what was between them? The way he felt? "Marry me." The words spilled out in a tumble, refusing to be contained for another second.

She stilled beneath him, eyes going wide.

"Be my wife. For real." He rolled his hips, pressing his point, and was rewarded with a needy moan from her lips. "I love you," he rasped, not recognizing his voice.

"For real?" she whispered back.

"For real." He thrust again, the ache at his center building as she clenched around him. "Make babies with me."

Two tears spilled out the side of her eyes. "Oh, Colt, me too."

He kissed the trail they left, pouring all his feeling into every movement, every push of his hips as they joined.

She raised her head, bringing her mouth to his. "Yes," she

said against his lips before kissing him. "Yes."

Her words acted like a key, turning a lock that caged in the deepest part of his soul. As they spiraled higher together, the first stirrings of happiness sprang to life inside him – new, and fresh, and perfect. The sensation carried him to another plane, where every touch, every caress, every thrust their bodies made together, held deeper meaning.

And as their cries mingled with the night frogs and other woodland sounds, Colt's heart filled to bursting. He rolled to his side, pulling her with him as they floated back to earth. "Will you tell me now? What's been bothering you?" He tugged on a lock of her hair before brushing it off her forehead.

She gave him a rueful smile, fingers tracing the tape on his ribs. "It doesn't matter, now. I was afraid to tell you how I felt. Worried you'd feel pressure to change our agreement. And I realized I'd rather take a fake engagement over nothing at all. I love you so much, Colt," her voice grew misty. "I want to spend my life being your wife. Even if we have to be apart for long stretches."

He placed a finger over her lips. "Hush now. We'll figure it out. Heck, we're figuring it out." He crooked a finger under her chin, lifting so he could kiss her.

"Seeing you with your niece–"

"Seeing *you* with my niece," he answered with a laugh. "When do you want to start making babies?"

"Seriously?"

"I'll be ready… in about five more minutes." He winked and thrust his hips, already half-hard for her.

"There's this small thing called my boot company," she protested.

More like a big thing. How could she care for an infant

keeping the hours she did? But no way was he going to point that out to her. "We can discuss babies whenever you're ready. We have more pressing matters."

"Like what?"

"Like getting you a proper engagement ring."

"No." She shook her head. "I want this one. You picked it out."

"But I picked it because it's gaudy and I knew it would horrify you."

"You still picked it out. And it's grown on me," she added with that half sexy smile he loved so much.

"I can pick you out something I know you'll like better," he offered. "I don't want you wearing something you don't like."

"*No*," she said fiercely. "I want this one."

CHAPTER 31

H ER MOTHER WAS pouting. She could hear it over the phone. "I don't know why you and your sister are so against the Posse doing something for you," Dottie groused.

Lydia rolled her eyes as she wove through the crowded exhibition hall in Miles City, Montana. "How about you hold a luncheon at the diner? Now that you have a back room, why not break it in?" She still missed the Formica counter and vintage booths of the old diner, but when her mother had rebuilt after the tornado, she'd done it with an eye toward the future.

"When will you be home?"

"We'll be home late tomorrow night. Colt's last ride is this evening."

"Then three days from now will be okay?"

"Colt's insisted I take the week off from boot making. Something about him being worried my hands will be too swollen for the wedding ring. We'll both be home all week."

"Smart man."

"Mama, I have to go, there's someone waiting in my booth."

"Dinner will be waiting in the kitchen for you tomorrow night. Love you, sweetie pie."

"Love you too, mama." Lydia clicked off and hurried the rest of the way down the aisle, shoulders tensing when she recognized Sammy Jo Carter.

She tried to keep her voice warm. "Hi, Sammy. How are you?" She failed. The woman set off all the warning bells in her body. And while she'd never admit it to Colt, she hated that there had been something between the two of them. Even if it was years ago. Sammy Jo knew a piece of him that she'd missed out on because Colt had left Prairie. She was determined not to be one of *those* women, so she made an effort to be as gracious with Sammy as she was with everyone else. But the woman didn't make it easy. In fact, it seemed like she went out of her way to send little darts Lydia's direction whenever she was within earshot. "Can I help you with something?"

Sammy Jo's eyes went straight to her engagement ring, just like they always did. Giving in to the devil inside her, Lydia angled her hand so she could see the whole thing. Just in case she needed a reminder about who Colt belonged to. Sammy Jo's eyes flashed. "When did y'all say you were getting married?"

"Did you not receive the wedding invitation? It's next week." Was Sammy Jo playing her? Colton had invited all his sponsors. And while she didn't like it, she agreed it had been the right thing to do.

"Are you sure you know what you're getting into, where Colt is concerned?"

"Quite sure." White hot anger shot through her. She didn't have time for Sammy's digs and twisted barbs. Not today, not ever. "Thank you for your concern. Was there something else you needed?" she asked coldly, not caring that Sammy Jo was responsible for a huge division of Carter Holdings.

"I know your type." Sammy Jo's voice dripped with condescension. "I've known Colt for years, seen it all before. You think you can reform him. That your gentle hand will bring him to heel and that he'll become your everything." She shook her head. "Wild like Colt can't be contained. And you'll get burned if you try."

Lydia stood a little taller in her boots. Sammy Jo might have been a flavor of the week years ago, but Colt loved her, and nothing would get in the way of that. Especially not Samantha Jo Carter. "I think you're jealous that you were the wrong person for him, and you can't stand that he might be happy with someone else."

Sammy Jo lifted a shoulder nonchalantly and traced a finger over the embroidery on one of the boot tops on display. "Suit yourself. Just remember, I know where all his skeletons are."

"That so?" Let her think that. She knew where the older, darker ones were, and she'd never ever in a million years use them against him. "If you'll excuse me, I've got real customers to take care of," she said with a dose of saccharine, ignoring the tendril of doubt that sprouted in her mind. Turning her back, she approached the man hovering in the corner of her booth, admiring her newest sample, a bedazzled, embroidered ladies wedding boot. "Looking for yourself, or someone else?" Lydia asked with a smile. The man wore pressed denims and a custom-made suit jacket, but his boots weren't quite up to Lydia's standards.

He extended his hand. "Treat Wilson, CEO Trinity Apparel."

"I love your brand," Lydia answered excitedly as she took his hand. "Your ladies wear has ended up on my inspiration board for a number of my designs."

"That so?"

"What can I help you with today?"

"Can we sit?" He motioned to the chairs she kept in the center of her space. "A friend of mine ordered a pair of your boots earlier this spring in San Antonio."

"Oh? Who was it?"

He sat, stretching his legs in front of him. "Adam Hawkins. We attended Harvard Business School together."

"I remember him." A thrill ran through her at the thought of her first referral. She made a note to send Adam a bottle of wine if Treat made a deposit. "Python vamps, black tops with python inlay."

He grinned at her. "Excellent memory. Said they're the best fitting boots he's ever owned."

She flushed from the compliment. "I'm happy to hear that. I take a very personal approach with each client. As you know, a custom-made pair of boots is special. I want each pair I make to reflect the unique qualities of its owner."

"I like how you think Ms. Grace." He nodded, as if checking off a mental box. "Tell me, what's your turnaround time these days?"

She had to keep herself from bouncing in her seat. This was why she wanted to cultivate more referrals. They were already sold on her boots before they stepped inside the booth. "Sadly, you're looking at about twelve weeks right now. My business has exploded, which is wonderful, but I'm committed to never cutting corners. I want every one of my clients to have my best work."

Treat Wilson's eyes lit up, and he nodded again. "Do you know that Trinity Apparel is a family-run company, and that we personally train every employee on every aspect of our garment construction?"

"I knew that you were family owned."

"We're very aware of the high rate of repetitive stress injuries in the garment industry, so we never let an employee do one thing for more than a few hours."

"And the switching hasn't impacted your productivity?"

"It's improved it."

"I'm impressed." Maybe when she had time to hire help, she could do that too. Her hands ached constantly.

Treat leaned forward. "I confess, Ms. Grace, I didn't come here for a pair of boots today."

Lydia's heart plummeted to her boots, and she struggled to keep her smile in place. She'd have enjoyed collaborating with him on a pair of boots. Already, she could see him in embroidered black calfskin. "Well, please give my regards to Adam. Tell him I'm glad he's enjoying his boots." She moved to stand, but he held out a hand.

"I shouldn't have been coy, Ms. Grace, but I had to vet you in person."

"I don't understand?"

"Trinity Apparel has been looking to bring a boot maker into our fold for the better part of a year. But we have high standards, and haven't found the right company to partner with yet. Adam spoke so highly of you, and after researching what I could of your online presence, we'd love to talk to you further if you're interested."

A laugh escaped her before her blood turned to ice. "I'm sorry, but I'm not interested. Thank you so much." She moved to stand again.

"Wait. Obviously, it would take some time, and more conversation, but we're prepared to make you a very generous offer. And we'd keep the Grace name. We could guarantee you the same quality of boot, but with our facilities and staff, you could expand into ready-made, as well as take on more custom orders."

"That's very generous of you, Mr. Wilson, but I'm not interested. I've poured my heart into this company, and I could never imagine giving it up."

His eyes drifted to her hands, and Lydia resisted the urge to hide them. "We started off small, too. Bootstrapped and grew in inches and fits. Worked long hours for days on end. I had the help of a sister and brother, but my sister developed arthritis in her hands and wrists from too many hours of stitching. There's an easier way that won't ruin your body in the long run." He reached into his coat pocket and handed her a business card. "You wouldn't have to give it up. We'd need someone to continue designing and managing the brand. Keep my card. If you change your mind, I'd love to talk to you."

CHAPTER 32

COLT COVERED THE length of the small room right off the chapel in four steps. Leave it to Mr. Punctuality to be late this afternoon. "Where have you been? Wedding starts in five minutes."

"Calm down, we're here now," Travis called from the doorway, a proud smile lighting his face. "You clean up good, little brother."

"We had to change Avery's diaper." Dax wrinkled his nose. "Again."

Colt would laugh if he wasn't so nervous. "You have the ring?" He tugged at his collar, not used to having his shirt buttoned all the way up, but he'd wanted to wear a tie today. For Lydia. She'd insisted it didn't matter, but he was determined to do things by the book. And that meant wearing a tie with his starched shirt and denims.

Travis patted his blazer. "Right here in my pocket."

Pastor Ericksen stuck his head in. "We're ready."

"About time," Colt muttered under his breath. The hours since before dawn had crawled by at a snail's pace.

"Anxious much?" Travis teased.

"Let's just say I'll be glad when the pastor says I can kiss my bride." He stepped out into the sanctuary and took his place on the steps as Gloria McPherson finished playing the prelude. At the back of the church, Lydia's twin, Lexi, and her younger sister, Carolina, signaled they were ready to walk down the aisle. As the organ began the wedding march, the congregation stood. Colt stopped breathing when Lydia appeared on her father's arm. His throat squeezed so tight his eyes watered. "You are beautiful," he mouthed silently.

Her smile widened. "I love you," she mouthed back.

Her dress floated around her as she walked down the aisle, but she could have worn a feed sack for all he cared. He couldn't take his eyes off her face. The rest of the church fell into the background as she moved forward and took his hand. His heart only started beating again when she stood on tiptoe to kiss his cheek. "Lookin' mighty fine, cowboy. Wanna get hitched?"

He kissed her back. "Hell, yes," he whispered in her ear.

Pastor Ericksen cleared his throat and began. Colt didn't hear any of it, he was lost in the most beautiful pair of blue-green eyes to grace the planet. Only when they clouded with concern did he come out of his fog. Murmurs came from the congregation as people shifted in their seats, some turning and looking to the back of the church.

"Wait," called the last voice in the world Colton wanted to hear today. "You can't marry *her*, when you have a baby due any day."

The congregation let out a collective gasp as Sammy Jo Carter, eyes glittering, flanked by her daddy and her uncle, strolled down the aisle with a very pregnant woman he'd never seen before, at least he didn't think he'd ever seen her before. Beside him, Lydia went stiff as a board.

He muttered a curse under his breath. He should have known better than to invite the Carters, but he'd invited all his sponsors. It was the right thing to do. He took Lydia's hand, giving it a squeeze, eyes darting from the horrified looks on her sister's faces, to Dottie and Teddy's glower. His stomach lurched sickeningly. "What is this?" he bit out, voice like ice as he clamped down on the white-hot anger surging through him. What kind of sick game was Sammy Jo playing? And how dare she pull this on Lydia's wedding day.

"I think it's pretty obvious, don't you?" She turned to Lydia. "Still think he's all that?"

The stricken look on Lydia's face nearly brought him to his knees. Taking Lydia by the elbow, he turned his attention to the Carters. "Come with me. *Now.*" He ushered them into the room where less than ten minutes before he'd eagerly waited for Pastor Ericksen to tell him it was time. He pulled shut the door, standing in front of it, ensuring no one would leave until he said so.

"What in the *hell* is going on? Did you know about this?" He glared at Hal, who shifted uncomfortably and cleared his throat. "You did, didn't you?" he roared, a breath away from losing his shit completely. Forcing himself to lower his voice, he continued. "And you waited until my wedding was in full swing to bring this to my attention?"

Sammy Jo crossed her arms. "I've been trying to talk to you for weeks."

"*Bullshit.*"

Harrison stiffened. "Don't you talk to my daughter that way, son."

"It's time you wake up and see what kind of person is. What kind of *psycho* pulls this shit at a wedding?"

The pregnant girl started to sniffle. "You don't remember, do you? How you promised you'd take care of me?"

"Sorry, darlin'. I don't recall ever seeing you before."

"Of course you don't," Sammy Jo snapped. "How could you, when your bedroom was nothing but a revolving door?"

He stalked to her, crossing his arms to keep from punching something. "Is that what this is about? The fact that you and I were bad for each other and you could never let it go?" He swung his gaze to Hal and Harrison. "And *you*. Always looking the other way. How many lives does she need to ruin before you recognize she's sick in the head?"

Harrison's face became mottled. "There's... there's, noth–"

"Is she an actress? Did you hire her?" he bellowed, coming perilously close to losing his shit entirely.

"*Enough*," Lydia hollered, eyes flashing. "Everybody *out*." She stamped her foot and thrust her bouquet toward the door.

"Sweethea–"

"*Not a word*," Lydia cut him off.

Colton opened the door and stood aside, glaring at each one of them as they filed out. As soon as the door snicked shut, Colton turned. "I–"

"Uh-uh," Lydia shook her head eyes flaming, holding up a hand. "Is it yours?"

He'd never heard her sound like this. Harsh and angry. Voice lashing like a bullwhip. He shook his head. "No. I swear. I'd been celibate for months before I returned home at Thanksgiving."

She made a harrumphing noise in the back of her throat that sounded just like her mother. He loved her for it. "But what about the blondes in the hot tub?"

"Didn't even kiss them."

"Or any other blondes?" She narrowed her eyes suspiciously.

"Not before Thanksgiving, and definitely not after. I've only had eyes for you since then." She *had* to believe him. He'd never do anything to jeopardize what they had. He held out his hand, desperate to convince her. "Have I ever lied to you?"

Her mouth thinned, but she shook her head.

"Have I ever presented myself to you as anything other than I am?"

"No," she whispered, eyes filling with tears. The anguished expression on her face sent an arrow straight to his heart. He *hated* that he was the cause of her sorrow. And that her wedding day had been ruined. Anger spotted his vision. He would take the Carters to account for this. As soon as he got everything squared away.

"Will you believe me then? I swear to you, I am not that child's father."

She drew in a ragged breath, but didn't say anything. She was slipping away. Somehow he had to convince her. "Look, give me five days to sort this all out. I swear, I've never seen this woman before in my life. Sammy Jo's gone over the edge and managed to drag her father and uncle with her. I swear, I'll make this all up to you."

"Why five days?"

He pinched the bridge of his nose, staring at the ceiling. "This ain't my first rodeo, sweetheart," he answered quietly, shame exploding across his chest and heating his face. "It takes five days for a paternity test to come back." Of *course*, his past would come back to haunt him on his wedding day. He'd been an idiot to think he could ever move beyond it.

Lydia's eyes grew wider. "Have you—"

He shook his head. "Never. I have no children. You are the *only* person I've had unprotected sex with. Ever. But I'm a rodeo personality, hon, and some people would... like to profit from my success," he finished. The door burst open, and Travis rushed in closely followed by Dottie, Teddy, and Lydia's sisters. "For fuck's sake," he shouted. "Can we have a

Goddamned minute of peace?"

THE ROOM EXPLODED in a circus of sound and gesticulations, everybody shouting at once. If it wasn't so awful, the scene before her might be funny. For starters, Lydia'd never seen her mother apoplectic, or Travis murderous.

"Colton Kincaid, I don't care how angry you are," blustered Dottie. "You will *not* swear in church."

"What did I tell you about breaking her heart?" Travis thundered, looming over Colton.

Lydia stared down at her new boots, arguably her best work yet, willing the floor to swallow her up. This was all too much. She needed time to think, to sort this out with Colton. In private, not in front of her family and friends who'd appointed themselves judge and jury. But she couldn't hide from this, and she darned well wasn't going to leave Colt to fend for himself with this crew.

Across the room, he stood his ground, jaw tight, eyes flashing. His was not the face of a guilty man. It was the face of a man who'd been unjustly slapped around one too many times. Her heart went out to him. She brought her fingers to her lips and let out the deafening whistle she'd perfected in New York to hail a cab.

The cacophony stopped abruptly as everyone turned to stare. Icy calm came over her, and she looked her sisters, her parents and Travis in the eye, one by one. "Mama, Travis, *back down*." She let the iron in her voice sink in before she continued. "Colt has every right to clear his name."

The room exploded with opinions, head shaking, and more shouting. She couldn't hear, she couldn't *think*.

"*STOP TALKING*," she screeched above the noise and

throwing her bouquet against the door.

Again, the clamor died down, but not before she heard a voice muttering. "Calm down."

"*Calm down?*" She was on a roll now. "Your wedding wasn't just ruined by a jealous harpy. Your fiancé wasn't just accused of fathering someone else's baby *in front of the whole town*. Don't tell me to calm down." She glared at everyone. "For what it's worth, I believe Colton." She held up a hand. "Uh-uh-uh, don't even start." She turned her gaze to Colton and nearly lost it. But she would not cry. Not now. Not in front of her family. Her throat closed, all prickles. Colt's face was the picture of devastation. His eyes bleak and hopeless. She crossed her hands over her heart. "I believe you, Colton. Maybe I shouldn't, and I'll come out of this looking like a fool. But I do." She held his gaze, tuning out the rest of the room. "I believe you. But I'm not going to live in limbo while I wait for the results of a paternity test. I'm going home to Mama's and staying there until I hear from you in five days' time"

Colton's face crumpled. "Please don't go," he pleaded.

For a second she wavered. But she knew herself. She needed space to think and to pull herself together. Her sisters knew her well enough to run interference where her mother was concerned, and no one from town would dare cross Dottie once word got out she wanted to be left alone. Opening the door, she stepped into the sanctuary, head held high, walked herself down the aisle – alone – and out into the brilliant afternoon sun. Only then, did she let the tears come.

CHAPTER 33

I T TOOK EVERYTHING Colt had inside him not to chase her down the aisle. But at the moment, he had bigger fish to fry. He swept his gaze across the crowded room. Meeting his brother's eyes. And Teddy's. Next, Dottie's, then Lydia's sisters, who glared daggers at him. "I've never seen that woman before today. And I certainly didn't contribute to her state."

His declaration was met with ominous silence.

"I understand that my reputation is less than stellar. I made mistakes, big mistakes, when I was a kid. But you have to believe me when I swear to you I love Lydia with all my heart, and I would *never* betray her."

"You offered to undergo a paternity test?" Travis's question sounded more like an interrogation.

Colt fought the urge to lash back defensively. "Of course."

Teddy, normally taciturn in the presence of his wife and daughters, spoke up. "I'm sure Doc Winslow's over at the clinic. We can head there now."

Colt hid a smile, sure that if they'd been at the Grace ranch, he'd have been polishing his shotgun. Teddy was a quiet man, but when he made up his mind, there was no changing it. "Yes, sir."

"But you'll need the lady to consent to a blood test too," said Lexi.

"I wouldn't call her a lady," Colton retorted.

"I could write a letter," she offered, ignoring him. "Most of the time a scary legal letter is enough to get someone to comply."

Lydia had mentioned Lexi was a lawyer. He'd gratefully accept any help he could get right now, especially since his own lawyers were in Colorado.

"How fast can you put one together?"

"I have letterhead in my bag."

"You carry it with you?" Always prepared, these Grace twins. For a split second he wondered if Carolina and Cassidy were the same way.

She nodded. "And a printer. All I need is an internet connection."

"The diner has Wi-Fi," Dottie said. "We added that in the rebuild."

"Great. I'll head to the clinic and then meet you at the diner."

Halfway down the aisle, Lexi caught up to him. "For what it's worth, I believe you too," she said quietly, heels clicking on the wood floor.

Colt stopped and stared, blinking hard, because she looked exactly like Lydia but with longer hair. It unnerved him. "Thank you," he murmured, needing to look away. Looking at her was too much.

Lexi continued. "My sister always sees the best in people, and if she believes you, it's with good reason. Besides, I can tell how much she loves you." She pointed to her head and then her heart. "Twin thing."

"Thank you," he said again, clinging to Lexi's words like a lifeline. "I'll see you at the diner."

Hopping in his truck, he drove to the edge of town where

the Warren G. Hansen Memorial Clinic had opened a few weeks previously. It was a surprisingly large facility for the size of the town, funded by the community in the wake of a killer tornado a little over a year ago. With grim determination, he marched into the small waiting area and rang the bell.

A moment later a beautiful young woman with a blonde ponytail pushed through the doors, a warm smile on her face. "Yes? Can I help you?"

"Uh, hi. I'm looking for Dr. Winslow?"

Her eyes lit. "That's me. How can I help?"

Colt's stomach dropped like he'd just jumped off a cliff. Taking a deep breath, he started, face flushing. "I need a blood test. For a paternity test."

Dr. Winslow looked nonplussed. As if she dealt with things like this every day. "Of course. Test results take about five days. Will a lady be coming in as well?"

"That's where it gets complicated."

"Would you prefer to sit?" she asked gently, reaching for a clipboard behind the desk. "I've got some paperwork for you to fill out."

Colton found himself pouring out the whole sordid story as he followed her back to an exam room. She responded with sympathetic noises and no judgment. By the time she wrapped the rubber cord around his arm before taking the blood, Colt felt surprisingly hopeful about the whole situation.

Dr. Winslow, labeled the vial of blood and put it on a tray. "Since we'll only need a blood sample from the mother, if you don't want to bring her all the way back here, I can print off a label with a barcode, and any clinic in Manhattan can draw the blood and mail it to the lab." She gave him a sympathetic smile. "That might be a little less stressful for you?"

Two hours later he strolled into the Bison & Bull Inn in downtown Manhattan, scanning the lobby for any signs of the Carters. Sure enough, they were relaxing by the fireplace, cocktails in hand. Tightening his grip on the envelope Lexi had given him he strolled over and flicked the letter to the table.

Three pairs of startled eyes jerked up to him. "Where is she? Did you bring her with you or is she local talent?"

"That is no way to talk about the mother of your child," Sammy Jo snapped.

"That baby is no more mine than it is yours." He braced his hands on the table, lowering himself to eye level. "Why'd ya do it? Didn't have the balls to fire me to my face? Or is this because if you couldn't have me, no one could?"

Harrison pushed back from the table. "Don't you threaten my daughter, son."

Colt righted himself. "Suck it, Harrison. Your daughter is a liability to your brand far more than I am."

Hal cleared his throat nervously. "You don't know what you're saying."

"The hell I don't," he growled. "I should have parted ways with you years ago, and that's on me. I was too chicken shit to tell you to fuck off the first time you tried to get me to marry Sammy Jo."

She gasped audibly, going pale. Harrison turned purple.

"And then for some stupid-ass reason, I had a misguided sense of loyalty to your brand because you were the first to take a chance on me. But no more." He pointed to the envelope. "This is a letter from my lawyer demanding your pregnant actor, wherever she is, undergo a blood test for a paternity test. You'll be receiving another letter from my legal team, dissolving our contract effective immediately."

"You can't do that," Hal sputtered. "You have obligations."

"Those ended the second you showed up to my wedding with an uninvited guest. Now, we can do this the easy way – quietly. Or we can do it the hard way – in public, with lots of press and lots of lawyers. You decide. And in case you're on the fence about it, I can guarandamntee you that if you choose the latter, it will be your name dragged through the mud. Not mine."

He swiped the whiskey cocktail sitting in front of Hal and drained it in one gulp, slamming the glass down so hard, the table shook. "You have two hours to get the lady to a clinic for a blood draw. Everything you need is in that letter." He glared at each one of them. "Don't even *think* about not complying."

Spinning on his heel, he stalked out of the lobby and back to his truck.

THE FIVE DAYS crept by with the slowness of a snail climbing a fence post in February. Colton paced in front of the fireplace at Resolution Ranch.

"Coffee?" Travis offered from the kitchen. "Why don't you have a sit? You've been pacing like a caged animal."

Colt stopped, bracing an arm on the large fieldstone mantel. "You have no idea. I've been doing everything I can not to go out of my mind."

Travis let out a wry laugh. "Hate to break it to you, little brother, but you're already there."

"Shit. I'm sorry." He stared up at the ceiling for a count of ten. "I can get out of your hair. See if the Sinclaires have space over at their hunting lodge. Or go to Manhattan."

"Hell, no," Travis said, pouring him a cup of coffee.

"You're gonna park your ass on the couch and talk to me." Travis rounded the large farm table that stood directly behind the couch, holding out his hand. "Here. Have a seat."

"Since when did you get all domestic?" Colt grinned over at his brother.

Travis's eyes lit. "Marriage and family. What can I say?"

"You wear it well." Colt stared into his mug, letting the steam warm his face. "I hope to know something about that soon."

"When does the test come back?"

"Sometime today, I hope."

"And then what?"

Colt shrugged, unease twisting his insides. "Wedding tomorrow."

"And after that?"

He knew where this was going. Travis had tried to return his Resolution Ranch investment as soon as he'd learned that Colt had drop-kicked the Carters and Carter Holdings back to Texas. "Back on the road."

"No honeymoon?"

"Said the man who didn't take one." Colt shrugged. "Lydia and I talked about going somewhere after the last qualifier in mid-October. But now that I've got an offer on the table for the ranch, we'll probably head to Steamboat." Even coffee couldn't wash away the bile in his throat. He loved his ranch, and it killed him to let it go, but with his liquid assets tied up in Resolution Ranch and Grace Boots, he didn't see how he could keep it. And at the end of the day, he'd rather be dirt poor with Lydia than rich without her.

Travis grew determined. "I wish you'd let me return the money you fronted us."

"No," he said flatly. "Not open for discussion."

"You took a bet on us, and I'll always be grateful for that."

"Keep it. You know you need it."

LYDIA PAUSED OUTSIDE the entrance to the church, heart pounding. She shouldn't be this nervous, she was more than ready to see Colt. Keeping herself from him the last week had been sheer torture. She'd lain in bed counting the hours as the moon tracked across the sky, willing herself to not cut across her property to his, to not meet him in the barn for a midnight tryst.

Cassie's hand came to rest on her back. "Do you have the check?"

"Are you sure about this?" Lexi asked.

"As sure as I know my own name," Lydia answered with conviction.

Carolina wrapped her in a fierce hug, putting on a brave face in spite of the lines of grief still showing around her eyes. "Then go get your man. Will thirty minutes be enough? I saw Gloria McPherson sitting in the parking lot."

"Fifteen will be plenty."

Cassidy pulled open the heavy oak door and gently pushed her through, letting the door creak shut behind her. Lydia stood at the back, blinking as her eyes adjusted to the dim.

"Lyds?"

A figure stood at the front, and slowly Colt came into focus. Tears wet her eyes as soon as she saw him, and forgetting her plan, she hurried down the aisle and launched herself into his arms.

He swung her around, holding tight. "I missed you so much," he said, voice husky. "I'm never letting you go."

"Never." She nodded, tilting her chin to receive his kiss. The second his mouth touched hers, the tears fell and a sob lodged in her throat.

Colt pulled away, panic flickering in his eyes. "Sweetheart, what is it?"

"I'm happy, I swear," she laughed, through her tears. "Kiss me again."

He complied with a fierceness that left them both breathless when they pulled apart. He brought his hands to her face, wiping her tears with his thumbs. "Have I told you how much I love you?" His eyes, brimming with love, told her all she needed to know.

"I'll never get tired of hearing it."

"I promise to tell you ten times a day. Twelve." Holding her shoulders, he took a step back, perusing her with a sultry tip of his mouth. "Look at you. You're stunning. But that's not the same dress you wore last week, is it?"

She turned in a circle, showing off Emmaline's miracle work. "The other one left a bad taste in my mouth, so Emmaline helped me change it this week."

"For the record. I'd still want to marry you if you wore shit kickers and a feed sack. You look beautiful in anything." He pulled her close, wrapping an arm around her, hand splaying across her hip. This time, when he kissed her, she sensed the need, the urgency.

With a sigh, she opened to him completely, receiving his offering as his tongue licked and flicked her lower lip, slowly stoking the fire building between her legs. "Can we just get married now?" she whispered when they parted.

"The next time you walk down that aisle, it'll be for good," he murmured back. "But first, I need to give you something." He pulled an envelope from his pocket and handed it to her. "Paternity results, showing I'm one-hundred-percent not the father."

"You didn't need to do this." She handed it back. "Your word was good enough."

His eyes flashed gratitude. "I still wanted you to have it."

She cupped his cheek. "I love you. And I trust you. Always." His hand covered hers as their gazes tangled, adding weight to the moment. "I have something for you, too," she murmured, pulse kicking up like she was chasing down a taxi.

"Oh?"

She raised her brows wickedly, then slowly slid a hand down the vee of her dress.

Colt cleared his throat. "I'm not sure we should have a quickie in the church, sweetheart."

Her chest shook with laughter, and her smile broadened as she continued her slow tease.

Colt's eyes went dark with desire, then widened in surprise as she pulled out a folded envelope from her bra. "What's this?"

She handed it over, heart in her throat.

He opened the envelope, making a noise in his throat before folding the check and holding it out. "No," he said flatly, shaking his head. "I'm not taking this. I already have an offer on the table for my ranch. We'll be fine once I sell it."

"But you have to. I sold Grace boots. This is your initial investment plus the interest we agreed upon."

"*What?*" He stared incredulously as her words sank in. Then he sprang to action, pacing in front of the altar. "No. I can't let you do that."

"It's a little too late."

He whirled, fixing her with a glare. "Then get it back. It's your dream. I'm not going to be the one who made you give up your dream." He sliced his hand across the space. "Absolutely, unequivocally, no." He stalked halfway down the aisle, then back. "You've worked too hard on this, it's too important to you."

"Colt," she laid a hand on his arm. "It's done."

"But *why*?"

She didn't think it was possible to love him any more than she already did, but his reaction expanded her heart to giant-sized proportions. "I got approached by Trinity Apparel a few months back and said no."

His jaw went slack, and hurt flashed in his eyes. "Why didn't you tell me?"

"Because at the time, it wasn't that big of a deal. And I wasn't even sure they were serious. Honestly, they asked and I laughed, and didn't think about it again."

"What changed your mind?"

"Running a boot company by myself was a great idea, but I had no idea how hard it would be, or how hard it would be to find qualified help." She held up her hands. "You were right to be concerned about me trashing my body. The CEO talked to me about the toll repetitive motion took on his sister's body. The more I thought about it, the more I realized I didn't want that to happen to me."

"But I don't want you to feel like your only option is to be... what'd you call it? A camp-follower?"

"I won't be. Grace Boots will go on as the signature line of Trinity Apparel. I have a contract that gives me full artistic control and quality control. Trinity will use a portion of their factory in Texas to build the boots. They have quality machinery, and people already trained in boot making. It's still a family-owned business, which I like. And I get to do what I do best, which is design." She made a face. "And since

I flat-out refuse to marry you if you have anything to do with Carter holdings, it seemed like the best thing for our future, was to pay back your investment and then some."

He dropped his head, laughter ringing from the rafters. "You don't have to worry about Carter Holdings anymore, sweetheart. They're history." He looked at her with wonder. "I don't know what to say."

She held out her hand, and laced her fingers with his as she pulled him close. "Say you love me and that you'll marry me as soon as my sisters let everyone in the church."

"Yes, to all of that," he rasped, picking her up, mouth brushing hers with such sweetness an ache ballooned in her chest. "So you can join me on the road?"

She nodded, happiness settling in her bones. "I'll still be speaking for Grace Boots, so they're happy to have me represent wherever you are."

"And you won't miss making them? The boots?"

"I'll still make shoes for my friends and family, but my hands are killing me."

"And they're too perfect to hurt all the time." His mouth brushed hers again.

A thrill of attraction raced through her. "And if I'm not working seven days a week churning out orders..." She kissed the corner of his mouth. "We'll have time for other... more *family-oriented* endeavors." She giggled as a growl started low in his throat and his arms tightened around her.

"Oh, we'll have plenty of time for that," he murmured against her mouth. "I'll make sure of it."

Anticipation raced through her veins. "I love the sound of that."

The heavy door creaked open. "Hey, if you two would stop making out, maybe we could have a wedding in here," Lexi called.

EPILOGUE

December – National Finals Rodeo, Las Vegas

C OLT CHECKED THE tape on his arm a final time before slipping into his shirt. Chaos raged around him, but his focus was laser tight.

"Here, let me," Lydia said softly. "Shut your eyes and see your ride. I'll finish the buttons."

He snaked a hand around her neck. "Kiss first, wife," he growled. He'd swear on a stack of bibles her kisses had added thousands to his earnings this year. Something about the way the energy ripped through his body when her mouth went soft under his. It kept him hyper-aware, perfectly balanced, like he was one with his ride.

"You're gonna be late," she laughed breathlessly when he pulled away.

"They're not gonna send Candy Corn out into the arena without me, darlin'. Now button me up and get out to your box so I can see you before I ride."

She gave him a grin that held more mischief than a funhouse on the midway.

"What you got up your sleeve, sweet thing?" he asked, guard going up. "You change my ringtone again?"

Her laugh sounded like music to his ears. "Of course." She winked up at him as she finished the last button and held out his vest.

"What else? You're workin' on something. I can tell." He shrugged into his vest, while she centered his neck protector.

Her grin widened. "You could say that."

He pulled her flush against him. "Don't make me kiss it outta you," he rumbled.

"Ooh, promise?" Her eyes lit.

He gently smacked her ass. "One more kiss and get outta here, darlin'."

She stood on tiptoe, and gave him a kiss that curled his toes in his boots. "That's it." He grinned down at her, still surprised by the lightness that swept through him at unexpected intervals. "That's the winning kiss. I ride eighty-six, and I win tonight."

Lydia's eyes grew soft. "You're already the best in my mind, Colt. No matter what happens. See you in the arena." She turned with a saucy sway of her hips and left him to walk the final yards to the chutes on his own.

Back behind the chutes, he tied his glove, rubbed the palm with glue, and climbed over the rails at the signal from the flank men.

"Ladies and Gentlemen, all the way from Steamboat Springs, Colorado, give it up for a man who's been in the hunt for best All-Around Cowboy, Colton Kincaid."

The roar in the arena made his ears ring, but Colt was focused on jamming his glove into the rigging and getting his body balanced just right.

"Ready?" asked one of the flank men.

He scanned the box, searching for Lydia and raised his arm when they made eye contact. Keeping his eyes on her, he set his spurs, and just as he was ready to nod, she raised a sign with the words *RIDE HARD DADDY!*

He dropped his arm as the words sank in. "What?" he

shouted over the cheers of the crowd as the announcer picked up on their exchange. She nodded vigorously pointing to her belly. He couldn't wipe the grin off his face as joy like he'd never felt before burst inside his chest. Didn't want to. "I love you," he mouthed, throat tight with wonder.

"We love you," Lydia mouthed back, hand over her heart.

With more determination than ever, he raised his hand and gave the nod, body moving in slow motion as Candy Corn bolted from the chute.

There was nothing left to do but hang on for the ride of his life.

THE BEGINNING OF HAPPILY EVER AFTER

Did you like this book? Please leave a review! Independent authors rely on reviews and word of mouth. If you enjoyed this book, please spread the word!

Want more? Sign up for my newsletter to get notifications about A Hero's Home, the next story in the Heroes of Resolution Ranch coming in June 2018

tessalayne.com/newsletter

And while you're waiting....

Will a shared passion be enough to help these polar opposites find true love?

COMING JUNE 26TH – A HERO'S HOME

When Army Ranger Jason Case accepts an invitation from his closest friend to join Resolution Ranch, the last thing he expected was to be a hero to Prairie's resident hippie, Millie Prescott. He's no hero, and he wants to be left alone.

Millie knows she and Jason have a cosmic connection – he saved her from certain death. There's only one problem...

- He Loves Bacon – She Loves Tofu
- He's a hardened warrior – She's a peacemaker
- He's the man of her dreams – She's a thorn in his side

Neither Jason nor Millie could have predicted the blistering heat that erupts between them, and in a moment of lust-fueled insanity, the grouchy vet agrees to help Miss Sunshine save her struggling vineyard and put Prairie on the map for heirloom wine.

But trouble comes to Prairie when Jason's family decides they'll stop at nothing to bring Jason back where he belongs, running the Case wine empire. And Jason must decide how far he's willing to go to ensure the woman he's fallen for doesn't become collateral damage.

MEET THE HEROES OF RESOLUTION RANCH

Inspired by the real work of Heroes & Horses... Chances are, someone you know, someone you *love* has served in the military. And chances are, they've struggled with re-entry into civilian life. The folks of Prairie are no different. With the biggest Army base in the country, Fort Riley, located in the heart of the Flint Hills, the war has come home to Prairie.

Join me as we finally discover Travis Kincaid's story and learn how he copes in the aftermath of a mission gone wrong. Meet Sterling, who never expected to return to Prairie after he left for West Point. Fall in love with Cash as he learns to trust himself again. Laugh with Jason and Braden as they meet and fall in love with the sassy ladies of Prairie. Same Flint Hills setting, same cast of friendly, funny, and heartwarming characters, same twists and surprises that will keep you up all night turning the pages.

A HERO'S HONOR – Travis Kincaid & Elaine Ryder
(On Sale Now)
A HERO'S HEART – Sterling Walker & Emma Sinclaire
(On Sale Now)
A HERO'S HAVEN – Cash Aiken & Kaycee Starr
(On Sale Now)
A HERO'S HOME – Jason Case & Millie Prescott
(Coming June 2018)
A HERO'S HOPE – Braden McCall & Luci Cruz
(Coming 2018)

Help a Hero – Read a Cowboy
KISS ME COWBOY – A Box Set for Veterans
Six Western Romance authors have joined up to support their
favorite charity – Heroes & Horses – and offer you this sexy
box set with Six Full Length Cowboy Novels, filled with
steamy kisses and HEA's. Grab your copy and help an
American Hero today!

WHERE IT ALL BEGAN:
THE COWBOYS OF THE FLINT HILLS SERIES

Sizzling, Standalone Stories with HEAs, Sassy Heroines, and
Cowboys you want to Cuddle

PRAIRIE HEAT – Blake Sinclaire & Maddie Hansen
(on sale now!)
PRAIRIE PASSION – Brodie Sinclaire & Jamey O'Neill
(on sale now!)
PRAIRIE DESIRE – Ben Sinclaire & Hope Hansen
(on sale now!)
PRAIRIE STORM – Axel Hansen & Haley Cooper
(on sale now!)
PRAIRIE FIRE – Parker Hansen & Cassidy Grace
(on sale now!)
PRAIRIE DEVIL – Colton Kincaid & Lydia Grace
(on sale now!)
PRAIRIE FEVER – Gunnar Hansen & Suzannah Winslow
(coming in 2018)
PRAIRIE BLISS – Jarrod O'Neill & Lexi Grace
PRAIRIE REDEMPTION – Cody Hansen & Carolina Grace

Coming this fall!
PRAIRIE FEVER
(Book 7 in the Cowboys of the Flint Hills Series)

Playing doctor has never been so sexy.
Confirmed bachelor Gunnar Hansen, has successfully resisted the matchmaking efforts of Dottie Grace and her posse of granny wannabe's. There's no room in his life for love, or for starting a family of his own. Not when his hands are full running Hansen Stables and heading up the board of Prairie's new medical clinic. But everything turns upside down when the socialite who ditched him at the altar years ago turns out to be Prairie's new doctor.

Four years ago, fresh out of medical school, Suzannah Winslow took a gamble on a sweet-talking cowboy who left her high and dry... and pregnant. With her residency behind her, and an offer to become Prairie's first and only physician, she can finally provide her daughter with stability she's longed for. She has no interest in taking a second chance on a silver-tongued cowboy full of empty promises. Even if his smile still melts her panties.

But Gunnar has other ideas, and when he mounts a full-scale campaign to win back the woman he lost, will little Lula Beth become his unlikely ally or the wedge that drives them apart for good?

Subscribe to my Newsletter for updates and release information for Prairie Storm and the rest of the Cowboys of the Flint Hills Series.

tessalayne.com/newsletter

Join my reader group on Facebook – The Prairie Posse this is where I post my sneak peeks, offer giveaways, and share hot cowboy pics!

facebook.com/groups/1390521967655100

ACKNOWLEDGMENTS

Writing this book was so much fun! It made me fall in love with my rodeo roots. Growing up in Colorado meant that January was National Western Stockshow & Rodeo Month. I can't tell you how many years we walked the stock show pens in the snow! So tell me... do you like rodeo? I sense another cowboy series coming to Praire... maybe this one focused on rodeo ☺ Drop me a line and tell me what YOU want more of!

Many thanks to my amazing cover designer Amanda Kelsey – Colton is my favorite cover yet!

Many thanks to all my readers and fans in the Prairie Posse! You make writing so much fun, and your encouragement on the hard days helps me keep going.

Thank you to Posse Member Stephanie Perrow, who helped me pick out the perfect bad-girl name!

My heartfelt thanks to Kimberley Troutte, I'm so grateful for your steady encouragement. You've taught me well and this book showed me I could fly on my own ♥ I never would have gotten here without you.

Thank you Genevieve Turner and Kara for always being willing to tell it like it is. You make my books better.

Lastly, to Mr. Cowboy, Tiny & Teenager: Check your phones, I might have messed with your ringtones!

Made in the USA
Columbia, SC
19 July 2018